She had to be hallucinating. She [barcode: D1267947]
to her best friend's ghost...

"Let go, Rae. Let us go."

Never in a million years could she mistake that voice. Never did she not believe that she wouldn't see Ginny Grover standing on the steps behind her, looking beautiful and benevolent against the glowing backdrop of white stone.

"Ginny?"

It wasn't a cry of denial but rather a plea that it be true.

But of course it couldn't be. Ginny was dead.

A mistake. Had it been an awful mistake? Had some other unfortunate been killed upon the tracks and wrongfully identified as her best friend because of the belongings scattered nearby?

Her mind told her no, but her stubborn heart wanted to hang on desperately to the notion.

"It's too late for you to make amends, Rae. You've got your own life to live. You had your chance to make it up to me. Four years, Rae."

"But I never had a chance to say I was sorry," she cried in her own defense. "I never had a chance to tell you I was wrong."

"You just did. Go home. Let us rest."

"I can't, Ginny. Not until I know what happened to you."

"What difference does it make now?" came a sadly spoken truth. "You can't change what's happened. But if you don't leave things alone, you'll join us. Is that what you want? To be like us? Is that the price you want to pay for the mistakes you've made?"

"No."

Even as she said the word, Ginny's beloved features began to dissolve into the horrifying remains of a track accident. As she spoke, the flesh fell away from the crushed side of her face, leaving an unrecognizable mess of shattered bone.

"Don't make us come after you, Rae. Mind your own business. Your pride and guilt are denying us the peace we deserve."

Midnight Masquerade

***

Nancy Gideon

ImaJinn
Books

MIDNIGHT MASQUERADE
Published by ImaJinn Books, a division of ImaJinn

Copyright ©2001 by Nancy Gideon

ISBN: 1-893896-48-X

10 9 8 7 6 5 4 3 2 1

PUBLISHER'S NOTE:
This book is a work of fiction. Names, characters, places and incidents are products of the author's imagination or are used fictitiously. Any resemblance to actual events or locales or persons, living or dead, is entirely coincidental.

Books are available at quantity discounts when used to promote products or services. For information please write to: Marketing Division, ImaJinn Books, P.O. Box 162, Hickory Corners, MI 49060-0162, or call toll free 1-877-625-3592.

Cover design by Patricia Lazarus

ImaJinn Books, a division of ImaJinn
P.O. Box 162, Hickory Corners, MI 49060-0162
Toll Free: 1-877-625-3592
http://www.imajinnbooks.com

PROLOGUE

There.

There it was again.

Clutching her purse with its woeful $38.57 in folded bills and change inside, she glanced over her shoulder without slowing her step. As before, the sidewalk behind her was empty.

Despite the sweltering July heat, hair prickled up on the nape of her neck, creating a cold trickle down her back.

No one there. Just her imagination.

Quickening her pace to match the increased rhythm of her heartbeats, she hurried toward the transit opening. She loved everything about her new job except the evening hours. Walking the nearly abandoned D.C. streets gave her the creeps and aptly described the type of people she usually brushed past in her rush for home. Driving her car through the snarl of traffic when she was a brisk three blocks from the Metro seemed foolish during daylight hours, and she was trying so hard to maintain her new air of financial responsibility. Her father would approve. And so would her dyed-in-the-wool common sense friend, Rae. But when the pulsing energy of the working world became the seeping shadows of evening, it seemed far less foolish to toss off her desire to make those two role models proud and spring for the extravagance of a cab. Especially with her heart hammering in her chest and her paranoia galloping full tilt at every sound. Then it was harder to live up to her new life of respectable frugality.

Close to midnight, crime statistics had an annoying habit of haunting her.

But then her father and her bold former friend were afraid

of nothing – not of daily challenges to behave as responsible adults, not of the constant struggle to live within the wages earned, not of the uncertainty of carving out a new life alone. But she was getting braver. Even Rae would be impressed by her sensible outlet store clothing and strict regime of healthy habits.

She concentrated on the destination rather than the journey, on taking off the tight new sandals that had looked so snappy on the shelf but felt like an Inquisitor's boot when her toes swelled up at mid-day. A pint of rainbow sherbet and the caress of the air conditioner beckoned at the end of her fifteen minute ride. Rewards for a long day and a silly fright. Eager to shake them both off, she started down the steps of the Metro tunnel, anticipating the cool that came with subterranean travel.

She paused at the top of the escalators as that shivery feeling crawled along her arms and marched in an uneasy ripple down her spine. A quick glance showed an empty stairway and the night sky above.

Chuckling softly at her case of hyperactive nerves, she stepped onto the escalator and began the descent into the bowels of D.C.

The Metro system was a boon to tourists and employees alike, providing cheap, reliable transportation every five minutes during the rush hours to just about anyplace one needed to go. Once you got used to the transfer stations, carrying correct change and the color-coded lines, it was sit back and leave the driving to them. She knew the underground system better than the streets above and felt comfortable riding the rail . . . once she got to it.

It was that first step that always got her.

Of all the stops, this was the only one that made her hold her breath as if she were taking an e-ticket excursion straight to hell.

The escalator plunged into darkness, its pitch so steep, its drop so far that one couldn't see top nor bottom to gage a final or starting destination. Suspended in some eerie Twilight Zone where one could only guess at the world where one would finally emerge, the ride went on forever.

Too much late night TV, she thought with another chiding chuckle as she glided deeper into the earth.

That's when the lights flickered out, and the metal step beneath her shuddered to a stop.

Darkness. Complete and cold.

She spoke a soft explicative. Annoyance settled before alarm. Now what? Start climbing back up and foot the expense of a cab or continue down and hope this was an isolated failure and that the train would be there for its twelve-minute interval. She couldn't see the bottom of the escalator to tell if the lights were on below, and the idea of feeling her way down into that black oblivion held no appeal.

Well, it was onward and upward and the cost of a cab.

Taking a deep breath in anticipation of the climb ahead and a tight hold on the rubberized rail, she turned. And stumbled back several steps.

Above her in the dark were twin pindots of red, like lasers shining in the blackness.

Repair technicians.

Her breath expelled in a relieved rush.

"Thank goodness. The lights went out," she called to the figure above her. "Do you know if the train's still running?"

Her questions echoed and hung unanswered.

The fiery dots began to descend smoothly, as if the escalator was still moving.

"Hello? Can you help me?"

Silence. No sound of footsteps on the metal risers.

Hair stirred to attention upon her nape again.

Briefly, she thought of abandoning her cramping shoes and running down into the tunnel. She considered sliding down the separating steel between the up and down escalators then recalled the upraised metal studs embedded to prevent such mischievous behavior. No help there.

Remembering the credit card-sized flashlight her father had given her to attach to her apartment keys so she could locate her door lock after dark, she fumbled in her purse as the glowing twin dots came closer, closer. Her breath gusted loudly, the only noise in the chill tunnel until the clatter of her lipstick and car keys against the grated steps. She dug more frantically, beginning to retreat, backing down the immobile escalator as sobs panted from her. Her fingers closed on the flashlight. She jerked it free, her purse falling from her shaking hands. She heard its contents spill into the void of blackness below.

Holding the flat pocket light in both hands, she pressed down on the sensor pad. A thin beam shot upward, wavering wildly, illuminating steps, blank walls, impotent lights . . . and then a sight so terrifying all logic fled her.

Thin lips pulled back from horrible fangs.

She dropped the light and raced downward toward hope of possible salvation, slipping on the strewn contents of her bag as she ran.

A sudden push of air, cold and silent, descended upon her.

Her scream trailed down into darkness, thinning then stopping all together.

After a long moment, the lights blinked back on. The escalators began their efficient humming, until steps splattered with crimson disappeared beneath the bottom plate.

ONE

Umbrella tops crowded together like mushroom caps growing in the shadows of a slated sky. After a morning of continuous drizzle, puddled walks provided a challenge for the stylishly dressed groups hurrying toward their luxury cars to get out of the weather and away from the dismal scene. No one liked to linger in a graveyard, even on the best of days. On this one, only the heavens remained to weep for the one they buried. The heavens and Rae Borden.

She'd arrived too late to hear the comforting words of a life eternal spoken over the casket of her best friend. She'd only heard the news six hours before and was still reeling from shock and denial. She'd taken the first plane out of Detroit and still held her hastily packed overnight bag as she watched an indifferent grounds crew begin to disassemble the drooping mourners' canopy. Flowers hung limp and skewed from the weight of the water as a heavier rain pelted a baleful tympani off the metal folding chairs. Only as the loneliness of the scene struck her did Rae really begin to believe.

Ginny Grover was gone.

Her best friend, her pseudo-sister and soul mate.

Dead. And now buried.

And she hadn't had the chance to say good-bye.

There was no reason to remain as the rain swept down in merciless sheets, soaking the freshly turned earth, fluttering the ribbons of the graveside wreaths bearing the grieving words, *Beloved Daughter*. There was nothing more to be done here, nothing she could do for the body of Ginny Grover encased in satin, brass and mahogany for her eternal sleep underground.

But if there was something she could do to make her friend's memory rest easier within her heart and soul, she would see it done before saying her final farewell.

That was the graveside promise she made in place of a prayer.

***

Memories came rushing back as she piloted her rental car up the wide horseshoe drive of the Grovers's country home. Some of those remembrances, like that of two young girls learning to drive a stick shift and ending up in the azaleas, made her smile briefly. But others were too painful to embrace without breaking down completely. Those she would cherish when she was alone, taking them out one by one to examine then store away as if they were delicate Christmas ornaments wrapped in a protective tissue of emotion and bittersweet recall.

And then there was her last memory—that of driving away from this home, this family, in anger and disgrace. It was that moment that made her doubt her welcome, that ugly parting that made her ache for a place she could no longer call home, for these people she should no longer think of as family. For four years she'd been waiting for a reason to come back, hoping for an invitation. But when the invitation finally came, it wasn't to mend those damaged fences but to bury forever her last chance for forgiveness.

She needed to know how Ginny Grover had died. And why.

An accident was what the report had read. She'd had it faxed to her and had agonized over every detail it hadn't explained. Like how Ginny had fallen from the platform in front of the oncoming train. There'd been no witnesses other than the horrified conductor who'd had no time to stop or even slow. Like why, if it was an intentional suicide, her purse and its scattered contents had been found at the escalator instead of where she had died.

Unless she hadn't died in the fall.

Unless someone had been chasing her.

The unfortunate thing about trains was that they left so

little evidence behind.

Except one odd piece that had puzzled her when reading it. One strange, unexplained observation that gave her a moment's pause.

Ginny Grover's body had been a nearly bloodless corpse.

Was she the only one who wondered why?

First, she would pay her respects to the man who'd been like a father to her. Then she'd bulldoze her way into the local investigation to get at the real facts of the case.

Rae hadn't been inside the house since that last disastrous evening four years before. There'd been subtle music and well-dressed guests and long tables of catered food at that event, too. Only today, they weren't celebrating a future about to unfold. That truth wedged hotly in Rae's throat on the edge of a sob. At any minute, she expected to hear the slightly bawdy laughter ringing a bit too loudly over the subdued conversation. If she looked up, would she see the willowy figure in designer clothes and tennis shoes descending the slow curl of the staircase...or sliding down its polished bannister? The ache of knowing neither of those things would ever be a part of her world again swelled hurtfully within her breast.

How could Ginny be gone? How could one senseless, violent act end such a vibrant presence? One that still shimmered with firefly incandescence through the conservative rooms?

"Rae, so glad you could make it."

This was the moment she'd dreaded, this confrontation with those she'd humiliated so publically upon her last visit to their home. As much as she yearned to reach out to share in the terrible pain of loss and mourning, she held herself back, unsure of her reception.

"Thank you for calling me. I'm sure that wasn't easy for you...considering." She'd tried for a neutral tone, but her voice wavered. Just as Bette Grover's polite smile wavered.

"Don't be ridiculous, Rae. Of course we'd call you. You were her best friend, regardless of how things ended. That's what we'll remember. The rest just isn't important anymore."

Not quite open-armed acceptance, just a weary truce. She'd

take it.

Struggling for control against the tidal force of gratitude and grief, she presented her cheek to the soft, scented press of Bette Grover's, murmuring, "Where is he?"

Bette, still remarkably unlined for all her fifty-three years, as if age or gravity wouldn't dare disturb such beauty, was ever the perfect hostess. Even in the waning hours of her step-daughter's funeral, she remembered to ask after Rae's flight and to commend her paltry luggage and wet coat into the care of one of the hired crew. Then the facade wavered slightly as she beheld her daughter's friend through welling eyes. Her voice shook as she finally addressed her question.

"He's in the study. It'll do him good to see you. The last few days have been...difficult."

How could they have been anything else to a man for whom the sun rose and set upon his only child?

The study had been father and daughter's refuge. They'd celebrated the addition of each trophy in the wall-to-wall glass case, whether it be for forensic speaking or scratch golf or the sixth grade science fair. They'd wept on the big leather sofa as Ginny's mother struggled upstairs in a losing battle against cancer. They'd discussed math problems and boyfriend problems and college choices across the big teakwood desk as if making global policies. And Rae had been a part of it, like family.

Thomas Grover stood before that wall of glass studying the polished plaques engraved with his daughter's accomplishments. He didn't turn to address her but rather acknowledged her presence by speaking as if she hadn't just arrived.

"I told her that horse was too big for her, but would she listen? She proved me wrong, didn't she? And she and that big brute...what was his name?"

"Charlemagne," Rae supplied softly.

"Yes. Charlemagne. She wouldn't admit that he was too much for her until after she'd won the trophy. Because you had told her she could do it, and she was afraid of letting you down. Stubborn child, like her mother. What am I going to do without her, Rae?"

She walked to him then, slipping her arms about a figure that had just started to relax into a heavier middle as the result of success. With her head resting against his broad back, with her hands crushed up in his big, callused palms, she finally admitted, "I don't know."

"She missed you, Rae. All she could talk about was making you proud. Your opinion meant everything."

Rae shuddered with remorse and whispered, "I was proud."

They stood like that for a long while, until a tap on the door brought them back from their private well of misery.

"Thomas, our guests are asking for you."

"In a minute, Bette."

Wordlessly, his new wife withdrew. He'd waited almost eight years after Ellen died to remarry. The mourning period had been almost operatic. Then Bette—bright, efficient, loving Bette—had forced his life back on course. Only to have it steer astray once more with this new devastation. His sigh was tremendous, overwrought with pain and sorrow.

"What happened?" Rae asked at last.

Never in all their years together had Thomas Grover been less than completely honest with her. Never until this moment.

"I don't know, Rae. An accident. A tragic accident. How could it have been anything else?"

Indeed. How could it have been?

All Rae's professionally honed instincts came into play, reading between those carefully tendered lines to find unspoken volumes of guilt and evasion.

What wasn't he telling her?

"I know this isn't exactly the best time—"

Grover pulled away from her embrace to stalk to the sideboard, splashing a large quantity of rarely consumed Scotch into a tall glass. He drank it down neat in two big swallows. "Is there ever going to be a good time to discuss a daughter's death?" His voice grated rough with the burn of liquor and regret.

"Do you think it was suicide?"

"Ginny?" A harsh laugh. "Ginny loved life. She loved her new job. She was in love. The idea of her killing herself is as obscene as her death."

"No money troubles, no man troubles, no emotional troubles—none of that?"

"No." Said quietly. "No." With more force of conviction. "An accident," he repeated, as if trying to convince himself that it was true.

Neither of them believed it for a minute.

Grover reached for the decanter, then his hand hung, trembling, just shy of grasping it. Finally, he lowered it and murmured, "I should see to our guests. You'll be staying, of course." Not a question.

"Yes. For a few days."

For however long it took to discover the truth.

The truth Thomas Grover was hiding from her.

***

He'd never get used to riding in style. He was an old, beat up Camaro with a rumbling muffler kind of guy. If folks looked his way, it was because he was breaking sound ordinance laws and leaving four feet of rubber on the ground. They'd shake their heads, thinking he'd be in jail by the time he was thirty. Wouldn't their eyeballs just pop if they could see him now, leaning back into seats of butter soft leather so form fitting they almost swallowed him whole, wearing shoes that cost more than that first fast car, sporting a haircut that would have taken his first paycheck and change. When people stared now, it was because they were impressed by the pewter-colored limo with its mysterious tinted windows. Inside they'd expect to find a success story in Italian loafers, not a hellraiser from a poor parish outside Baton Rouge. How amusing to be both at the same time.

He stared out through the bulletproof glass at the upscale Maryland countryside rolling past the window and purely marveled at the fortuitous turn his life had taken. Perhaps some day he'd live in one of these sprawling estates and raise pedigreed dogs and children of his own where they could run wild and free. They'd never have to smell the stench of poverty, see hopelessness in the eyes of those they loved or know loneliness that sank, cold and sharp, all the way to the bone. Or fear. A fear of failure. A fear of never being able to escape. Of losing the spark of ambition in one's own eyes. The way it had extinguished in his own father's gaze.

"We're here."

The quiet statement pulled Nick Flynn from the dark direction of his thoughts. He glanced ahead as their limo glided into the U-shaped drive of one of those enviable brick mansions. The drive and part of the immaculate lawn beyond were crowded with luxury vehicles.

"Looks like we'll be interrupting a party."

His companion smiled slightly. "Something like that."

"Are you sure this is the right time?"

"Timing is everything. And I guarantee you, the time is right. Mr. Grover will be expecting us." And again the small, mirthless smile.

Everything about his employer, Kazmir Zanlos, was as enigmatic as that smile, from the accent that was impossible to pinpoint to the expressions that were impossible to read. The flat onyx of his stare reminded Nick of a shark's. The comparison would have amused the owner of the largest legal firm in the Capitol area. Perhaps that's why he'd taken such a shine to Nick, whose charismatic dazzle reflected off his own smooth surface. For whatever the reason, Nick was grateful. He was about to close on his biggest deal ever, with a percentage that brought all his dreams to fruition.

Life was good, and he wouldn't question the whys and wherefores.

As the two of them entered the big house, there was no music or cheer associated with a celebration. The somber tone alerted Nick to the fact that all was not right in the Grover household. He was about to mention his observation to Zanlos when his scanning gaze caught upon one of the guests and could not break away.

She stood apart from the others, by choice rather than design. Her comfort with that isolation made his attention pause that extra involving second. While those around her were carefully coifed and purposefully subdued, she stood in their midst, unapologetically underdressed and seething with intensity. Her rumpled, khaki-colored vest and shorts held a slept-in softness next to the knife-edged creases and silky stockings of the other guests. Her features were equally unprepared for the occasion—her eyes smudged, her dark auburn hair shaped into flattened geometrics by the rain, and her face naked of artifice in both cosmetics and emotion. She was a raw nerve, a flame-thrower in a room of mellow tea lights. And Nick was mesmerized, not so much by her striking appearance as by her aggressive attitude—her stance one of coiled energy, her gaze ever in motion.

She had as much business in this crowd as they did.

Then their stares locked in an instant of combustible awareness. Her eyes were green, as glittery as fresh-struck emeralds. Then several couples passed between them, severing that visceral contact and allowing him to release the suspenseful breath he hadn't known he'd been holding. And then she was gone.

"Ah, there's our host," Kaz murmured, drawing his focus away from his search of the gathering to the man who stood at the end of the hall. Kaz approached like a money-seeking missile.

"What are you doing here?"

Thomas Grover's growl made them feel as welcome as dog doo on a white rug.

Without a break in his bland facade, Kaz reached out his hand. Nick supposed it was to shake the other man's, but then he saw Kaz's palm turn upward to reveal what looked like a credit card. Then he saw it was a thin, touch pad flashlight holding a single key. Grover stared at it blankly at first, then with a horror that built like a tower of cards to a dangerously wobbly height.

"Where did you get that?" His voice quavered.

"Just a little something to shed light on our negotiation. Are you ready to talk business now, Mr. Grover?"

Like a creature caught in a soul sucking quicksand trying to warn others from the same threat, Grover cast his gaze about, but his guests were too far away to have heard their words or to have noticed him in the shadowed doorway to his study. Then he glared at the two of them through eyes shiny with pain and shock.

"Have you no decency at all?"

Then Nick understood. This was a funeral gathering.

"I'm afraid that's not one of my better qualities," Kaz admitted with a mildly amused candor so out of place with the circumstance that Nick rode out a shuddering chill from head to toe. He touched his boss's arm.

"Perhaps we should come back later."

Zanlos's black stare fixed upon him with a cyclonic intensity, but still he smiled. "Nonsense. No time like the present. Mr. Grover's put off this moment a bit too long already, haven't you Mr. Grover?"

His features ashen, Grover made a tremulous gesture to the room at his back. "In here. We won't be disturbed."

"Excellent. I knew you could be a man of reason."

***

"Rae, let me take you up to your room."

The interruption of Bette's voice jerked her from her gravitational pull toward the dark stranger, and when she glanced back, he and his equally slick and enigmatic friend had disappeared.

Who was that guy?

She'd never felt such immediate attraction and...alarm. Not only because he was the most jaw-droppingly handsome man she'd seen this side of a pinup calendar but because she'd felt the punch of his presence all the way across the room and was still tingling. And since she'd been taught never to play with a downed power wire, she was understandably cautious of that potentially deadly surge of...what? Desire? Lust? Need? She was feeling particularly needy at the moment, and perhaps that Darwin thing had just kicked in, coaxing her to find the best the species had to offer. And wow, had he come through for her.

"Rae?"

Pulled once again from her odd musings, Rae smiled up

at the other woman. "Thanks for putting me up."

"I'm just glad you're here."

Again, warning bells jangled. There was more than just the stress of the circumstances in Bette Grover's voice. A genuine snag of desperation reached out to her.

What was going on? Why had Bette Grover called her after a painful four-year exile? Not to wax sentimental. Not to forgive and forget.

Then why?

Did she suspect there was something wrong in the way her stepdaughter had died?

Suddenly, Rae was eager to leave the milling crowd and the intrigue of the dark stranger to pump Bette Grover for information.

The upper floor of the house was quiet and cool, just the thing after the chaos of travel and mugginess of a D.C. rainstorm. The stir of air against her skin was almost as good as a cold shower for waking up her senses.

Who was that guy? The prickly heat of awareness wouldn't go away.

"You can have your old room, of course. It's been given a facelift, but you should still feel right at home." Bette was chattering away with a frantic cheerfulness, the 'nothing's wrong' smile pasted awkwardly over whatever else lurked beneath.

Rae stepped inside and stepped back in time. The colors had changed. Gone were the screaming pinks and limes of her teen years, replaced by a subdued mauve and forest green. But there was the same canopy bed under which she and Ginny had shared secrets and dreams. There were the casement windows that opened onto the roof below. And from there just a short drop to the plush lawn and an evening's freedom. Her carry-on case was next to the armoire where they'd tucked one of Ginny's more aggressively amorous suitors when the first Mrs. Grover had come to say good night.

How could this be so reminiscent of a time that was forever past? How could the spirit of Ginny Grover, preserved so perfectly within this room, be no more?

Sorrow swelled up on an engulfing tide that Rae could only forestall with a barrier of anger.

How dare someone take her friend's life and all the memories they had left to make between them?

"Bette, what's wrong here?"

The older woman looked startled, then afraid. Such an odd yet strong reaction. Rae knew she hadn't been far off in her intuitions. She held up her hand to stop the expected platitudes.

"Please. This is my family. Didn't you think I'd notice?"

Bette released a tremulous breath. "I was hoping you would, almost as hard as I was hoping you wouldn't."

"Is it Ginny? What happened to Ginny?"

"It goes back before Ginny. There's been something going on with Thomas. He's been so preoccupied, so...distant. For a time, I even thought he was having an affair." A soft, bittersweet laugh. "How I wish he had been. I could have survived that much easier than this."

"This what, Bette? What's been going on?"

"I don't know. He won't tell me anything. There've been sudden trips into the city, phone calls late at night that leave him upset and...and frightened. And then Ginny's death. Rae, I'm afraid something terrible is going to happen."

And as if that hushed sentiment was a harbinger of things to come, the explosive sound of a shot punctuated it.

TWO

Nick hated the whole scene. Strong-arming wasn't his thing, not when a glib tongue and a big, white smile could get him where he was going. Where this was going was downhill fast, and he couldn't put on the brakes even if he knew how. For God's sake, the man was hosting a funeral in his home!

Zanlos had misled him, telling him it was Nick's show. The minute the curtain went up, Zanlos was center stage with his unique brand of silky intimidation.

Nick didn't like it, but what could he say? He was so new at Meeker, Murray & Zanlos that he hadn't even taken half of his shirts out of their packages. He wasn't keen on the idea of being shipped back to Baton Rouge because he'd failed to display the necessary aggressive attitude to get the job done.

The thought of that small, airless office over the local pharmacy on Carver Street was the prescription needed to cure his qualms about Zanlos's methods. Maybe he just didn't understand how things were done here in the Big Leagues. He needed to sit back and watch the master at work. Listen and learn, Marvin Meeker advised him on his first day. So he'd hang back and observe unless Kaz called him to the forefront. And he wouldn't let a little thing like scruples screw up the best opportunity ever to come his way. His last opportunity if he wasn't careful.

Adopting a solid but silent presence, he took one of the two chairs on the guest side of Grover's desk and waited for Zanlos to make his move.

Grover took the opposing chair. Nick was sure he'd put up an impressive front on most occasions. Grover was a big man with a big reputation behind him. As big and impressive as the Viet Nam mementos housed in a case on the wall behind him. Nick recognized the Purple Heart and Bronze Star from John Wayne movies. Those awards, as well as his personal ambition, had him in charge of one of the industrious leading competitors for government contracts. That didn't make Nick feel any better being a part of what was beginning to resemble a shakedown.

"Mr. Grover," Kaz began with the ripple of his South African accent that so perfectly conveyed both civility and menace. "By now you've had a chance to thoroughly research the offer, and I believe you are wise enough to realize that it will make you a very wealthy man. I know you value integrity above gain, and I believe we've been able to convince you that your honor will not be soiled by the association. I think we can make this marriage of convenience work."

"I've already been soiled by the association," came Grover's strained reply.

Kaz smiled wide, a flash of white, predatory teeth beneath those flat black, soulless eyes. "Then there is no need to protest before getting into bed, is there? I have come to you in good faith on more than one occasion. I have offered my hand, and you have refused to take it. You have hurt my feelings, Mr. Grover."

"Hurt your feelings?" Grover stared at him, astounded. "Why should I care about your feelings?"

"Because I am a man who holds a grudge, Mr. Grover. I think you have a clearer understanding of that now, do you not?"

Any color Grover may have had left in his face drained away. His uncompromising gaze weakened then swam with a backwash of unexpressed grief and horror. Before Nick sat a shell where a vibrant, heroic man had once resided. Unable to witness the complete destruction, he averted his eyes. He looked instead at the mementos sheltered on shelves of glass. Trophies, plaques, and pictures. He squinted at one in particular. At Grover between two teenage girls in formals. One was dazzling and sleek—obviously the father's daughter—and the other somber and...and the younger image of the woman he'd seen in the other room.

Then the conversation pulled him away from his study of Grover family history. Kaz was closing in for the kill.

"Now, one last time, I will extend my hand, and I will remind you of what still remains at stake and of how much you still have to lose beyond your precious integrity. I trust you will do the right thing and that you and I will enjoy a long and profitable relationship."

Nick glanced over in time to see the last spark of resistence crushed out beneath the grind of Zanlos's heel. Grover regarded them with a blank, broken expression. Kaz took silence for acquiescence.

"Very good. Mr. Flynn has the papers for your signature. That's all I require of you today. Just your name on a simple document, nothing more. Then we will leave you to return to your guests with our condolences."

A brief flash of emotion flared in the deadened gaze. Kaz didn't see it because he was reaching down for Nick's briefcase.

"Mr. Flynn, would you be good enough to see that Mr. Grover understands the terms of the contract before he signs his name? We would not want to take advantage in this time of mourning. That would be quite unprofessional and...unethical."

Forcing himself to act as that professional, Nick retrieved the contract he'd labored over for long nights to give birth to a document without a loophole, creating government sanction and impunity for an import company in his home state. He laid it out on the desk before the shattered businessman and readied to explain the fine print while Kaz sat back with a slight smile. Zanlos was too much the professional to gloat.

"We've added a protective addendum on page seven," Nick began, turning to that ironclad clause.

"Just a moment," Grover interrupted. His voice held a renewed tensile strength. "I need my glasses."

Grover reached into his desk drawer. Instead of a 20/40 prescription, came up with a snub-nosed .38.

Nick froze.

Beside him, Kaz looked momentarily startled from his smugness just before Grover pulled the trigger.

"No!"

Nick surged up from his chair, lunging across the desk in an effort to halt the concluding action. The report of the pistol echoed through his head even as he reared back from the dampness splattering his face.

"Son-of-a-bitch," Zanlos growled, jerking the papers away before they could be contaminated by Grover's defiant response.

Nick collapsed into his seat, staring at the ruin of the man before him. And as he sat, dazed and disbelieving, he watched Kaz stuff a pen into the limp fingers to scrawl out an obviously practiced signature on the final page. Then he returned the contract to Nick's briefcase and looked to him impatiently.

"Let's go. We got what we came for."

Nick had gotten much more than he'd bargained for.

What kind of firm was he working for?

He sat in the back of the plush limo not sure how he had gotten there except that they had exited through the patio slider even as the locked door to the room rumbled under pounding fists. Shock at what he'd seen, at what had been done, quaked through him.

On the seat next to him, Zanlos was carefully examining the pages of the contract for signs of the violence they'd left behind without a backward glance.

"Nick," he said conversationally without looking at him. "You have blood on your face."

Taking the white square from his employer, he blotted his cheeks and brow. His stomach did a slow somersault when the linen handkerchief came away splotched with crimson.

A man had died. And he'd just walked away.

It grew increasingly difficult for him to draw a decent breath.

Kaz opened the wet bar and poured a generous glass of bourbon, offering it with a "Here, this will make things go down a little easier."

Forgetting his pledge to abstain, Nick took the glass in

one hand, needing to stabilize it with the other. He took a big gulp then another, letting the conscience-soothing elixir burn down his throat on its way to his seething belly.

A man had died. And he'd just walked away.

It wasn't like it was the first time.

He shut his eyes, clutching the glass in both hands, letting Kaz fill it twice more as they rode in silence to the city. Kaz was right. Just what the doctor ordered. He let his mind go numb until they pulled up outside his hotel. There, Kaz regarded him with a satisfied smile.

"I'm going to take these and get them filed. You did good work, Nick. You've made us proud. That bonus check will be on your desk when you come in tomorrow morning. Get some rest. You look like hell."

He'd looked into hell, and he'd seen his own reservation.

He entered the elegant Wardman Park Hotel on auto-pilot, crossing the spacious lobby on his way to the piano bar area for the solace of a few more bourbons. Since he'd decided to backslide, he might as well enjoy the whole journey.

"Afternoon, Mr. Flynn," called the young black man at the concierge's desk. "How did your meeting go?"

Unconsciously, he stood a little straighter. "It went fine, James. Did you have any doubts?"

"Not a one, Mr. Flynn. You the man."

"I'm the man," he repeated with a flash of his cocky grin.

A drink in the smoky bar area lost all its appeal. He kept walking, past the big screen television where the Senators were up at the bottom of the fifth, forgoing his usual stop into the gift shop for a nice glass-tubed cigar and his copy of the *Wall Street Journal,* and down the long glass hall to the old section of the hotel to the exclusive bank of elevators that would take him to his upper floor. He rode alone, still numb from the shoulders up.

The wide hall was empty in the late afternoon hour. The only sound was the hum of a vacuum cleaner and the contagious thump of salsa music turned up loud enough for the maid to hear it over her sweeper. Nick went straight to his suite, sagging briefly against the door as it locked behind him.

A man had died . . .

He jerked off his tie and let it drop to the plush carpeting without a second thought. He paid housekeeping well to pick up after him. He was an important man with his mind on better things than worrying about hanging up his jacket before the expensive summer-weight wool wrinkled.

He slipped out of his coat and shoes, padding in his socks and shirtsleeves into the spacious bathroom. Stoppering the sink, he began running cold water, scooping it into the well of his palms and submerging his face into the icy reservoir.

And then he happened to glance up at his reflection in the mirror, his eyes making contact over the cup of his fingers. His gaze looked old and empty.

He looked closer, brows knitting in concentration.

There, just below his left ear, smeared along his jaw line was a smudge of Thomas Grover's blood.

He had only a second of rumbled warning, just enough time to lean over the porcelain bowl before all that unsettled bourbon came roaring up in a scorching diatribe.

The taste of success.

***

It was late.

Instead of stretching out beneath the canopy upstairs, lost to reminiscing, Rae sat stiff and still on the living room sofa. She'd been perched there for the past four hours watching the first patrolman on the scene, followed by EMTs, investigators and finally the coroner arrive and disappear into the back room. Bette sat beside her, sniffing occasionally as the powerful sedatives she'd been given finally kicked in enough to quiet her hysterical sobs. The invited guests had been interviewed by the uninvited ones, and now the former were gone. The quietly efficient hired staff took away the food no one had a taste for and were quickly collecting the padded folding chairs onto their rolling rack.

The gurney rolling from the front door toward the study woke Rae to action.

As she started to stand, Bette clutched at her.

"I'll be right back," Rae soothed, patting the desperate hands until their grip lessened. "I want to ask some questions."

Leaving Bette to her woeful sniffling, Rae strode down the hall, winding her way through the retreating detectives until faced with the zippered bag being wheeled out by the stony-faced coroner's crew.

Her eyes teared up briefly as her fingertips trailed along the heavy gage plastic, then her resolve firmed to a hardened purpose. She pushed through the gaggle of crime scene staff and into the study.

Even without the sight of Thomas Grover slumped back in his chair with the top of his head missing, the grisly scene made Rae pause. The glass trophy case doors would need a good cleaning, and the center one would need to be replaced.

"Ma'am, you shouldn't be in here," came a gentle, cautioning voice from beside her.

She glanced at the young officer whose finger-raked rock star blond hair and neon-colored silk shirt featuring a comic book hero contrasted with the badge suspended from a cord around his neck. His gaze was steeped in regret. A newcomer still capable of empathy.

"This is a crime scene," said another older man, obviously the one in charge from the way he elbowed his way over. "You'll disturb evidence."

"Not any more than the chorus line that's paraded through here in the last couple of hours." She reached into her handbag and displayed her own shield. "Any conclusions yet?"

"Death by his own hand. That was pretty much what was written on the wall."

"Detective Palmer," the younger man interjected quietly. "Ms. Borden is a friend of the family, so go a little easy."

Palmer brushed off his concern with a gruff, "I know who she is. I served with her father and with the deceased. I don't think Ms. Borden will be unduly shocked by anything I have to say, will you?"

The man had known her father. A small world. She was too focused to react with any surprise.

"Nothing I haven't heard before," came her weary reply. "You're saying suicide?"

"He just buried his only daughter. His wife states he's been on edge and not himself for weeks. The weapon was in his hand, and he was alone. All the other guests have been interviewed and their whereabouts verified."

Something clicked in her memory. "What about those two men?"

"Which two men?"

"I noticed them in the hall just before I went upstairs, and I saw a limo leaving right after I heard...the shot."

"You think they were with the victim?"

"I don't know. One was carrying a briefcase."

"Kind of a bad time to be conducting business."

Rae didn't argue.

"We didn't find an appointment calendar," the younger officer put in.

Rae returned to the living room, the two detectives trailing after her. She knelt down beside the grieving wife and step-mother.

"Bette, where did Tom keep his appointment book?"

She looked blank for a moment then said, "He kept all his business on the computer."

"Do you remember if he'd been scheduled to meet with someone today? I mean before Ginny's death?"

Her expression puckered slightly, then brightened. "Those lawyers. I think those lawyers were supposed to come. Thomas was upset because he'd tried to call and cancel and couldn't get hold of them."

Lawyers?

Rae returned to the study and bent over the computer, pausing before touching the keyboard.

"It's been dusted," the younger man told her. "His were the only prints."

Rae brought up the main screen, trying to ignore the pattern of red dots peppering the monitor. She opened his dayplanner and read aloud.

"Meeker, Murray & Zanlos. Are those lawyers?"

"Only the biggest firm in the D.C. area," the rumpled blond told her as if she should know that already.

"You need to check and see if they own a dark silver limo. If they do, they may have been the last to see Thomas Grover alive."

"Thank you, Ms. Borden. We'll take your suggestion under advisement."

"It's Detective Borden."

The young man touched her arm to confide, "I'll check."

She smiled faintly, grateful for his cooperative attitude. The other man just plain had attitude. She looked at Detective Palmer, trying to place him.

"You say you knew my father?"

"Well enough to know he took the same way out. Kind of ironic, don't you think?"

Refusing to be baited, she replied, "I think it's a waste. Will you keep me up to speed on the investigation? As a professional courtesy?"

Palmer had negative stamped on his lowered brow, but the rock star detective asked, "Where can we reach you with any news?"

"I'll be staying here."

The young man put out his hand. "Gabriel McGraw. Nice to meet you."

He had a good, firm grip.

"Under other circumstances," she concluded.

He nodded. He was just the sort Ginny would have flipped over, she thought sadly.

"Just don't get in the way, *Detective* Borden," Palmer warned. "We know how to do our job. We don't need outsiders stepping in to mess up the process."

So much for professional courtesy. She wouldn't mess things up. If she had her way, they'd never even know she was there.

Finally, there was just Bette and ©©her and the remnants of the longest day she could remember. Rae sat beside her, enfolding her easily in her embrace.

"I can't believe this has happened. What am I going to do?"

Funny. Hadn't Thomas Grover said the same thing to her

several hours earlier?

"You're going to get some rest, and then I'm going to help you with the arrangements."

Bette gazed at her through welling eyes. "I'm so glad you're here."

Rae would have rather been anywhere else than burying the only two people she loved in the world.

And as Rae tucked the exhausted widow into bed, she asked, "What kind of business was Thomas doing with lawyers?"

Bette sighed. "I'm not sure, dear. I didn't pay very much attention to business matters. I'm not much help, I'm afraid."

Rae smiled tightly. "That's all right."

"But I do know that Ginny introduced them. She was dating one of the lawyers. She was quite secretive about him, and I remember hoping it wasn't because he was married. Ginny didn't always have very good sense about those things."

"No, she didn't."

And no one had been there to protect her against those foolish mistakes. If only she'd been here....

But her being here hadn't kept Thomas from taking his life in despair.

An accident and a suicide.

A murder and a suicide.

A terrible sense of deja vú overwhelmed her.

"Thank you for staying, Rae," Bette Grover told her with a fragile gratitude. "I couldn't manage on my own."

"You won't have to. I'll take care of everything."

Starting with the lawyer boyfriend.

THREE

"So that was your vehicle seen leaving the Grover residence?"

"Have I denied it, Officer Stanton? I gave my statement to a Detective Palmer first thing this morning. Didn't you bother to read it?" Kaz Zanlos leaned back in his throne-like chair to regard the investigator with an amused impatience just shy of contempt. Not a great way to inspire trust in the local law enforcement community. Most had no sense of humor.

"We had scheduled a meeting with Thomas Grover several weeks earlier. We were merely keeping an appointment," Nick interjected with a non-threatening smile followed by just the right amount of regret in his sigh. "We didn't know there'd been a death in the family. No one had called to cancel the meeting. When I suggested we make it another time, Grover insisted we not put it off. It was just a formality. We just needed his signature, and then we left."

"Out the back door?" The officer arched a suspicious brow.

"We didn't want to intrude any further upon the family."

"And after you left?"

"I dropped Mr. Flynn off at his hotel, and I returned here to see the contract properly filed," Zanlos concluded. He shook his head sadly. "We didn't hear about Grover until that other policeman called this morning. Dreadful business."

"How did he act when you were with him?"

"He'd just come from his daughter's funeral." Kaz's tone implied, *You moron, how do you think he felt?* "He was distracted, but I didn't think particularly despondent. Not so that it would alert us to what he meant to do."

"So he signed your contract then blew his brains out. Good thing you were on time, or you would have been out how much money?"

Zanlos's brows lowered like a storm-slated sky. "I do not care for your insinuation, sir. There was nothing good about what happened. We were hoping for a long and prosperous association with Mr. Grover and his company. His death did not in any way please us. Is there anything else, Officer?"

Looking chagrined, the investigator flipped his notebook shut and stood. "No. That's everything I need. Thank you for your time."

Now that the interrogation was over, Kaz became more indulgent with his good will. He stood, waving a magnanimous hand, "It was the least we could do. Has a date been set for the funeral?"

"Tomorrow, I believe."

Kaz tsked. "Two funerals in one week. The poor widow. I must offer my condolences."

Something in the way he offered his sympathies made the hair creep along Nick's arms. He also stood and put out his hand to the policeman, shaking it firmly with a dry, steady grip before showing the man to the door. Once he was turned safely over to Kaz's secretary, Nick released an expressive breath.

"Very nicely played," Zanlos remarked, well pleased with the situation. "I knew you'd be an asset to this firm."

Not feeling rewarded by the congratulations, Nick offered a thin smile before voicing his misgivings. "Now what? With Grover dead, that leaves a lot of our plans hanging."

What he really needed to know was now that Grover was dead and the business in New Orleans was complete, was there any reason for them to keep him on?

Tenting his long, elegant hands in front of him, Kaz considered the problem for a moment. "Not necessarily. Control will go to Bette Grover and after two tragic losses, my guess is that she'll welcome some kindly offered guidance from one of her husband's friends. It's the least I can do."

A shudder trickled coldly down Nick's spine, but none of his distaste revealed itself upon his face. The bonus check was in his wallet...more money than he'd ever had at one time in his entire life. A check of that size could overcome the most distasteful of circumstances. At least that's what he was hoping once this uncharacteristic fit of conscience dissipated.

"Perhaps I'm being optimistic," Kaz mused, "but why don't you draw up power of attorney papers for Mrs. Grover to sign. No sense she trouble herself over the particulars of her husband's business at a time like this, eh, Nick?"

"Plan ahead, I always say."

Kaz made a thoughtful noise. "I wonder if Grover planned that little surprise for us, or if it was spur of the moment. If he'd wanted to keep his family and his fortune secure, he should have planned a little more carefully."

And then Nick said what had been on his mind since wiping the blood off his face in the car. "The Grover girl's death was just an accident, right?"

Kaz stared up at him through those black, fathomless eyes. His tone was steeped in sincerity. "A tragic yet timely accident. Unless your suddenly delicate sensibilities object, I think the occasion calls for a celebration. What do you say, Nick?"

"I'm just a party animal," was his dry response.

"I'd heard that about you."

The chill swept through Nick again. His boss's comment could have meant nothing...or everything.

"Tomorrow night," Zanlos decided. "After I take the poor Widow Grover out for dinner. Be ready at nine."

Ready, but not so terribly willing anymore, Nick nodded.

***

Noir de Nuit was open from dusk until dawn and open, as well, to anything a patron desired. Situated in the nightlife nexus of Georgetown, its open to the public basement dance club drew the college crowd while its proximity to the peaceful C & O Canal had it rubbing elbows with the sophistication of its members-only clientele gathering in its exclusive rooms upstairs. Elegantly upscale on the surface, with a pale underbelly of excess, it drew the prominent and jaded of D.C.

to its flame of discreet decadence, inviting them to beat their wings against the temptation of their choosing. The clientele was exclusive and powerful, and a policy of absolute privacy allowed them to roam and romp to the limits of their imagination and credit account. Music, food, dancing, gambling, women, drugs—all the favorite deadly sins under one tin-punched ceiling, between wood paneled walls if one could afford a membership.

In his present state, the booze appealed to Nick more than any of the other distractions. He left Kaz to a bevy of lovelies at the door and beelined for the wall-to-wall mahogany bar. A couple of bourbons would make this place go down better.

He wasn't sure what it was about the *Noir*. He was no choirboy, and pleasures of the flesh never provoked him to take the soapbox stance of a zealous Wednesday night deacon. But there was something about this place, these people, that put the hair up on the back of his neck. He recognized many of the politicians who were regulars and didn't care if they preached family values on the front pages then broke them all behind the thick velvet curtains that enveloped the dining nooks into private paradises. It was none of his business if they wanted to be seen with a gorgeous creature on their arm while they drank and lost money on cards and dice. And the women were spectacular. He'd never seen such a stable of stunning females. Each unique, each exquisite, each eager to please. Even though he wasn't a man of any particular influence or power, the women noticed him as all women noticed him and he probably could have gotten more than his share of on-the-house entertainments.

But the truth of it was, the *Noir* women gave him the creeps. They were too perfect, too good to be true. Too aggressively sexual and blatant in their appetites. Hungry. Yes. That described them. Hungry as wolves circling through plump fowl seeking whom they could devour. Not him, thank you very much. If he got a yen for companionship, he could tune in a ball game or flirt with a counter girl from the deli down the block. These man-eaters were out of his league, and he didn't mind admitting it.

Until he saw her.

The surprise of it stopped him dead in his tracks.

The woman from the Grover's house. How could he mistake those incredible green eyes?

He hadn't thought her particularly glamorous at their first meeting. At the Grovers's she'd looked like a long night on the Red-Eye. But here, under the muted pseudo-candle glow of the *Noir*, she sparkled like a jewel reflecting flame.

He hadn't remembered her as being particularly tall. Perhaps it was the dress, a sheath of liquid bronze cut to the navel and slit up to the hip bone, in combination with stiletto heels, or the unashamedly broad shoulders bared and equal to carrying any burden, or the blazing glory of her hair, teased up to the envy of any country singer and highlighted with a dusting of winking glitter. But despite the statuesque build, the eye-popping display of bosom, the legs that went on longer than most new television series and the glam clothes, there was a hint of vulnerability in the pale shade she'd chosen to shape the refined line of her lips, a fragility to the porcelain fairness of her skin even as it soothed over nicely defined muscle. And there was a glint of the dangerous in those constantly moving emerald eyes.

Here was a woman he wanted to know.

She saw him, and he watched her go through the same strange paralysis of the senses. She stared, scarcely breathing, finally moistening those pale pink lips with the tip of her tongue.

And though the clothes said it and this place said it, there was something about her that didn't say call girl for hire.

But that was for him to find out.

She didn't move as he approached nor did her gaze ever leave his, but locked solid as if in challenge. She did none of the usual body language things women did when he drew near—none of the subtle thrusting of the chest, sultry pouts or inviting droop to her thick lashes. She waited with a combative readiness. A Green Beret in a Givenchey gown.

His interest meter hovered at the breaking point.

"Hi."

"Hi, yourself."

Her voice was low, softness disguising steel.

"This isn't a pick up line, but we've met before. Not really met, I guess."

"At the Grovers. Yes, I remember you. Someone said you were a lawyer."

She'd asked about him. Heat flooded through his groin in an embarrassingly powerful surge. "Yes, I am. Nick Flynn. And you are?"

"Rae."

"As in Ray of Hope or Ray of Sunshine?" He gave her his best dazzling smile only to have it collide with the deflector shield of her indifference.

"Whatever."

"So," he continued, trying not to feel as flustered as a high school boy trying to score with an upperclassman, "what were you doing at the Grovers?"

"I wasn't working, if that's what you mean."

Her tart tone actually brought a flush to his cheeks. "That's not what I meant."

"I knew Ginny Grover. A long time ago. I was paying my respects. Did you know Ginny?"

"No."

She nodded slightly and seemed to run out of things to say. All sorts of things came to his mind, crazy things like "You drive me crazy," "I can't think straight when you look at me," and "What's a classy lady like you doing turning tricks?" Wisely, he spoke none of those things aloud.

Instead, he picked a safe alternative.

"Can I buy you a drink?"

"I don't drink."

"Anything?"

Her mouth quirked, holding back a smile. "Club soda."

"Wait right here. I'll get you one." And then they could talk about this thing...this whatever kind of chemistry thing that they had between them.

He went to the bar. As he started to order a bourbon for himself, he changed his mind, making it two club sodas with twists of lime. Like the lady, bubbles with a bite of sass.

Glasses in hand and anticipation percolating like the effervescent drinks, he turned. And went blank with dismay.

She was gone.

Normally, he would have felt like a fool to have been so easily brushed off, but with this woman, it was a sense of disappointment, a feeling of regret for what might have happened that made him go all flat inside.

Damn.

Rae, what?

He hadn't gotten her full name.

***

When she saw him, Rae knew his punch to the gut effect on her hadn't been a fluke or exaggerated over the past two sleepless nights. He was simply the most astounding man she'd ever seen—a dark, dashing cross between Gable and Grant, swarthy, sinfully gorgeous and sexy as hell. For a moment, she forgot to breathe.

Until she told herself that this man might have been involved in Ginny's murder.

She wasn't thinking accident anymore. Not since Thomas Grover had taken his own life. Sorrow wouldn't have made Grover pull that trigger. But guilt would.

It had something to do with the slick, high-powered lawyers who were the last to see her surrogate father alive. What kind of deal had gone down behind those closed doors? Had Ginny served as an example of what would happen if compliance wasn't obediently given? Had Tom been involved in a shady deal gone sour and, when he tried to pull out, Ginny was sacrificed as his punishment?

Who were these two men?

One of them had been having an affair with Ginny.

She'd gotten that much out of the girls at the accountant firm were she'd worked. Dark and exotic, they'd told her, Ginny's mystery man of no name. She'd introduced the law firm of Meeker, Murray & Zanlos to her father, and what a price she'd had to pay for that association.

Rae had done some snooping. Dark and exotic. Marvin

Meeker was retirement age, balding and soft around the middle. The Murray part of the firm was female and was said to be working in offices overseas. That left Kazmir Zanlos, the third partner, who was sleek, deeply tanned and South African. And Nicholas Flynn, equally dark and delicious, from the sultry heat of Louisiana. The rest of the firm's employees were women or didn't fit the profile.

Zanlos or Flynn. One of them had romanced a naive Ginny Grover to get close to her father's business. She'd learned that Zanlos had a quiet partnership in the classy night club *Noir de Nuit* that catered to kids below and passed out call girls above, and she'd paid one of the D.C. patrolmen a healthy sum to call her the minute he or Flynn showed up there. She wanted to get an up close and personal look at them without them knowing she was doing the looking. When the call came stating both were expected in house that evening, she was on scene, dressed for sin to catch a sinner. She'd slipped inside the private club by dazzling some myopic congressman with her attention. Once past the doors, she'd hoped to escape notice by pretending to be a visiting member of the same sisterhood as the ladies plying their age-old trade inside. But as she drew their curious then territorial looks, she realized she'd have to work fast to find out which one of the handsome lawyers had manipulated Ginny to her death.

And when she saw him across the room, all dark and debonair, she knew she didn't want it to be Nicholas Flynn.

Okay, so his approach wasn't terribly unique, but it was delivered with style and sizzling charisma. She could have lost herself for days in the dark liquid of his stare – like black satin sheets. She liked that he maintained eye contact when most men would have been delving down her cleavage. And she liked his voice, a silky drawl on the surface with the rough cut of whiskey sluicing underneath. He made a woman think of those sheets all rumpled the morning after with him still between them. And that wasn't the way she usually thought about men at first sight.

Rae got the feeling that she might have to look pretty hard to find a reason to dislike Nick Flynn.

Unless, of course, he'd arranged for her best friend and her friend's father to die.

As much as she wanted the combustible meeting to go on indefinitely, the second he denied knowing Ginny, she forced herself to abandon the unlikely fascination.

She believed him about not knowing Ginny. When men told a lie, they usually said more than they had to in order to appear innocent. Flynn's simple "No" told her all she needed to know for the moment.

Kaz Zanlos was the one she was after.

She sent Flynn for drinks and ditched him. From the shadowed fringe of the crowd, she couldn't pretend his wounded surprise at finding her gone didn't nudge a chord of regret.

Another time, Nick Flynn. But not tonight.

She found a secluded alcove from which to watch Zanlos without being observed. And as she followed his trail of seductive overtures from one flustered woman to the next, a granite block of loathing massed within her breast. Slick described Kaz Zanlos. Good looking in a dangerous, pirate-like way, with his dark complexion, piercing black eyes and regally hooked nose, he had an agelessness about him, though she guessed him to be in his forties. If Flynn was a dashing Mark Anthony, Zanlos was a hawklike Caesar. While he had none of Flynn's spontaneous charm, Zanlos exuded an air of inescapable conquest and control. There was nothing playful or flattering about his agenda. She didn't even think it was the sex as much as it was the power that he was after. He liked being in charge, dominating weaker wills with a cold effortlessness that was truly frightening.

Just the kind of man that made her blood run icy.

Ginny hadn't stood a chance.

And from the looks of things at Thomas's funeral that afternoon, neither would Bette.

After Ginny's drizzly sendoff, her father's burial was awash with sunlight and fragrant breezes. Arlington, always an emotional sight with its endless white markers and aura of heroism, embraced Thomas Grover in a way it hadn't her own father. Both had died at their own hands, but Frederick Borden's sins went far beyond that last selfish act earning him, instead of a triumphant exit, a coward's burial, alone and unmourned in a small, insignificant plot in an unremarkable suburb.

Thomas Grover exited with pomp and circumstance. He would have enjoyed it. He'd loved serving his country, both in its foreign confrontation and at the helm of government contracts. And he'd loved his family even more.

Rae didn't weep as the final words were read. She supported a sobbing, black-shrouded Bette Grover and stared suspiciously at the handsome lawyer who watched the two of them from the other side of the open grave. Inevitably, he approached them to offer somber condolences and then, somehow, it was his arm about Bette Grover and his comfort she leaned upon. Smooth operator didn't even come close.

He'd taken her out to dinner. The invitation had been extended to Rae, but she was no fool. And she knew she wouldn't be welcome as a third wheel.

Bette Grover didn't know how to survive without a man in her life. She was the perfect hostess, an exemplary helpmate but she hadn't a clue how to function on her own. She clung to Kaz Zanlos like a drowning woman to a life preserver, swept away by the attentive flattery of the younger man. And Rae had to wonder why the man offered to keep her afloat.

So she'd called in favors back in Detroit after finding no help at the local level. To her dismay and disappointment, she discovered the D.C. police had already marked both cases "Case Closed." Her inquiries met with a solid wall of resistence. She faxed one of the women in the Metro records department who'd taken her self-defense class. The woman swore to repay her after the techniques she'd learned stopped a car jacker cold. In minutes, the information came humming across the lines, and Rae learned everything there was to know about the elegant South African while he was out wining and winning over the not-so-distraught-any-longer widow. She'd discovered he had left his homeland under a cloud of suspicion and disgrace just a step ahead of the law. And he'd quickly reestablished himself in the same illicit and most likely illegal doings here in Washington. Everyone knew it, but no one could prove it.

Having had no sleep for three days and reeling with the

one-two punch of loss, Rae, unlike the D.C. police, didn't need proof to know the truth. Kaz Zanlos was responsible for taking her loved ones cruelly away. And for that, he would pay.

She waited for her opportunity and was rewarded at last. Alone, he left the merriment, heading down a long, dimly lit corridor toward the rest rooms. And Rae followed. She waited until he went inside and for two other men to exit. Then, after surveying the surroundings and finding them all clear, she reached for the thigh holster, for the small but still deadly caliber pistol strapped where it wouldn't ruin the sleek line of her gown. With the comforting weight of retribution in her hand, she pushed the door open just far enough to see inside.

Kaz Zanlos stood at the sinks, rearranging his tie as he hummed a Broadway tune. He looked like a man who was confident in his control of his circumstances.

Rae thumbed the safety off.

He was wrong.

Just as she started to shove open the door to confront the man who'd destroyed her only claim to family, a hand clamped over her mouth to silence any outcry. A strong arm banded her waist, lifting her bodily, turning her into the hall and away from the image of Zanlos primping in the mirror, totally unaware of what had almost happened.

Rae struggled. She didn't wriggle ineffectively the way most women would when grabbed by an attacker. She knew how to fight back. But this enemy seemed to anticipate and evade her every move as he carried her easily down the hall and out the fire door into the darkness of an alley. There, he released her, and she spun about, all clenched fists and fury.

To face an empty street.

Perplexed, she did a full circle, only to find herself alone.

What the – ?

"Forgive me if I hurt you."

The quiet words were spoken right behind her where a fraction of a second ago no one had been standing. She turned, too alarmed and surprised to offer resistance. As it happened, she had nothing to defend against. The man she confronted was not an enemy.

And then he offered a startling proposition.

"If you want to get Kazmir Zanlos, I can show you a better way."

FOUR

They rode into the night and, after a while, Rae was too tired to try to figure out where they were. South. Towards Alexandria, was her guess.

Looking even more like a rock star in his studded leather coat and dark glasses after dark, Gabriel McGraw offered little in the way of conversation. He responded succinctly to her questions.

"Are you really a policeman?"

She caught his small smile.

"For longer than you know."

"Where are we going?"

"That's not important."

"What were you doing there tonight?"

"Keeping you out of trouble."

"Why?"

He glanced at her briefly. "Because I was told to." His grin flashed mega-watt bright. "And because I like you."

"It's good to have friends." She leaned back into the all too comfortable rolled and tucked seat of the big old Mercury convertible he drove. She didn't know street rods. She guessed this one had at least twenty years on her in age, but it rode like a dream. She should have so much class when she was an old dame.

"Let me ask you one?"

She didn't open her eyes. "What's that?"

"Would you have killed him?"

Her smile was Mona Lisa mysterious. "I guess that's not important now, either."

He chuckled softly, and that was the last of their

conversation.

Sapped of energy from fatigue and the adrenalin ebb, Rae wondered herself if she would have pulled the trigger. Had she planned to burst into that restroom to force a confession, or to end a life? She wasn't sure. Now that the intensity of the moment's emotion was over, her actions surprised her. How had anger and frustration so quickly gained the upper hand? Usually, her level-headedness and self-control were legendary.

But no one had snatched her stability away before...or at least, not for a very long time.

She must have dozed off because the gentle jerk of the hot rod coming to a stop brought her up in the seat. It was too dark to get a fix on their location. She got the sense of a building, and she could smell the waters of the Potomac. Then Gabriel was opening the door for her, leaning down to help hoist her from the low-slung seat. Standing on the wharf with the chill seeping in off the river, she realized how much of her was left bare to the night breeze and to her escort's scrutiny. But thankfully, he appeared disinterested in her state of undress. Now that they'd reach their destination, his mood became one of focused intensity.

"This way. And watch your step."

He glanced at her, and for an instant what little light there was outside on the uncomfortably cloying evening flashed across his gaze turning his eyes a sudden, incandescent silver. An unnatural fire burned behind them.

Before the shock could settle, he turned away.

Just fatigue. Rae shook off what she'd seen as a play of imagination before following him toward the warehouse. She asked no questions, intuiting that no answers would be given. At least, not from him.

Her footsteps echoed through the large empty storage space, a tap tap tap of needle-sharp heels on concrete. Oddly, his boot heels made no sound at all as he led the way toward the back of the building. A chill took her. Just the scanty dress and the night air, she told herself. But deep down, she knew it was more than that. She responded instinctively to the aura of danger. Her senses sharpened, reached outward for evidence of threat. Her muscles bunched and readied as she continued toward she knew not what.

Gabriel opened a door at the back of the warehouse. Muted light pooled out, illuminating him, haloing his spiky blond hair, basking his lean figure like some hallowed gatekeeper opening the way to the beyond. Beyond what? She wouldn't know until she stepped across the threshold. He moved back, giving her room to go ahead of him. She proceeded with caution into what appeared to be an office with desk, filing cabinets and a big leather couch. One wall of windows was shuttered off from the view by tightly closed blinds. Inside the room was uncomfortably hot, airless.

"Ah, Miss Borden, good evening."

The deep, lightly accented voice greeted her from the shadows. The accent was French, and the speaker unknown to her.

"It's been a long day. I haven't slept for over thirty-six hours. Cut the pleasantries and get to the point. Why have I been brought here?"

"She speaks her mind, Gabriel. Not unlike my daughter. But is it bravery or foolish bravado? That we need to discover."

Her host stepped into the light of the room. He was dark and strong of build, broad shoulders straining the bulky knit of his sweater. Why wasn't he perspiring in the heavy garment within the pressure-cooker hot room? Then she forgot about his wardrobe as his gaze affixed hers. His eyes were black yet bright with some inner light that glimmered just there behind his stare. Like Gabriel's when he'd turned to her in the doorway. Strange, compelling eyes. She couldn't look away.

"My name is Marchand LaValois. You will not know it and others will not recognize it. I have been careful to keep my anonymity. Please sit down, Miss Borden."

She sidled over to the couch on her treacherously high heels and sat, keeping a cautious eye on LaValois and upon Gabriel who still lingered at the door, a silent sentinel. "What do you want with me?"

"Such directness. I like that." LaValois perched on the corner of the desk, posture relaxed, but Rae felt a pulse of constant movement and energy from him. As if this composed mien was for her benefit alone. "I had Gabriel bring you here because we could not be of help to one another if you were in jail for shooting Zanlos tonight."

She felt her jaw drop. *How did he know?*

"How did you know?"

"Gabriel told me."

But when had Gabriel had time to do that? She hadn't seen or heard him make a call. Perhaps while she was out of it in the thrall of that unnaturally heavy and sudden slumber. "Why should you care what happens to me? I don't know you."

"True. But I know you. Raelene Borden, 34, lives alone, prefers to work alone, unmarried, unattached and apparently uninterested."

"What is this, the dating game?"

"You enjoy kickboxing, you like to read Haiku and hard-boiled detective fiction, you're rated a marksman with a pistol and expert with a rifle."

"I make a mean chocolate trifle, I like squirrels, walks on the beach and men who aren't afraid to say they're sorry— preferably before they smack you."

LaValois continued, ignoring her tart remark. "You got interested in police work while teaching self-defense at a local women's shelter. You worked domestic assaults, until you sent a battering husband to the ER with three broken ribs and a concussion."

"If I'd sent him to the morgue, he wouldn't have smashed his wife's collarbone with an aluminum bat three weeks later." Her bitterness over that episode still prickled in her tone. Where was all this going?

"After you got off suspension because no charges were filed, you were put into vice."

"A nice place to meet men you're interested in dating."

"Your colleagues don't want to work with you because you won't let go of something once you start. It becomes a personal vendetta." He tented his hands and regarded her over them thoughtfully until she wondered what sort of assumptions he was forming. She didn't feel like making any explanations in her own defense. Then he surprised her by saying, "We are strangers to one another, Ms. Borden, but friends of the same cause."

"What cause?" Her tone relayed her caution. "Revenge?"

Marchand smiled narrowly. "Revenge and justice. A satisfying combination when taken together. But the first can be self-destructive if pursued alone." He sighed somewhat sadly. "I have seen your record. It speaks of valor and distinction, yet you were ready to throw it all away by acting against the system you believe in. Why is that? The first time, I can understand considering your past."

Rae tensed, ready to strike out verbally or on foot if he pursued that path. Again, he threw her off balance.

"You are a fine officer, Ms. Borden, who can't abide a wrong being done once it's brought to your attention. But with Zanlos, you have no evidence to prove the man has committed any crime."

"I didn't need any. But then no court would arrest or convict on my gut instinct, would they?" Her reply was flat and factual. "Kazmir Zanlos killed my best friend and her father."

"Probably. Or had it done."

"And you're saying I should do nothing about it?"

A low chuckle. "Oh, no. That's not what I'm saying at all. Men like Zanlos deserve what they get."

"Then why did you stop me tonight?"

"Because you do not deserve what you would get if you pulled that trigger. Haven't you heard the expression 'Revenge is a dish best served cold'?"

"While I wait for it to cool, he gets away with what he's done."

"And that injustice infuriates you, does it?"

"Yes."

"Good. Then let me help you do something about it."

She did a quick top-to-toe assessment of him. "You're not a cop."

"You are right. I am not the law. The law can be bought

and paid for by a man like Zanlos, which is why he has escaped it so many times before. I have been a soldier, and I have always served the rights of mankind—at first on my own and then with the assistance of a chosen few. That number has grown as the crimes against mankind have grown."

"You're vigilantes."

"Nothing quite so mundane as that. We adhere to laws. Those of our kind."

She glanced between him and Gabriel. "And what kind are you? Some sort of paramilitary group? Are you working for the government?"

"Some factions of the government are not unaware of us."

They were covert-ops. But what were they doing working on U.S. soil? Rae knew she had to tread carefully. These people could often be more dangerous than those they pursued for reasons not always sanctioned by the law.

"Are you after Zanlos?"

"No."

"Then we have nothing in common, and I'd like to go." She didn't have time to be drawn into some spook operation. She had her own agenda to attend.

"No. Not directly," Marchand clarified. "But he works in conjunction with the one we are after, and striking at one may well bring both down."

Rae leaned back into the couch's obliging cushions. "I'm listening."

"You are a smart girl. But are you ready to step into a danger so great you may not survive?"

"Zanlos murdered what was left of all that I held dear. Surviving without them isn't as important as punishing the one responsible for taking them away."

He studied her, and she could see he was impressed with her words. Yet she intuited he was a man one had to impress with actions.

"Going after Zanlos tonight was stupid," she admitted at last. "I know that now. If you have a better way, I'll listen."

"*Bien.* Tell me what you know of Zanlos."

"He's a partner in a very high profile legal firm that handles contract law. He has the reputation of being someone who makes things happen."

"And how do you think he makes those things happen?"

"By hook or by crook, Mr. LaValois. Mostly by crook. I think he intimidated Thomas Grover into signing a government contract just before he died. I think he arranged the death of my friend and now is courting Grover's widow to seal the deal. I think he makes things happen by being unscrupulous and too clever to be caught."

"Not clever enough, if you and I know what he is. And you and I can stop him if we are prepared to be equally unscrupulous and clever. You say you want justice, Miss Borden. What are you prepared to do to see it done?"

"Anything."

"Anything within the limits of the law?"

She returned his somber gaze with an unblinking intensity. "Anything within the limits of my ability."

Where was the law when I attended two funerals in one week?

As she sat in Marchand LaValois's office, she purposefully, intentionally turned her back on all the things that motivated her career. Things like honor and duty and right and law. Those things meant nothing now because they meant nothing to a man like Zanlos, and she couldn't bring him down unless she played by his rules. And that meant surrendering herself to darkness.

She didn't know this man LaValois any more than she knew his servant, Gabriel McGraw. But she knew people, and she knew this was a man she could trust.

"What can I do for you?"

"Get on the inside of the *Noir de Nuit*. Move where we can't go."

"But I'm a policewoman. They'll know who I am."

"Not if we cover your tracks well. And believe me, we are experts in that area."

"What's on the inside?"

"Let me tell you what I know, and then tell me if we can work together."

"Tell me."

***

"What do you think of her, my love?"

Nicole LaValois curled into her husband's embrace upon their big, satin-covered bed as the dawn brightened in a world they would never see again. "I think she's angry and in pain."

"Can she be trusted?"

"I feel a strong sense of honor in her. She reminds me of our Frederica."

He sighed as her head pillowed upon his shoulder. "I was thinking the same thing. Am I wrong to send her against an enemy she doesn't understand?"

"What could you tell her that she would believe? Besides, she won't be alone. There are those on the inside to protect and watch out for her. But she's not the one I fear for. She's not the only one who stands to lose much by being kept in the dark."

"We've discussed this, Nicole. It is not our affair, not our family."

"It's like family to me, Marchand. Someone should tell him the truth and let him make up his own mind instead of forcing him to become a pawn to those of us who think we know what's in his best interest."

"We do, Nicole. The less he knows, the better. Considering what we know of *his* character, what do you think his choice would be?"

"That's unfair and unlike you. What really has you so worried?"

He hugged her tightly so that she could feel the tension vibrate through him. "Being this close to that demon. Have you forgotten?"

Her touch was gentle in its stroke along the side of his face, but her tone was tempered steel. "I've neither forgotten nor forgiven. You were right. The time has come to put an end to it. And if this Borden woman can be used as the tool of that destruction, I say use her."

Marchand caught his wife's hand and pressed a firm kiss upon its smooth, ageless palm. "How fierce you sound."

"When those I love are involved. I am tired of living with this ever-present threat hanging over them. If we strike now, much of the evil that's been done will lose focus and fall away."

"That's my hope. But promise me, my love, that you won't interfere." At her silence, he prodded, "Promise you will not go to Gerard. That would only bring him into the fray, and with his habit of recklessness and uncertain loyalties, we will lose our only chance to finally be rid of her. I've been a soldier all my life. I weary of the fighting."

"I give you my promise not to seek out my old friend. Make this your last battle, my love. Then the only skirmishes you'll have are those with me."

He rolled abruptly so that he was above her. "Ah, but those are the battles I enjoy."

"When you win them," she teased as her gaze invited an engagement.

"Win or lose, the result is sweet."

And he went on to prove it.

***

Rae had listened to Marchand LaValois until nearly dawn. Then, their bargain made, Gabriel drove her back to the Grover country home, speeding recklessly along the dark, empty roads to deposit her at the door. Sensing his hurry, she let herself out. As she shut the door, he leaned over to call, "Be careful, and don't pull your gun on anyone unless I'm there to watch your back."

Rae smiled wryly and flashed him a salute then stepped back quickly as his tires threw gravel in their bid for traction. After his taillights disappeared, there was nothing left for her to do but enter the silent house where memories waited like restless spirits to haunt her mind and torment her soul. They swarmed her, stinging with barbs of regret as she finally lay back beneath the canopy in the hug of a comfortable tee shirt.

Why had she stayed away for so long? Why had she allowed pride and her own painful past to separate her from those she loved?

And now it was too late to amend those mistakes. Now she would have to find a way to live with them, unresolved and aching within her heart.

And she would have to trust a stranger in order to see they rested with the peace of the vindicated.

She closed her eyes, trying to summon sleep, but her mind spun at a frantic pace refusing to be still. Within a few hours, the game would begin in earnest, and knowing that had her both anxious and anticipating. She didn't like the idea of using an innocent in the trap to bait Zanlos, but if Nick Flynn was working for him, how innocent could he be? He had been there minutes before Thomas Grover ended his life. He was privy to whatever drove that good and decent man over the edge and beyond redemption. And for that knowledge he would pay, as Zanlos would pay.

And she would do whatever was necessary to collect upon that debt. To the limit of her ability, she'd told Marchand LaValois, the intense Frenchman who may or may not be using her as well. She didn't care about that as long as Zanlos fell in their quest to get the party LaValois was after. Whatever means to the justified end.

To the limit of her ability. To the limit of her soul.

To the limit of her life.

FIVE

What had he gotten himself into?

The bourbon in his hand was the only thing strong enough to take that relentless question away.

He'd had one or two too many. He could tell by the way the pleasant numbness spread from his fingertips toward his brain. Good. That was good. Soon he'd be able to go up to his room and sleep without dreams. As it was, he could almost lift his gaze to meet his reflection in the mirror behind the bar without a spear of guilt and regret taking him to the heart. Almost. As he stared into the somber face, the jab was now a manageable twinge. And once he finished his drink, he wouldn't notice it at all.

He took a deep pull from his glass as his gaze tracked movement in the room behind him. The bourbon sat warm and tingling upon his tongue for a long moment.

It couldn't be.

Rae.

Even the overabundance of alcohol couldn't mute the effect those long, lean legs had upon him.

He finished his drink with a hasty, choking swallow and watched her in the mirror. A finger of unexpected jealousy crooked about his insides and jerked hard.

Who was she here to meet? That question gnawed at him.

He should have been asking himself why he'd care, but that logic never formed into a defense against the longing swelling within his soul. Not a yearning for sex, though the mere idea had him quickening with heat and anticipation. The mere sight of her made him yearn for something missing, something much more complex than an easily obtained physical relief. The relief he sought was on a more esoteric plane, and why he thought he could find even a piece of it with a high price call girl would have amazed him if the need wasn't powerful enough to engulf all common sense.

Or perhaps that was the bourbon talking.

The memory of her in the molten evening gown had delighted his imagination all day, keeping the mounting uneasiness about his job at bay. Now, here was the real deal more conservatively clad in a business suit. Some business. The turquoise jacket was cut in dramatic lines—big shoulders, nipped in at the waist and flaring over curvy hips, with low, overlapping lapels that displayed sheer lace over pale skin. A brief, snug skirt left miles of leg adorned in silvery colored silk. And shoes of the same bold, Carribean-waters blue boosted her height a good three stilt-like inches. A fever broke hot upon his brow. He didn't exhale until she wove out of sight behind the booth petition.

Disappointment and loss hit like a punch to the solar plexus.

If he were to take a quick peek around that paneled divider and find that she was alone, would he be setting himself up for another one of her ego-sapping rejections?

Tonight, on this lonely night, he deemed it worth the risk.

Leaving a large tip on the bar, he straightened his tie and tried to summon up his usual swagger. No need to look too desperately pathetic. Finally satisfied with the rather dashing gentleman he saw in the glass, Nick took a fortifying breath. Grateful that his steps were steady, he took a turn about that petition, hoping for a miracle.

His night for miracles.

She was alone in a back booth, staring idly out the window into the hotel's circle drive. But alone didn't mean available. She glanced up when he stopped at her table.

"Hi."

"Hello, again, Mr. Flynn."

She remembered. Crazy sensations did handsprings within his chest. He felt fifteen years old again.

"Expecting someone?"

"Not any more. I had an appointment cancel at the last minute, so I thought I'd grab a quick drink before grabbing a cab."

"I thought you didn't drink."

"Mineral water. Good for the skin."

"Oh."

He just stood there, floundering. Nick Flynn the lady killer, smiling like a fool with no amusing sentiments surfacing to save him.

Then she threw him a line.

"Would you like to sit down?"

"If it's not an intrusion."

She shrugged, the movement elegant and unintentionally sexy the way it made the front of her jacket gap, letting him glimpse the plump orbs of her breasts through the wispy lace. Or perhaps very intentional.

She wasn't wearing a bra.

He dropped onto the booth seat like a sack of cement.

"What are you doing here alone at this time of night?" she asked.

"I live here."

"In the bar?"

"Upstairs. I have a suite."

"You live in a hotel? Not much for permanence, are you?"

"It's just temporary. I just started a job a little over a month ago."

"Not sure it's going to work out?"

Talk about getting right to the heart of the matter. He fought not to grimace.

"Probationary period."

"You with them or them with you?"

"Both, I guess. And how about you?"

"Just in for Ginny's funeral."

"Oh." How dejected he sounded with that one single syllable.

"But I like it here. I might stay if I could find decent work."

"What can you do?"

"I'm...versatile. Just don't ask me to type. Not that I've

had many prospective employers sit me down at a keyboard."
The slightly cynical curl to her smile made him laugh. It was
the first time he'd laughed...since he'd come to D.C. It felt
cathartic.

"I promise I won't ask you to do dictation."

His hand found hers almost by accident on the tabletop.
His fingertips slid over the backs of hers, then lingered,
intrigued by the soft warmth of her skin. She didn't draw away.

"What would you ask me to do, Nick?" That quiet question
steeped with steamy innuendo.

His touch glided over her knuckles, stroking down her
thumb to slip under her palm, tracing the delicate whorls of
life and love fate had etched upon it.

"Nothing you didn't want to do."

Here it was, her chance to ditch and run or plunge boldly
ahead.

Rae was silent for a long minute, studying the man across
from her. He'd been in the bar awhile. She could smell the
bourbon, but it didn't seem to affect his coordination or smooth
speech. Nor did it put her on the instant defensive the way it
usually did. She was sure with his spectacular looks and boyish
grin that he had no problem picking up women but with her,
he seemed oddly uncertain despite his confident approach.
There was nothing practiced in his come-on. Nothing jaded
or expectant in his posture. His eyes convinced her. That direct
contact, staring straight into hers with a flattering interest. No
nonsense. Just like his conclusion.

Nothing she didn't want to do.

Her fingers closed about his. Nice hands, strong,
surprisingly burred from physical activity, and sensitive in
the way his fingers meshed through hers. Not possessive or
demonstrative but with a light, confirming pressure.

"Let's get out of here."

The minute she said the words, consequence dug in its
heels. She'd just said yes to sex with a stranger, or at least to
the opportunity for it to happen. She rarely said yes to sex
with men she'd known for ages.

Yet when Nick Flynn slid out of the booth, her hand still

cradled within his, she followed.

He guided her with the touch of his fingertips at the small of her back. No groping, no grabbing, just that light connection. Anything more might have sent her running. Her heart beat wildly. Her breathing quivered as much from excitement as anxiety.

Nick Flynn was exciting. Just the thought of where their walk might lead had her emotions rocking on a tightwire of nervousness. She was in control. She clung to that knowledge. Nick might promise nothing she didn't want, but if he tried to force more upon her, she was more than capable of saying no in many different—and some quite painful—ways. If she didn't think she could handle herself, she wouldn't have said yes to LaValois's suggestion. She wouldn't be here coaxing a strange man to his room.

But as Marchand had said, Nick Flynn was the weak link to getting where they needed to be to both get what they wanted. And right now was the time and the place because the handsome lawyer wanted her enough not to ask any questions. And she was just jazzed enough by the simmering tension between them to carry through on the plan.

Nothing she didn't like.

She canted a look at his dark, patrician profile. Could she trust him to keep that promise?

It was a long walk to the elevators. His suite was in the old section of the hotel, separated by a glass hallway studded with a scattering of antiques and replications. A ritzy place. He must have been pulling down pretty darn good pay to put himself up in such style. With his tailored Armanis and manicured hands, despite their sexy roughness, she couldn't exactly picture him in a motor lodge. This was bachelor nirvana—elegant, hedonistic yet with no commitment. Was that the kind of man he was? She wasn't sure she didn't lean more toward the motor lodge type.

He rang for the elevator that seemed to be waiting just for his call. The doors slid open, and Rae knew once she stepped inside everything about her life and her self-image would change.

She crossed the threshold boldly and waited for the doors to close upon her decision.

As the car vibrated upward, they stood side by side, more like strangers sharing the ride than soon to be lovers sharing much, much more.

"Rae, what?"

"Excuse me?" She glanced at him, but he was watching the ascending numbers above the door.

"Your last name."

"Just Rae."

He looked at her then. "How am I supposed to find a 'Just Rae' in the greater D.C. area when I want to see her again?"

She just smiled until he got the idea.

"Oh." He managed a deprecating chuckle. "I guess I deserved that. It's not like we're developing a lifelong relationship here. Is it?"

"What do you want it to be, Nick?"

This time his laugh was a tad strained. "I guess we'll have to wait and see."

Yes, they would.

And thankfully he shut up until the door opened to his floor.

He steered her down the twists and turns, his hand on her elbow, a bit more aggressive but far from demanding. She felt herself tensing with each step. She didn't have to be here, doing this. Getting to know Nick Flynn could have ended at that bar downstairs.

But this was the more direct, more certain way to convince him that she was what she pretended to be.

"Here we go."

She noted the brass numbers on the door, waiting with knees locked to keep them from trembling as he used his key card to open the way to no going back.

The room was dark, smelling of recent maid service and recycled air. Before turning on the light, Nick crossed the long living area to open the French doors that led out onto a decent-sized balcony. Rae was drawn to the sight of him silhouetted against the night sky, to where he breathed in its sultry, perfumed air as he leaned upon the wrought iron rail.

Giving her time to make the first move.

She joined him.

"This is nice."

"One of the perks of the job."

If she'd had time, she would have spent it trying to decipher the interesting bite to his words.

"The firm pays for your room?"

"Yes. They brought me up here from Baton Rouge to take care of some contract work for them. Louisiana still uses the old Napoleonic codes of law that their own lawyers aren't licensed to handle. But by the same token, I can't practice here without applying to the Bar. If the firm likes my work well enough, they'll take care of that hurdle for me. Consider this an engagement period."

"They're very generous in their engagement presents. You must be very good at what you do."

"I try to be very good at everything I do."

She thought she was ready, but when he turned toward her, smelling of bourbon, his expression sharp with desire, she froze. Paralyzed with panic, she lost herself in the smoldering darkness of his stare coming closer, closer as he lowered toward her. Her breathing stopped. Then he stopped.

"I owe you a drink."

He'd been ready to kiss her. The sudden statement threw her off guard. She blinked and tried to regroup.

"What?"

"At the *Noir* the other night. I went for drinks and you disappeared."

"Oh. I'm sorry about that."

He waited to see if she'd offer more in way of an explanation. When she didn't, he smiled thinly. "I think I've got some club soda around here someplace."

He left her there on the balcony to berate herself.

Coward, coward. Why had she come up with him if she couldn't go through with the plan? How was she going to convince him of what she was supposed to be if she got a deer-in-the-headlights look every time he got personal.

It wasn't personal. She had to remember that. It wasn't personal. It was for Ginny and Thomas Grover.

But even as she followed him toward the kitchen area, she found herself wondering what his kiss would be like. He had the confident look of a good kisser. If only she could relax and get past the taste of liquor on his breath.

He found that bottle of soda and placed it on the kitchen bar next to the ice tray and two glasses. But he hesitated before pouring. With the bar between them, she felt some of her own confidence returning. Enough to slip off her jacket and give it a casual toss over the back of the nearest chair. She knew there was nothing subtle or concealing about the cream-colored stretch lace camisole she wore, but instead of staring through its delicate patterned sworls to find the pucker of her nipples, he stared straight into her eyes.

A long second passed.

"You don't want to be here, do you?"

Taken aback, she asked, "Why would you say that?"

"Ever since the elevator you've had the look of the condemned about you. I'd hoped . . ." He reached out then, his fingertips grazing the curve of her cheek in a slow, sensory sweep. "I'd hoped you'd want to stay."

His caress ended at the side of her throat where he could test her galloping pulse and ride her bucking swallow.

"Why?"

Just for the sex? was what she didn't add but really meant.

"Because you're the first person I've met since coming here that I've made a connection with. And I'd hoped–" He broke off, his hand dropping away. When she continued to stare at him, saying nothing, he smiled regretfully. "I'll call you a cab."

The exquisite vulnerability in that honest claim broke through Rae's resistence. Acting from the heart instead of the head, she leaned across the counter, her hands bracketing his swarthy face when he would pull back in surprise.

The first touch of their lips stirred thunderous passions. The tentative slide of her tongue along the soft seam of his mouth sizzled, a bolt of pure desire.

Nothing you don't want.

Amazingly, emphatically, what she wanted at that moment was him. Nick Flynn with his charm-you-out-of-your-panties smile and those dark, soulful eyes changing from sly dog innuendo to puppy dog sincerity in a blink. Nick Flynn of the whisper sweet, soul-sucking kisses and unhurried touch that had her toes curling.

Nothing you don't want.

Was he kidding? She couldn't imagine him doing anything she didn't want at this emotionally-charged moment.

Except send a sudden splash of soda water cascading over the front of her when tipped by his elbow.

Crying out in dismay, she jumped back to survey the damage. The tropical sea color of her skirt now showed two dramatically different depths. Watching her brush ineffectually at the spreading stain, Nick's gaze had gone from a house on fire to the cold ash of regret.

What else could go wrong?

Nick wondered as she plucked the soggy lace of her tank top away from her skin. The briefly tasted heaven of her lips was now a rapidly evaporating hope. No sense in trying to recover from the comedy of errors performed at his suddenly inept hands. The flames of opportunity had been thoroughly doused.

"Want that cab?" he asked, trying not to sound as morose as he felt at that moment.

"I want your shower. I feel all sticky."

She was staying.

Elation swirled through his mind, slowing his response until she looked at him in question, all gorgeous and soaked through. And smiling a good sport smile that dropped his heart to his feet.

Abruptly as sweaty palmed as a kid, he nodded toward the bedroom. "In there. There's a robe on the door you can use while your things dry out. Then I promise to be a more coordinated host."

Her smile took a sultry bend. "I look forward to that, Nick."

Watching her sashay into his bedroom, impatience almost

had him following in a lather of anticipation and urgency.

Down boy.

Instead, as he heard the indescribably delicious sound of this particular woman running the water in his shower, he turned his restless energies toward mopping up his mess. Once that was done, he looked toward the wet bar, feeling suddenly, desperately dry. A drink would help get him through the next few moments...He started reaching....but would be a hindrance later on. He scrubbed his palms on his trousers.

Rae of the no last name was intoxicating enough for any man.

What was it about this one? Yeah, she looked great and the opportunity to see more had him chafing, but his needs didn't stop at a quick roll in the sack the way they did with the other women he'd met and mated. With her predecessors, he'd been impatient to bed them then even more impatient to have them gone. With Rae, he was looking forward to the "after." After the passion finished its tornadic roar and quieted to a manageable tempest. After the physical was satisfied, when the two of them could curl close together and share themselves.

He wasn't much for sharing. He hoarded his past and his emotions as zealously as he did his bank account, so this notion came as an out of left field surprise. Why would a sexy hooker want to linger in his bed listening to him spill his tawdry secrets? Why would she want to hear him talk about his lean years in Louisiana, when hopes and dreams seemed so impossibly out of reach? Why would she care to learn what was really on his mind? What he really wanted, needed, to confide in her was his dissatisfaction with that same dream. How could a woman like her relate to his sudden, irrational urge to flee from that finally realized goal of success and wealth?

And why did part of him believe instinctively that, of all the people he knew, she would be the one who would understand?

He didn't know her from Adam or Eve, but here he was, ready to spill his guts about matters of firm confidentiality and client privilege. Mr. Lonely Hearts searching for a sympathetic ear.

But she'd known Ginny Grover. She'd been there to witness his moment of shame and glory. Was that the attraction? Was he clinging to those circumstances, using her familiarity with the Grovers to punish himself for his part in their ruin? Looking to her for some sort of forgiveness?

Jeez, that was sick.

And he felt sick. Had felt sick since he'd watched Zanlos sign Grover's name with the man's dead hand and had said nothing.

Towels.

There were no towels in the bathroom. He'd tossed them into the hamper this morning for housekeeping and hadn't replaced them from the stash in the linen closet.

While the water still pounded within his tiled tub enclosure, Nick, his arms loaded with the generic whites provided by hotels around the world, slipped into the bathroom thinking to unobtrusively lay the stack on the sink and go. But as he set the towels down, his gaze was caught and mesmerized by the silhouette behind curtain number one—his prize of choice.

And while he stared dreamily at that languidly moving figure, red-tipped fingers grasped the edge of the curtain and pulled it open part way. Far enough to expose the bare arm and shoulder and wet head of his soon to be indignant guest.

"Yes?"

He gestured blindly toward the sink. "I brought towels."

"Oh. Thanks. But I was really hoping you were here to do my back for me."

"I could do that," he offered up a little bit slowly.

And before he could get all the way out of his jacket, she'd caught him by the tie to drag him toward the tub.

Nick had the presence of mind to step out of his shoes and toss his wallet to safety in the sink before surrendering himself to the jetting spray.

And surrendering his common sense to much, much more.

SIX

I'm in control. I'm in control here.

Nothing you don't want.

Rae let the water beat upon her back as the words beat upon her flagging confidence.

She couldn't convince herself of the first because of the seductive appeal of the second.

Truth be told, she wasn't in control, of the situation or her own emotions. Marchand LaValois manipulated the first and Nick Flynn the second, and here she was, the one with the most at stake, going with the flow.

Right down the drain.

She didn't like using Nick, because she liked him, genuinely enjoying his company and being here in his rooms. How easy it would be to forget her purpose and Marchand's plan to indulge in the passions of the moment.

And oh, with Nick Flynn, there was passion aplenty. Behind that first look across the room, beneath the clever banter of their conversation, within the slightest brush of his fingertips. It wasn't going to be a problem giving herself over to this evening's inevitable end. The problem was going to be in living with herself afterwards.

Think of it as undercover work.

Under the covers work was more like it.

Over the rush of the water, she heard the door to the bathroom open. All of her self-defense mechanisms immediately came on line. She started rinsing off, waiting for him to tear open the curtain and ruin everything.

But he didn't.

And as she waited in the billowing clouds of steam, her own temperature began to rise at the thought of him there on the other side of the droplet-dappled sheet of semi-opaque vinyl.

What was he waiting for?

An invitation?

Yes.

That's exactly what he was waiting for, and the notion had her steaming hotter than the spray.

Seeing him standing there, looking part sheepish, part predatory, his swarthy features already slicked by a sheen of moisture, created an instantaneous need. And since she couldn't go out to him, undressed as she was, she brought him to her.

She lifted her lips to him in silent offering. He kissed her, once softly, as if trying out something new and making sure he understood how everything worked so he wouldn't have to read directions later. Then, again, with the aggressive skill of someone who knew exactly how to manipulate every nuance of desire and need with the varying pressure and position of his mouth upon hers. A fast learner. As she stepped back, dragging him into the tub with her, he took her right to the tiled wall beneath the shower head. Grateful for the support, her knees in danger of collapse, she unbuttoned his increasingly wet shirt while his hot, seeking tongue made love to her mouth, sliding in and out in suggestive repetitions. An urgent, hungry sound growled up from her throat as she peeled down his shirt. After tossing it over the curtain rod, she traversed the sleek contours of his back and shoulders with hurried revolutions. Beneath her palms, he was rock solid, a stud, not a soft chair jockey, and she let him hear her approval with a rumbling purr of appreciation.

His one hand tangled in the heavy wetness of her hair while the other stroked down from her shoulder, fingers splayed wide. His thumb grazed the fullness of her breast, hitting her tightly beaded nipple as if it were a speed bump. Though her breath sucked in, he continued the journey, traveling along the curve of her torso to the gentle nip of her waist, skimming over rounded hip to claim a handful of firm cheek. He tugged her into him, rocking, rubbing, letting her get the full picture of how she was driving him crazy with need. That evidence strained the front of his trousers in impatient and impressive detail. Needing a first hand sampling, Rae insinuated hers between the press of their bodies, finding that rigid and ready sex that was more median divider than speed bump, and tormented him into a groan of objection with her not so gentle travels.

He tore away from the greedy suction of their kiss to stare at her as if in wonder, blinking water from his enviably thick lashes as he pushed her hair from her face.

"Eighty percent of all home accidents happen in the bath," he panted. "Let's move this someplace safer."

Not believing such a place existed as long as this fierce urgency pulsed between them, Rae nodded and reached back for the shower control, shutting it off. Her own control was way beyond the simple turn an on/off knob.

Once the water stopped pelting down and the steam settled, there were the two them, dripping and mostly undressed in the tub. And Nick still in his socks.

He stepped out, slipping slightly as he groped for the stack of towels. Swiping one over his face and damp hair, he let it lay about his shoulders as he assisted his guest from the tub.

She was Venus arising from a tile shell, her toned body glistening, naked perfection. He swaddled her in his bulky white robe, pulling the hood up over her wet head, buffing and blotting because he couldn't stop touching her.

And then her clever fingers hooked themselves through his belt loops, coaxing him up against her.

What was a man to do?

As her arms lifted to circle his neck, he cupped her deliciously taut bottom and picked her up. Long legs knit together behind his back. He almost walked them into a wall as she bent to kiss his mouth, his nose, his brow, his ear—where she lingered to elicit a mighty moan as her tongue charted the inner whorls.

He stumbled in a blind desperation toward the bed.

She hit the smooth surface with a bounce, pulling him over her. His open mouth dropped down on hers with a claiming certainty, and for a long moment they held a voracious dueling contest with their tongues. He let her win. There was something to be said for being a gracious loser. She tasted him, tempted him with light nibbles to his lower lip and chin, then sent his world spinning as the tip of her tongue danced across his tightly closed eyelids.

Then as she sucked at his earlobe, she whispered, "There's something we need to get out of the way first."

Damn.

She was going to talk about money.

He wouldn't have believed anything short of a nuclear attack could wither his rampant interest, but that did. He'd forgotten whom he'd brought to his room, to his bed. Her company didn't come free of charge.

No matter what he'd dared hope.

He eased off her, wondering where he'd left his wallet, when she snagged his belt buckle, undid it and yanked leather through the loops with an expectant zing. And that was followed by the rough purr of his zipper going down.

"You're all wet," was her only comment as she pushed his trousers and jockeys down.

She'd been talking about his wet clothes.

Momentum surged once more as he wriggled out of his sodden pants and sent his soggy socks flying. He sank back down on her luscious form.

"That better?"

"Mmmmm. Yes." And she wiggled within the confines of the robe, parting her knees so he could sink in more satisfactorily. The scrub of her palms quickly warmed the chilled flesh of his butt. The rest of him didn't need warming. He was on fire. She was gently biting his shoulder. He moved against her cleft, letting her know that he was hard enough to crack cement. She murmured in response, her hands gripping his buns to increase the pressure. A pressure that was going to blow sky high like a newly tapped vein of crude jetting out of the ground.

No time for finesse. He reached for the night stand, jerking the drawer out in his haste. The contents spewed on top of the coverlet, giving him access to the one thing he sought. Triumphantly, he brought the packet up to tear it open with his teeth. Perhaps a little too vigorously.

The both of them stared at the mangled rubber.

Nick's gaze darted to the bedspread where most of his worldly goods were scattered next to the Gideon Bible. Change, his keys, a comb, his phone card, breath mints...everything except a replacement for the damaged prophylactic dangling impotently from his hand.

"Sonuvabitch."

He was on empty. At least in the protective sense.

He stared down into her gorgeous, flushed face, stammering apologetically.

"I'll just be a minute. There's a gift shop downstairs."

"Nick."

The soft purr of his name short-circuited his runaway train of thoughts.

"I'm not going to give you anything you don't want. Can you say the same?"

"I'm– Yes. I'm fine. I mean I'm clean."

Her well-kissed lips pursed into a naughty smile. "After our shower, I would hope so. I want you inside me, Nick. Now, please."

With a sweep of his arm, the drawer, the change, the useless condom and all the rest clattered to the floor.

A long juicy kiss got things moving in the right direction once again. From there, Nick moved downward, parting the robe and giving his full attention to her breasts for the first time. Ripe, full, glorious. Her nipples had softened into coral-colored circles the size of fifty-cent pieces. He watched, fascinated, as the feather-light brush of his thumbs puckered them up into tiny distended volcanos of response no bigger than a dime. A sucker for geology, he lowered his head.

At the first sweet pull of his lips, Rae arched and grabbed frantically at his head, her fingers anchoring in the short dark hair just in case he thought of moving any time soon. Heat flooded in molten waves to the hard little nubs and lower, to where his unrestrained sex furrowed impatiently against her belly and the nest of reddish curls below. The fingers that weren't taunting her other nipple into new heights of sensation slid down between their bodies, seeking that slight mound where passion began to coalesce. He lifted slightly so his middle finger could glide like a heat-guided missile between moist folds to sink into ground zero with explosive results. Her hips bucked, twisting and grinding upward against the heel of his hand in an effort to appease the restless energy centering into a fiery pool.

He played her body with a master's respect for an exquisite instrument. Increasing the pull of his mouth and fingers upon the throbbing peaks of her breasts, he created soul-shaking music upon her nerve endings with each slow draw and inevitable return. She squeezed the walls of her body around him, trying to hold him there, to pull him in farther as seismic shivers began to quake along her thighs. She clenched them, locking her ankles in a effort to still their trembling. But as his palm moved in a tight rotation, never lessening the pressure, the epicenter burst, sending wave after wave of pleasure rumbling through her.

He lifted up to see passion infuse her features like a sunrise. Her eyes were tightly shut, but when his rigid sex replaced his finger in one deep, filling stroke, her gaze popped wide open to fix upon his in an unfocused daze of surprise and delight. Hot green seas a man could drown in.

Rae said his name, or she thought she did, in a low, urgent guttural. The fierce driving force of him kept chasing the thrill of her release higher, higher, until the breaths expelled with each smack of their bellies became a soft, desperate keening. Too much, too much. The intensity built, thickening, growing hotter, finally snapping to free tremors of unbelievable strength and longevity. The Big One, seismically speaking. Powerful enough to crumble and crash the last of her inhibitions. He swallowed her unrestrained shout with his devouring kiss then was swallowed up himself by the sweet violence of her San Andreas-sized response.

He groaned into her mouth, drenching the fires inside her with the sudden gush of his own reward.

As with any aftermath of an earth-rending event, a complete stillness followed. In that long evaluating moment, their ragged breathing slowed. The tension in their bodies transformed into a heavy lethargy, defying movement, forbidding thought as they recuperated from the stunning magnitude of what they'd just survived.

"Wow," Nick managed to summarize at last as he got his elbows under him to lever up.

"You bet wow," Rae echoed while wondering if the tiny shivers would ever quiet along her limbs. She felt ridiculously weak and vulnerable. And satisfied as hell. As the pad of his thumb sketched along her jaw, dampness sprang to her eyes, wobbling embarrassingly on the tips of her lashes. She tried ineffectually to blink them away, then he was kissing them away with the devastatingly gentle sweep of his lips. And she went to pieces all over again.

Good God, girl, get it together. It's not like you've never had sex before.

Not like this, came the seditious reply. *Not with a man like this.*

With a man she wasn't supposed to care about. With a man she was supposed to use heartlessly for her own purpose.

With a man who had her emotions in such a scramble of need and want and necessity, she just wanted to hang on tight and never let go.

She was a mess.

And she was crazy about him.

What was she going to do now?

Sleep wasn't the right answer, but it was what she settled for within the comforting and way too comfortable curl of Nick's embrace. She stirred drowsily when he got out of bed some time later, probably to latch the door and turn out the lights. Through slitted lids she watched him standing in the doorway for a long moment as if wrestling with some great indecision. Was this where he shook her, tossed her her clothes and said, "Thanks for the memory, baby"?

Maybe it would be easier if he did, instead of coming back into the room to pull the sheet up over her then slid under it himself.

She felt the heat of his lips against her brow. His arm skimmed the dip at her waist to curve along her spine, drawing her up to fit within the intriguingly firm highs and lows of his own form. And just when she thought that maybe she wouldn't be so adverse to another round of spectacular physicality, he tucked her head beneath his chin with his other hand and whispered, "Sweet dreams, lover." She rode out his big, well pleased sigh.

Now, she was wide awake and listening in an agony of guilt and forbidden fascination to the gradual deepening of his breaths into slumber.

Lord, how she wanted to lie right there all night, studying the pattern of his inhalations, steeped in the cocooning warmth of his nearness, to wake with him at dawn for coffee and conversation and perhaps more of that spectacular physical stuff.

But if she stayed, her job would be only that much harder.

As if it was simple now.

Carefully, she unwound herself from the tangle of his nicely furred arms and legs and escaped the room without a backward glance. Seeing him asleep and tousled on the sheets they'd so thoroughly rumpled would be too much like torture.

As quietly as she could, she rounded up her clothing then dressed in the dark of the living room where the security lights from outside provided just enough visibility to find what went where.

And as she wriggled into her jacket, the presence of a crinkly wad tucked into her sleeve gave her a moment's pause.

What the–

Unable to give more time or risk turning on a lamp to satisfy her curiosity, she had to settle for the cool, clinical brightness of the hallway as she trotted for the elevator carrying her shoes.

She glanced down at the paper crumpled in her hand and stubbed her toe.

Cash.
Hundreds.
Five of them.

SEVEN

"Give you a ride?"

She was almost too angry to be surprised at the sight of Gabriel McGraw sitting cross-legged on the hood of his bulky black hot rod.

She started to breeze right past him when a question came to mind. She confronted him, arms akimbo.

"What are you doing here? Spying through keyholes?"

His gaze gave her a slow once over. "My guess is I missed a good show. And here I was beginning to fear you'd burrowed in for the night."

"Hookers don't spend the night."

He frowned slightly at the harsh crack of her voice. "He bought it, then?"

She fanned the bills for his inspection. "Bought and paid damn well for it."

For a moment, he stared at her, his youthful expression a strange mixture of awe and regret. Then he slid off the car with a gruff, "No one said you had to–"

She cut him off with a wave of her hand...the one not holding the money a man had paid for the pleasure of having sex with her. "Let's just get the hell out of here, okay?"

He opened the door for her then wordlessly shut it once she'd tucked her long legs inside. The engine growled to life, and she didn't start feeling sick to her stomach until after they'd wheeled out onto one of the narrow side streets.

"Stop."

Gabriel glanced at her in alarm. "What?"

"Pull over at that corner."

He obeyed then waited with motor running while she

hopped out of the car.

A street person hunkered down on a camp stool beneath the weak pooling of a street light. He was so ragged and forlorn, he could have doubled for Emmett Kelly's sad clown. Leaning up against the rock wall beside him was a sign. Innocuous against the opulent backdrop of the hotel, the crudely lettered words entreated, "Help me feed my kids."

Vacant, hopeless eyes lifted when he heard her step. He lurched forward, expecting to be chased off the corner and into the shadows where no one had to be confronted with the tragedy he represented.

"Don't be afraid," she said quietly as she reached out to cram the currency into the faded Senators cap he had sitting like an offering bowl on the sidewalk beside him. "Go home and take care of your family."

She darted back to the car while he examined the bounty so unexpectedly thrust upon him.

And as Gabriel angled back into traffic, Rae heard a tear-filled voice cry out, "God bless you!"

I doubt it.

"Now what?"

She didn't look at the driver when she replied.

"Now we dangle the bait and get ready to set the hook."

***

Nick really didn't expect to find her there when his alarm went off at 5:30. But it would have been nice.

Wearily, but with just enough of that euphoria remaining to get him up and moving, he performed his morning rituals, grateful he didn't have to apply any actual thought to what he was doing. Going through the motions. That's what he'd been doing since he got here.

Until last night.

Those motions were indelibly inscribed upon his soul.

While his two cups of coffee for the road grumbled and groaned their way into the pot, Nick leaned upon the breakfast bar studying the paper in his hand.

Like a spy while she'd languished in his bed, he'd clenched a penlight between his teeth while he scribbled all that he could on the only available piece of paper he could find–his dry cleaning receipt. And then stealthily he'd replaced her driver's licence before it would be missed.

"Rae Borden," he said aloud, liking the sound of it, liking the feeling of familiarity and connection it gave him.

He would see her again.

She was getting soft.

A week had passed since Ginny's funeral, and she'd done zip in the way of physical exercise. Well, not exactly zip.

Fiercely, she sent her fist flying into the bag.

In Detroit, she started her day with a five mile run. Under Bette Grover's roof, she started off with a fifteen hundred calorie breakfast, and she was beginning to feel it.

She wished she didn't feel anything else.

She sent a furious combination into the barely yielding bag and followed up with a couple of hard kicks that sent a punishing numbness down her leg. She shook it off and continued the work out until her heart rate could jump start a fighter jet. Jab after jab, imagining the smug features of Kaz Zanlos exploding upon impact.

"Hey," Gabriel called out, anchoring the bag as it swung from the viciousness of her blows, "What did it ever do to you?"

"Got in my way, McGraw. It got in my way."

"I'll make sure I always give you plenty of space." Then he swayed with a mean one-two. "Keep your elbow up."

"Oh, an expert are you?"

"If you read my file, and I'm sure you have by now, you know that I'm division champion."

"Then let's go a few rounds, just for fun."

"Fun, huh?"

"Unless you're afraid of a girl." She grinned in challenge, goading him with a few half-hearted taps to his pretty face.

"You got it, girlie. Let me get some gloves on."

Rae continued to bounce lightly as she watched him tie on the gloves. He was a good-looking kid, and when he dressed down from his glam-punk attire to gym trunks and tank top, he looked positively lethal.

"I thought you were moving on a plan tonight," he said as he reached for protective headgear.

"I am." She gestured to the padded helmet. "That's for sissies."

"Yeah?" He grinned and tossed it aside. "Let's see what you got, girl."

They toed off within the elevated ring, drawing the attention of the few single cops who were getting their adrenaline pumped before the late shift. It wasn't much of a gym, not like the swank health club Bette Grover had a membership to. It was ragged, worn and smelled of old sweat socks and BenGay. And it was just what Rae had been looking for when she'd asked the nicely cut Gabriel where he worked out.

They touched gloves, and she sent Gabriel skipping back with an immediate jab. He laughed but at least he was taking her seriously now. They sparred lightly for a few minutes, weaving and exchanging taps.

"You're good, McGraw."

"Lots of time to practice."

She didn't have time to ask him to explain as she feinted away from his right hook.

"You're not so bad, yourself."

"For a girl." She landed a tight pop to his mid-section eliciting a surprised, "Oof!."

Gabriel backpedaled, rubbing his gut. "For a contender, Sugar Rae."

Now that he wasn't underestimating her, their contest escalated in intensity. Blocks and dodges became self-preserving necessity, and the select punches that managed to get through were definitely not for sissies. Gabriel was grinning around his mouthguard as he took her best and came back for more. He had great moves, so silky and swift. Now you see him, now you don't. Even as his blocked punches knocked her back, she sensed he was holding himself in, being careful about the amount of power he packed with each throw from close to the body. On occasion, she wondered if his feet even touched the floor as he glided away from certain impact. She remembered his disappearing act in the alley.

Just how good was this guy?

Then she saw it coming, a beautiful, right-from-the-shoulder jab. Just what she'd been waiting for. She took a breath, let her hands drop slightly and stepped into it. Pain exploded through her face. She met the canvas with her world rocking and rolling. For a minute, everything was black then spinning in pin dots of color.

"Rae? Rae? Damn, I'm sorry. I didn't mean to put your lights out."

Finally, she could focus on Gabriel's anxious expression as he bent over her. He'd pulled off his gloves to apply the wet towel someone had tossed from ringside to the shattering ache in her cheekbone. When he drew back the towel, he winced.

"That's gotta hurt."

"You more than me, pal."

Grinning, he helped her to her feet. "Didn't I tell you about keeping that elbow up?"

"Next time." She gingerly touched the side of her face, which was already swelling. "Now it's time to put my plan in motion."

***

It had been three days since he'd seen her.

He'd come to the bar each night...hoping. Normally, the disappointment of not seeing her there would have driven him to drink, not that he'd ever needed a lot of excuses there, but he sat on those three lonely nights, nursing his club soda in one hand and holding the slip of paper with her name and Detroit address in the other.

Rae Borden.

What if she'd already left town?

It was just a quick hop from National to Detroit Metro.

Then what? A happy reunion with a woman he'd paid to be with? He'd never paid to be with a woman before, but he didn't flinch at the idea any more than he had when viewing the sticker on the sports car he'd order that afternoon. High ticket items but worth the price and time for maintenance.

He had plenty of money. For the first time in his life, that wasn't the problem. The problem was his whole lack of logic concerning the subject.

He wasn't thinking. Pure emotion goaded him from minute to minute. The need to see her again ached like a cracked filling, distracting him from what he should be doing, should be feeling.

Man oh man, he was screwed up.

He tried to force the ruthless truth past the glow of the moment. She'd taken the money and run. What else had he expected? For her to seek him out for the purposes of a meaningful relationship? Was that what he wanted? He could picture it now, his high profile future going down the toilet when his wife was exposed as a former prostitute.

"Mr. Flynn, how did you meet the missus?"

"She was turning tricks in the bar where I was getting shit-faced drunk, and I picked her up. It was love at first sight. Of course, she only works on weekends now, just for a little extra spending money."

It was insanity.

And he couldn't seem to stop it from eating away at his mental faculties.

He took a drink, surprised by the bitey taste of the lime and the lack of alcohol. He stared at the glass as if he'd received the wrong order. He wasn't exactly a club soda kind of guy.

He was the kind of guy who ruined lives then turned his back on their pain.

Club soda wasn't making it. He started to raise his hand to get the waitress's attention. The gesture hung in the air, uncompleted.

If he'd been drinking, he would have called it a delusion.

As it was, the sight of Rae Borden in the open doorway wreathed by cigarette smoke and the white-hot aura of his desire, was a dream come true.

She was wearing a pair of bright patterned pants that looked spray painted on her long legs. A silky, sleeveless top tied beneath her breasts, leaving a patch of tanned and toned abs bare. Her mane of blazing hair had been braided back into a heavy tail, and her glorious green eyes were concealed behind a pair of oversized sunglasses.

She was alone.

Looking for him?

It was early, just after eight-o-clock. Businessmen and conventioneers crowded the bar stools and booths. Easy pickings. Before he could call himself a fool, he stood and signaled for her attention. Then, he experienced a wrenching deflation as she was met at the door by a balding man wearing a Rolex the size of a dinner plate.

He should have made reservations.

He was about to sit down and lick his wounded ego when Rae shooed the corporate crocodile away...and headed straight for his table.

"Hi, Nick."

"Join me?"

"Love to."

As she slid into the booth, he was taken with that graceless, sweaty-palmed urgency again. The kind that was clumsy and pre-pubescent. And damn, it felt good.

They sat, silent and staring at each other with all the awkwardness of a second date, while the noise and commotion about them faded into insignificance.

"I haven't seen you around."

Great opening line, Nick.

"I've been busy."

Just what he wanted to hear.

"Me, too."

"I've been looking for work."

He perked up. "Really? Doing what?"

He couldn't see much of her expression behind the huge oval glasses, but her mouth pursed ruefully.

"I don't exactly have a lot of marketable skills."

"Oh."

"There's that typing thing."

"I remember."

Silence again. Nick couldn't think of what to say. He

wanted to protest that there must be something...respectable out there for a woman like her who was gorgeous and witty and smart and . . .

He found himself staring at her blue, glittery fingernails. They matched her dangling earrings and the hint of a lacy bra that peeked from under the overlap of her blouse.

Not exactly executive wife material.

Where had all these references to wife come from?

He sat back and drained his club soda, wishing it came with a bourbon chaser. Then he glanced at the drink and felt like a clod.

"I'm sorry. Would you like something?"

"No. Thanks. I can't stay long. I really shouldn't be here."

She was toying with the sparkly bows of her sunglasses. They were cheap plastic, and it annoyed him the way they hid her expressive eyes.

He reached up for them. Rae reared back defensively.

"Don't."

"I was just going to take off those glasses. I like to see who I'm talking to."

"Well, you won't like to see this," she promised.

The wry tone and the reluctant way she removed the eyewear should have warned him. But nothing could prepare him for the shock of seeing her face.

"Sonuva—"

Her cheek was swollen by a rainbowed contusion promising a black eye to come.

The voice that growled from him was unrecognizable as his own.

"Tell me who did this to you. I'll kill him."

EIGHT

The intensity of his command frightened...because she believed it. A wild, panicky thrill ran through her. He was willing to throw off civility to defend her.

For the wrong reasons.

Rae pushed the sunglasses back on so he couldn't see the guilty remorse in her expression. Here was a man ready to sacrifice his decency for her honor, and she had none where he was concerned.

Nick gripped her hand. "Rae, tell me who did that."

She'd wanted his anger, his passion, to control him so that she could control him. That was the plan. And the plan stunk.

"Lower your voice, Nick. You're making a scene."

He blinked at her cool tone. Then his heavy brows lowered like an approaching storm front, the kind that blew in off the Mississippi where he'd been raised and raised hell with everything that got in the way. "Someone smacks the crap out of you, and *I'm* making a scene?"

"I don't know who it was, all right? Just a guy. An occupational hazard."

Her cold summation took him aback. He looked uneasy with her attitude, but that was all right. She needed him off balance.

And at that moment, with the gentle way his hand kneaded hers—a stunning contrast to the fierceness of his mood—she needed more from him than was allowed.

This wasn't working. This wasn't right.

She pulled away from the wonderful warmth of his touch and slid out of the booth. His gaze fixed upon hers, alarmed and objecting.

"I've got to go," she mumbled, then tore her stare away from the sight of him, her dark, avenging hero. She headed for the door before her emotional upheaval had her abandoning everything she cherished for the sake of a man she didn't know.

The humidity of the night hit her forcefully the second she stepped out into the drive. Her steps were wobbly. She couldn't see where she was going through the glaze of silly tears skewing her vision.

What was wrong with her?

Go back inside. You'll ruin everything! He'll get away. Zanlos will get away with everything he's done.

But the injustice packed in that claim couldn't quite overset the powerful image of Nick Flynn ready to do battle for her.

"Dammit!"

She stopped on the wide sidewalk to take deep, clarifying breaths, ignoring the strange looks she got from the bellhops and passersby. Her sides hurt from the feelings she was trying to suppress. She hugged them in denial.

She'd been a policewoman for eight years. She'd been in undercover work for three of them. This wasn't the first time she'd involved some innocent schmoe in the bigger scheme of things.

But it was the first time she'd involved herself.

"Are you all right?"

She nearly jumped out of her sandals, then turned with a trace of desperation quavering in her voice. "Walk away, Nick. No. Run away. You don't want to get pulled into this."

He couldn't possibly understand all the levels contained in that anguished plea. But he knew enough to dig in his heels.

"I'm not going anywhere until you answer the question."

His fingertips rested lightly on the back of her arm. The contact had her quivering all the way to her painted toenails. Upset, agitated with her own lack of discipline, with his inability to know when it was in his best interest to cut and run, she confronted him with the full brunt of her distress.

"No. I'm not all right. When is it all right for some guy to knock a woman around just because he can get away with it?"

She hated the anguish rattling through that sentiment, a very personal anguish that had nothing to do with him or this moment and everything to do with what motivated her. He didn't get it. She didn't want him to. She didn't want anyone to know that much about her.

"It's not all right," he told her quietly with a sincerity that melted down her barriers like a concentrated greenhouse effect on her own internal polar icecap. "It's never all right. And he shouldn't get away with it, Rae. I know people. Let me take care of this for you."

"Are you offering to bump him off for slapping a hooker?"

His stare grew positively frigid. "No. For making you cry."

She sucked a shaky breath, ready to throw herself into his arms. She exhaled in a helpless sigh. "What am I going to do with you, Nick Flynn?"

"Nothing you don't want to."

The reference poured through her like a jet of steam, making the wet, heavy air downright cool in comparison.

"I think I want to take a walk."

He glanced down, questioning the choice of her footwear. "Can those things handle it?"

"Honey, these feet have posted more miles than you could possibly imagine."

His features tightened ever so slightly. She'd meant walking one kind of beat, but he'd interpreted it as another kind altogether. She didn't set him straight. Better he believe the worst. With Nick at her side, she started to walk along the drive that circled in front of the hotel. She was very aware that his hand hadn't left her arm. The fragrance of the bedded flowers splashed along the curved walkway perfumed the evening, creating a mood of romance when it should be one of caution and control.

What was it about Nick Flynn that made it impossible for her to keep her mind on work?

Some of the fierceness left his expression as he escorted her down the narrow side street. As he relaxed, a certain satisfaction settled in its place, a contentment with their circumstance, with her on his arm. The bliss of the ignorant.

He had no idea what their circumstance was—that she was out to bring down his boss and possibly him in the process.

How much did he know about what Zanlos did?

"What's a nice Southern boy like you doing up in this boiling pot of political intrigue?"

He laughed softly, a husky sound that played over the surface of her skin like a smooth caress. Everything tightened.

"I wish I could say sheer skill, but it's more like dumb luck. My daddy wanted something good for me so he scrimped and saved and forced me through law school. I think he was envisioning thousand dollar suits and business lunches in Tokyo."

"Something like you have now?"

"Yeah. Something like that." And he sounded genuinely surprised by that truth. "I tried to give him what he wanted, a successful son he could be proud of. But he'd never say it in this lifetime. I got my degree and set up shop in our parish just doing nickel-and-dime stuff to pay the lease while I was studying corporate contract leases. I wanted to get in on some of the oil industry money. They're always getting dragged into court by somebody."

"So you were going to jump in on the side of the big guy and help them crush the little guy."

He glanced at her with a wounded lowering of his brows. "Rae, there are no good guys or bad guys in the legal profession. There are clients. And everyone's entitled to legal representation under our Constitution."

"Some are more deserving than others."

He chuckled at her staunch opinion. "All right. I'll concede on that one. But some are more able to pay their bills than others, and I'd been living off IOUs for too many years to let my own feelings get in the way."

"Sounds like we're in the same kind of profession, doesn't it?"

His wide-eyed glance of shock sank into a series of mirthful creases as he laughed aloud. He hugged her in close against his side. "Damn but you're honest, and damned if I don't like that about you."

The sidewalk took a steep downward pitch, so he kept her snug against him as she tottered on her high-heeled sandals. In the soggy heat of the night, she would have thought that close contact would have been uncomfortable, but it wasn't. Far from it.

"Yeah," he admitted good-naturedly, "We're in the same business, *cher*. But we do what we can to get by, even if it goes against the grain."

"You don't like your job?"

"I didn't say that."

He didn't deny it, either.

"Go on with your story."

He didn't continue right away. In the ensuing silence, the gaiety seeped from his expression like watercolors in the wash of a sudden summer storm. She could see him calculating his answer, debating on what and how much to tell her.

"I got my chance. I got an interview with a big firm in New Orleans. They loved me, and I loved what they were prepared to pay me."

Silence, again. "So?" she prompted.

"So I got sidetracked and never made it back for the second interview. Maybe that was meant to be because a few months later I got this offer from Meeker, Murray & Zanlos. One of their clients was embroiled in a bit of a legal struggle over some land rights on the Gulfside, and they ask me to fly up and consult with them. I don't know where they got my name. I was too busy packing my bags to ask them."

"So this is the happily-ever-after part?"

His smile took a crooked turn. "Maybe. Or maybe this is where our professions get a whole lot more alike."

Before she could ask him to elaborate, they'd reached the busy street that ran below the hilltop-set hotel. Traffic whizzed by on its way to join up with Connecticut Avenue and the race downtown. The sidewalks running in front of the narrow store fronts were crowded with tourists shopping for bargain tee shirts featuring everything from the Washington Monument to the WWF, or seated in the clutter of café tables sampling cuisine from Thailand, France or India. Scents and sounds were rich and varied, adding the chaos of input upon the senses.

"Want something to eat?"

Rae patted the flat front of her Spandex leggings. "Gotta watch my girlish figure."

And as they walked, Nick couldn't help noticing the way every man they passed seemed eager to watch it as well. It wasn't as much for her flamboyant clothing as it was for the confident sexuality in the way she moved. Very subtly, he tightened his arm, staking his claim in an unmistakable male fashion that all but growled, "Look but don't even think about touching."

One brave soul ignored that blatant No Trespassing sign. Nick didn't expect challenge to come from such an odd and raggedy source.

"Miss. Ma'am."

Nick glanced over at the homeless man who shouted at Rae from where he'd set up shop on the corner. Rae glanced, too, but quickly averted her face, as if she didn't want to recognize the man's dire situation.

Or be recognized?

When she didn't respond, the beggar left his post to approach them. Instinctively, Nick swept Rae behind him with the brace of his arm, intending to chase the panhandler away before he tried to extort sympathy and cash. But the man paid no attention to him or the threat he represented. He was smiling wide, his focus on Rae.

"Ma'am, don't you recognize me from the other night when you were in that fancy car with your other friend?"

Nick bristled up, walking faster to discourage pursuit. "You're obviously mistaken. Go away. We're not going to give you any money for booze."

But the fellow kept up, running slightly, trying to peer around him to catch Rae's attention. "I just wanted to thank you, ma'am. I wanted to let you know how much good that $500 did for my family."

Five hundred . . .

Nick stopped. Could it be that much of a coincidence?

Rae stepped out from his protective shadow. She smiled

tightly at the beggar. "Why aren't you with them?"

"This is what I do, ma'am. I look for work during the day and find what money I can for food here each night." His expression took on a strange mix of anguish and defiant pride. "What you did for us took my family off the street, at least for awhile, and put new clothes on their backs. I just wanted to thank you, not to ask for anything more." He glared at Nick for thinking that.

Rae put a hand upon the raggedy man's arm. The genuine concern softening her features was too much for Nick. He reached for his wallet and drew out two things. The beggar looked at the hundred dollar bill and the business card pressed upon him, then up at Nick with a suspicious hope.

"Get some new clothes for yourself and go to that address in the morning. Tell them I sent you, and they'll find you work. Be there tomorrow."

The beggar blinked then clutched at the card and the cash. His voice quavered. "Yes, sir. I will be. I won't disappoint you."

"Don't disappoint your family," Rae interjected. "They're the important ones."

"Yes, ma'am." He bobbed his head in thanks, his eyes swimming with humble tears.

"Tomorrow," Nick reminded before taking Rae's elbow and beginning their walk again.

The man glanced at the card and called, "I'll be there, Mr. Flynn. Thank you."

They walked in silence for a time, then Rae's arm stole about his middle for a brief squeeze.

"That was very nice."

Nick snorted. "I figured I already had an investment in the man. You gave him my money, didn't you?"

She wouldn't meet his gaze. "I didn't feel it was fairly earned."

He could have argued that but didn't. Something about her not keeping his money had his head and heart doing crazy things. And suddenly, he had to know.

"I've shared my boring life story with you, so suppose

you tell me what a smart, clever lady like yourself if doing in your current occupation." He steered her over to one of the sidewalk café tables then waved off the approaching waiter, earning a scowl for his trouble.

"If I was clever, I'd be doing something else. Anything else." Her small smile was rueful as she settled into the wire mesh chair adjacent to his. "You might say I fell into it out of necessity, and it got me where I wanted to go. My parents died. I didn't have a lot of options. I won't bore you with the rest."

He didn't think he'd be bored but he didn't think he was prepared to hear the rest of her story. Not yet at least. "You don't like your job?"

"I didn't say that."

He noted with a chuckle the sassy return of his own words.

"But I do like it here," she added. Her gaze canted up to mingle briefly with his own. "I like some things about it very much."

"Let me help you, Rae."

"You want to give me one of your cards, too, Nick? Am I another pro bono cause you need to rescue?"

"That's not how I think of you," he protested. "I just don't like thinking of you out here on the streets where you could get hurt...or worse." He stopped, and his fingertips grazed the swelling on her cheekbone. "Let me help you."

She caught his hand and clutched it tight. "I'll be fine, Nick. I'm a survivor. I just need some protection, then I'll be fine."

"You mean like a gun?"

"I already have a gun." That blunt statement took him aback. "I mean like friends who'll look out for me. Powerful friends in my business. Do you know any of those kind of friends, Nick?" Her tone chided him for his offer of charity. "I didn't think so."

And he chafed at the spot she put him into because his influence didn't spread into her circles.

Or did it?

"Rae, I need a number where I can get hold of you." At

her wary look, he added, "Just in case I run across any of those right kind of friends."

Rae picked up one of the cardboard mini-menu cards. "Got a pen?" He supplied it, and she scribbled a number. "That's for my cell. I'm kind of mobile at the moment."

He hadn't thought of that. "Where are you staying? I mean do you have a place?" Another crazy thought came to him, that of offering up his own suite.

Waking up to Rae beside him in the morning...The idea tantalized.

"I'm staying out at Ginny's mom's place for now. I'd rather you didn't try to reach me there. Mrs. Grover doesn't exactly know what career path I've chosen, if you know what I mean."

He tucked the card into his pocket. "I'll use this number."

She nodded gratefully and returned the pen. Their fingertips touched. The unexpected contact created a chain reaction of desire. Then just as unexpectedly, she was pushing back out of her chair.

"I've got to go, Nick."

"Go where?" he asked before he could stop himself. The notion that she'd leave him to meet with another man wadded up in his throat.

"Back to the Grover's. Bette asked me to help her go through some of Ginny's things."

And the poignant misery in her quickly averted gaze stirred up a host of guilty conflicts.

What if she knew of his part in her friend's family's destruction? He'd have to make sure that never happened.

"Can I get you a cab?"

She shook her head. "I've got a loaner a train stop away."

The reality of letting her walk away hit hard and with a surprisingly visceral objection. But since he could think of no reasonable objection, he stood as well.

What was he doing? What was he thinking? The woman was a prostitute, and here he was offering to put out a contract on some john who'd hit her. He'd been angry enough to take on the job himself, and now that he considered it in retrospect, he was sure Zanlos probably had some of the right connections to make the heavy-handed bastard sorry for what he'd done. Maybe not permanently, but the thought of a busted kneecap gave him a particularly grim satisfaction.

Was that what he'd become? A man willing to employ such means to get things done? A man like Zanlos?

He glanced at Rae's profile. He could just make out the puffiness riding her cheekbone.

Maybe there were times when such actions were warranted. Times like now where this woman was concerned.

They walked side by side but not touching to the train stop. Once at that opening to the underground, Nick reached for her hand, reminding himself not to hold on too tightly.

"I'll be calling."

"Okay."

Her smile wasn't exactly doubting.

"I will."

"Okay."

That was said softer, almost in invitation.

And who was he to turn down an invitation of any kind.

He bent, giving her plenty of time to evade his purposeful descent. She didn't try.

Their lips touched and melded together with an unplanned intensity. Though joined only at that one tender, seeking spot, the sense of oneness overwhelmed them both, the sense of rightness, of inevitability. Of need, sweet and all-consuming. He kept it simple, no dramatic tongue-tangling or tonsil-wrangling. If he tasted her any deeper, he wouldn't let her go.

And he had to let her go. At least for now. Now that he had her phone number tucked safely away and a plan cooking in the back of his now not quite so focused brain.

The light brush of her fingertips along his jaw ended their lingering communion. As he lifted back, he lifted her glasses. Her gaze drew him in with its complexity of rapid-fire questions.

Are you going to hurt me, Nick?
Are you playing straight with me?
What's in it for you, Nick?
What's in it for me?

Because he couldn't answer those questions or ask his own right here in the middle of the busy sidewalk –the question burning foremost in his heart and soul being *Would you come back to my room with me?*—he increased the distance between them. She leaned slightly, as if helplessly drawn after him by the pull of a magnetic force, those questioning eyes continuing to lock with his. He almost gave in. Almost.

"I'll call."

"You'd better."

And he liked the growly, rather fierce way she declared that.

"Here." She glanced down at the coins he pressed into her palm. "For the Metro," he explained. "You'll let me do that, at least, won't you?"

Her fingers curled around the coins, and in an erotic, misplaced flash, he recalled in vivid detail the feel of those long fingers curling about him.

The speaking eye contact continued.

Come back to my room with me.

Ask me, Nick.

"Good night, Rae," was what he said at last, freeing her to take a breath that she didn't seem to realize she'd been holding.

"Thanks for the offer, Nick. No one's ever . . ." She broke off the husky admission then darted toward the stairs. She didn't look back.

Thanks for what? he wondered. For offering to take out the creep who hit her? For the subway fare? For wanting to sweep her up and take her away, to keep her selfishly for himself?

Thanks for what, Rae?

The memories?

His hand touched his pocket, feeling the comforting square of cardboard residing within.

Not as long as he had her number and her name and the means to find out more.

***

Rae needed the increasing cool that came with the escalator ride downward. Things had gotten too hot, too fast a moment ago. The way they always seemed to get when Nick Flynn was involved. She closed her eyes and struggled to draw an even breath. A difficult feat with the way her heart pounded.

Why hadn't he asked her back to his place? And if he had, against all logic, all common sense, would she have gone?

Yes.

The quiet truth whispered through her with the force of the speeding trains traversing the tunnels below.

Yes.

"Either you're the best damned actress on the planet, or you're losing your perspective, Borden."

Gabriel's claim, spoken so unexpectedly against her ear, startled her into stumbling forward on the steps. Her balance faltered, only to be steadied by his hand on her elbow.

"Sorry. Didn't mean to scare you."

"Sorry won't give me back those threes years you surprised out of me." She put a hand over her galloping heart and turned to glare at the young man riding on the step behind her. She must have been deeply engrossed in her daydream not to have heard his approach. Usually her protective instincts were at full strength when she traveled alone at night. Particularly since Ginny's death. Especially considering their location.

"Is this guy getting to you, Rae? If he is, tell me now."

His calm command was just the shake she needed to wake her to her duty to her friend and pseudo-family. She gave her chin an arrogant tip and pronounced, "You can tell LaValois his wait's almost over. I've got my way in."

NINE

Kazmir Zanlos's corner office shimmered with chrome and reflective surfaces, reminding Nick of the man himself. It dazzled the eye, but the mirrors allowed no hint of the depth behind that polished exterior. Or the decay. As a boy, he'd thought to wade out into still, clear waters trying to catch a frog only to find himself mired in the deadly quicksand it concealed under the deceptively placid illusion. He felt the same way now. Only Kaz Zanlos wasn't sucking at his feet, he was devouring his soul. And like that child stuck in the bog, he wasn't sure how to extricate himself.

"Good morning, Mr. Flynn."

Naomi Bright, Zanlos's executive secretary, was a beacon of innocence within the corrupt center of Meeker, Murray & Zanlos. Nick wondered how she held to her sunny outlook within the grim interior of the firm. Did she know what went on behind her boss's glossy doors? She had to, didn't she, since she handled the calls, the paperwork, the evidence of what the firm was up to. And yet she could still smile and greet him as if each day at Meeker, Murray & Zanlos was a pleasure.

While he sank deeper and deeper in the quagmire of its evil.

"'Morning, Naomi. Is he in?"

"Let me buzz and see."

While he waited, Nick glanced about the surroundings that had so impressed him upon his first interview. The obvious wealth, the scent of success, the reflection of everything he desired—for a price he hadn't known he'd have to pay. Or had he been naive to think such trappings would come without that expected cost?

Who was he trying to kid? By the time Zanlos had come to him, he'd already sold his soul for success. Who was he to throw stones? If he hadn't known what Zanlos was from the get-go, it was because he hadn't wanted to know. Still didn't want to know, even though that truth beat at him like a morning-after headache. He couldn't condemn Zanlos because they were birds of a feather. Those birds were vultures, he supposed, circling in search of ripe carrion.

"Nick, Nick, Nick." Kaz greeted him with typical effusiveness, spreading those dark wings to swoop down upon him. "Come in. Miss Bright, some coffee please."

A wash of blinding sunlight seared the eyes as it flooded through the all-glass corner room to glint off metal and glass. A helluva a place to come with a hangover, Nick thought as he took one of the wing chairs in the office's conversation area. Like most of the affectations of status and style, Nick found the seating as uncomfortable to the body as it was inviting in appearance. He suspected Kaz liked to keep his company off balance.

His boss was smiling as he assumed his own rigid chair.

"How good to see you, Nick. I've been meaning for some time now to call you in for an informal talk. I wanted to let you know personally how pleased I've been with your performance, especially over the past few weeks."

Since he had watched a family be destroyed through intimidation and possibly murder and said nothing.

Nick managed a smile. "That's good to hear."

"But what about you? Have you been enjoying your work? Have you found it as challenging and rewarding as you had hoped?" He leaned forward as if truly interested in hearing his answer. That was what made Kaz so good at what he did.

He made everything personal. Nick had liked that about him from the first. He knew every employee's birthday and surprised them with gifts. From the mail room to the board room, he made each and every one feel special and appreciated. When he chose to. He'd made Nick feel immediately valued and at home in the firm family. When one of the family did well, Kaz was generous with his praise and all shared in the celebration. And when they strayed, Nick imaged he'd be just as severe in his chastisement and as quick to hold them up as an example. Heads hung on the lobby wall as incentive to succeed? He didn't care to have his own there.

"Well beyond my expectations," he assured his boss. That much wasn't a lie.

"Good. It would hurt my feelings to discover that you were unhappy and said nothing to me." Was there a rumble of warning beneath that mellifluous purr? "So, my friend, what brings you to me this morning? Problems with the new case?"

"No. Everything's going smoothly. I should have the paperwork ready for signature by later this afternoon."

"Excellent." He lifted a haughty brow, waiting.

"It's a personal matter."

"Oh? I am flattered that you would come to me. Whatever I can do to help, you need but ask." And it was that simple. With a snap of his fingers or a flick of his ball point, Kaz could make things happen. A traffic ticket disappear. A hefty insurance co-payment written off. A closet full of expensive suits and shoes, no problem. And the bigger problems, too. Want someone rubbed out for smacking a hooker? No big deal. Just ask. Nick intuited that Kaz could handle just about anything without creasing his brow with effort.

And that's why he'd come to him, reluctantly yet expectantly.

It was more difficult than Nick anticipated to frame the problem tactfully. "It's about a lady friend of mine. She's a working girl, you know . . ."

"A prostitute."

Nick winced. How unsavory that sounded said with such matter-of-fact bluntness. "Yes. I don't like her having to work the streets. I know you have an interest in the *Noir* and wondered if you could help me arrange for her to get a job there as...an escort."

Kaz never so much as blinked in surprise at his request. "She is attractive and well educated, your friend?"

"Yes."

"And you can vouch for her personally?"

"Yes."

"To what degree?"

"Excuse me?"

"You will take full responsibility for this woman, for her character and guarantee her cooperation?"

"Yes."

"Excellent. When can I meet this young lady and introduce her to my partner?"

"Tonight?"

"I will pick you up at your hotel at ten-thirty. Is there anything else?"

"No. That's it." It was that easy. But what was the price of this quickly tendered favor? That was question. But when he thought of the swelling around Rae Borden's eye, price didn't figure into the equation.

"Excellent. Consider it done. I will let you get back to your contracts."

"Thank you, Kaz."

"What are friends for?"

In saying that, he smiled, that flat gesture bringing no light into his shark-like eyes.

And Nick wondered if he'd just made another bad, bad choice.

From his own office, he overrode his misgivings long enough to place a call. The sound of her voice, that simple connection, was like a Red Cross worker to battlefield wounded. He relaxed and let go of his doubts.

"Rae? About that job opportunity. Can you meet me at the piano bar in my hotel at ten tonight? Great. I'll see you then."

Once he'd replaced the phone on its cradle, the uncertainty crept back like a stain on the rug that wouldn't go away no matter how vigorously one scrubbed.

Was he doing the right thing?

He tried to focus upon the marring bruise on Rae's face, letting his anger and upset build. This way he'd no longer be helpless. He could get her out of that dangerous environment.

By placing her in a worse one?

He thought of the women at the *Noir*, of their hungry, soulless gazes, of their sleek, unnatural beauty. But he wouldn't think beyond to the work they did for Kaz and his unseen partner. That was Rae's business, not his. He was the last one to set up a meeting tent to preach salvation. Not with all the sins resting upon his soul. This was the best he could do for now to help her. A place to work in her chosen field, a safe place that paid well and took care of their own, where no one would strike her and get away with it.

A place where he could always find her.

And once he knew she was safe, maybe then he could start working on her typing skills to wean her into more...what? Respectable work? He chuckled to himself as he considered the paperwork awaiting his attention. Respectable went beyond the eye of the beholder. No one would look at him in this posh office, wearing his imported suit and reach any unsavory conclusions.

If they only knew.

Was he making more problems for the woman he wanted so desperately to protect by placing her in the care of a man he knew he couldn't trust?

Rae was a smart girl. She could take care of herself. He was just presenting her with an opportunity.

How hollowly that conviction weighed upon his conscience as he went back to work.

"Who was that, dear?"

Rae tucked away her cell phone and smiled at Bette Grover. "Just a friend. We're going out this evening."

"Friend as in male friend?"

"Yes, if you must know." She kept her tone light and teasing because Bette Grover needed a little lightness in her life. And if Bette wanted to imagine her involved in a romance, she wasn't about to burst that balloon.

Even though she wasn't involved. Not with Nick Flynn.

The news made Bette smile, and that made the lie okay in Rae's book.

They were in the Grover's bedroom sorting through

clothing, deciding what to save and what to donate to charity. It wasn't a job she'd let Bette do alone even if the task was nearly as hard on her. She found herself clutching at a ratty old cardigan sweater, unable to let go. She remembered Tom wearing it when he went to her softball games as tournament play lingered into the cooler temperatures of fall. He never missed one. Not one.

But how she was going to miss him.

She took a shuddering breath and set the sweater aside, turning her emotions to a more stable area.

"And speaking of 'going out,' you've been seeing a lot of that lawyer, what's his name?"

"You know what his name is, Rae, and don't make it sound as if I'm doing something improper."

Rae quickly soothed the other's sensibilities. "I know you're not, Bette. There's just something about that man that I don't trust."

"How can you say that? He's been wonderfully supportive since Tom died. I don't know how I would have managed to make the right decisions if not for his advice."

"Advice?" Rae struggled not to betray her alarm. "Professionally?"

"Just as a friend of Tom's."

"I didn't know he was a friend of Tom's."

"I didn't think so, either, but Kaz explained it all."

Kaz. Rae's stomach clenched at the familiarity.

Bette continued, unaware of Rae's dismay. "Apparently, Tom made some rather risky investments that didn't pay off, and Kaz was trying to help him recover from the loss. That's why Tom was also so upset when they met. He didn't want me to know he'd made some terrible mistakes in the market."

Rae's teeth gritted together. Thomas Grover had never made a risky or ill-advised move in his life. Except for allowing Kaz Zanlos close to his family.

"How kind of him to help Tom deceive you."

"Now, Rae, that's not what happened. Thomas always kept me sheltered from the business. That's just the way he was. And I'd be drowning in all the decisions I have to make if not for Kaz's input."

"He's advising you on the business? Bette, is that wise?" What else could she say? Is that wise to trust your husband and step-daughter's killer? "Come to me if you need advice, Bette. I can help you. I know what Tom would have wanted."

Bette leveled a surprisingly pointed stare. "But how could you, Rae? You've been out of his life for a long time. You know nothing about what he was involved in and made it quite clear that that's the way you preferred it."

That truth speared through her heart. Rae blinked against the sudden, awful pain of it and looked away. Her voice roughened with hurt and regret. "And I know it's probably too late to step in now. But I'm worried about you, Bette. I want to make sure you're well taken care of. Tom would have wanted me to do that. No matter what you might think of my motives, I owe Tom Grover. He stepped in when I needed it, and now I mean to do the same."

The sudden fierceness of Bette's embrace startled Rae. Not one for emotional displays, she sat stiffly for a moment before she was able to respond with a gentle pat to the now weeping woman's shoulder.

"I didn't mean to shut you out, dear," came the sniffling confession. "I know that's not what Tom would have wanted. He was always so proud of how smart and resourceful you were. As proud as if you were his daughter, too."

Tears burned against Rae's closed lids and seared all the way down her throat, making it difficult to speak. She forced the words past the wadding of remorse. "Then let me help you now, Bette. Please. For Tom's sake and my own. Don't make any decisions, business or personal, without talking to me first. Can you promise me that?"

Bette nodded against her shoulder, and relief poured through her. For the moment.

A sudden worry made her ask, "What has he asked about me?"

"I told him you were one of Ginny's school friends."

"Did you tell him what I do for a living?"

"He didn't ask, dear, so I never said."

"Don't say."

"But I don't understand."

"Bette, this is important. I don't want anyone here to know who I am." She leaned back so she could impress the importance upon the other woman with the intensity of her stare. "The D.C. police may have closed their investigation, but I haven't. I'm doing a little poking around on my own, and I'd just as soon no one know about it. Okay? It could make trouble for me."

The notion of her career in jeopardy sobered Bette's expression. "I won't say anything, Rae. But you be careful. Don't do anything rash or reckless."

"I won't."

She didn't underestimate Kaz Zanlos. Not for a second. They were now in a battle for Thomas Grover's assets, and one of them seemed to be his widow. She couldn't allow herself to get so wrapped up in her own personal pain and vendetta that she forgot to protect this woman whom Tom had loved. She had failed Ginny. She hadn't been here to keep her or her father safe. But she would shield Bette from the evil Zanlos brought into her life, and to do that, she would make whatever concessions necessary.

Even if it meant betraying Nick Flynn.

***

The address was a run-down shotgun house on a run-down street in a once respectable neighborhood. Stephen Flynn continued to live there, even though he boasted that his successful son was now sending checks regularly. Debts had to be paid before luxuries were afforded. That's what he'd tried to instill in his son, anyway.

But with Nick, he was never quite sure if the boy had soaked up the right teachings. Maybe it was his fault for pushing so hard. Maybe he shouldn't have driven the goal of wealth as a daily mantra. But it was the only way he could think of to keep his Nicky safe if temptation came calling. That dark temptation from their past. He'd resisted but, as much as he loved his only son, he didn't think Nick had the strength of character to use his principles as a shield and walk away. Too much of his mother in him.

She'd never understood his insistence upon making it without interference from her...family. Perhaps if either one of them had been able to give just a little, they'd still be a family now instead of him living just above the poverty level and her touring Europe somewhere with a personal trainer named Sven.

But she'd kept her side of the bargain. She'd stayed away, so he'd stayed quiet.

It wasn't as though he wanted to make their son's life more difficult as she'd accused in one of those angry parting volleys. He'd loved Nick enough to sacrifice the only woman he'd ever loved enough to wed. And he still loved Nick, even though he wasn't sure he liked the man his son had become. Wealth was supposed to have been the goal, not an all-consuming passion. Nick had lost sight of that in his single-minded plunge ahead.

But he was safe.

At least he was safe.

Or so Flynn assumed as he hoarded those checks sent from a bank in Virginia and altered his nightly prayers for his son slightly from "a success" to "a well-adjusted success."

An unexpected knock at the door after dark never bode well. Flynn associated them with his son's wild years when the cops would come to tell him Nick had been in an accident driving while drunk or was in jail for curfew violations. But it wasn't a policeman standing on the tiny porch decorated with peeling paint and a sad looking azalea.

"Mr. Flynn?"

"Who wants to know?"

The speaker's voice was low but definitely female, something he never would have gathered from the way her form was swaddled in an over-sized coat and shadows. She stood just outside the reach of the flickering light of his television set.

"Your son is in danger, Mr. Flynn."

The soft-spoken words sent a shaft of ice through his soul. "Nick? My Nicky? Who the hell are you?"

"A friend of the family."

Then she took a step forward, a step that nothing human could make because it involved no actual physical movement. She glided toward him, and he shrank back, understanding all too well.

"You're one of them."

"Don't be afraid, Mr. Flynn. I mean you no harm." She said that even as the faint light caught in the jeweled brilliance of her eyes, creating an unnatural dazzle. She came right up to the threshold but didn't cross it. Didn't they have to be invited in? His frantic mind grasped at that old folk tale. And just as he was feeling a little more secure, she advanced into his shabby living room. By then, his chest was chugging with terror.

"What the hell do you want?"

"I want you to save your son."

"What kind of trouble is Nicky in now?" His voice quavered with upset and a new, selfish anger to think that his son's irresponsible actions could bring this horror to his doorstep.

"The trouble isn't of his making. It stems from a vendetta long past. Long past."

He understood. His wife's relatives...the ones that should have but didn't die a normal death. The ones that hunted the night and precipitated his evening prayers.

"What is it that you want me to do? Call him? Go to D.C. and fetch him home? He doesn't know anything about that side of the family. He'd never believe me."

"I'm not asking you to go. There's nothing you could do against the evil he faces. He needs you to set aside your pride and ask for help from the only source who can give it."

"I won't go to them! Never! They're–"

She smiled, a small, serenely beautiful smile. "They're what? Demons, like me? Who better to ask to march into hell? Time grows short. Do what you must to save his soul. Do it quickly."

And she was gone.

No dramatic puff of smoke or flash of light in the best of

film-making tradition. Just gone.

Stephen Flynn stood trembling and alone in his living room. Hell was here to claim his son.

What the hell was he going to do about it?

These same frenetic thoughts had plagued him once before, when Nick was a toddler and they were living well off his wife's supposed inheritance in the Garden District of New Orleans. He hadn't believed the letter, hadn't believed in the things it told him. Until he showed it to his wife—thinking she'd get a good laugh out of it—and she'd turned pale as Cararra marble.

His whole life had gone to hell that day, but at least he'd had the satisfaction of knowing he'd done what he could to rescue Nick.

But he hadn't, had he? His noble parental sacrifice had been for nothing. They'd gone after him anyway. He dialed the phone with shaking hands.

"Nicky?"

"Dad? Is something wrong? Are you okay?"

He couldn't respond immediately to his son's expression of concern. And that delay lent a sharper edge to the insistent voice.

"Daddy, talk to me. Are you all right?"

"Fine, Nick. I'm fine. Can't a father call his son for something less than a heart attack?"

He could hear the gust of relief on the other end.

"Jeez, Dad. Don't do that to me. You know only bad news comes in phone calls at this time of night."

"A call from your father is bad news?"

"That's not what I meant. What can I do for you, Dad?"

Impatience. His son had so little time for him now. But that was okay as long as he was okay.

"How are you doing, Nick?"

"I'm doing fine, Dad. Didn't you get your check?"

Trust Nick to think it was about money.

"Yeah, I got it. How are *you* doing? Is everything okay with you?"

"It's good, Dad. I was just going out. Is there anything

specific you wanted to talk about?"

Flynn smiled wryly. *Cut to the chase, so I can get back to what I was doing.* "Just wanted to check in, that's all. Are you sure everything's fine?"

"Yeah, Dad, terrific. The job's good. I'm good. Life is good. Can I give you a call this weekend? Then I can fill you in on all the details."

"I'd like that, son." His voice trembled. Dampness filled his gaze as it fixed upon the graduation picture framed upon his faded wallpaper. A grinning, cocky Nick out to capture the world. Everything was fine and as it should be. Why was he so worried?

"Dad, I'm running late. I gotta go. Talk to you soon."

Then a click and the impersonal dial tone.

Stephen Flynn carefully replaced the receiver. There. Now he knew. Nick was fine. He took a jerky breath, then lowered his head to weep into his hands.

TEN

Nick's gaze cut through the thick screen of second-hand smoke, searching for one figure in particular amongst those gathered in the informal piano bar area.

"'Evening, Mr. Nick. Something I can do for you?"

"'Evening, James. I'm meeting a lady friend. You've probably seen me with her before. Is she here yet?" Considering how much the young concierge noticed, his request wasn't all that impossible.

"Ah, the leggy redhead. Yes, sir. She's right over there."

"Thanks, my friend."

James quickly pocketed the folded bill and grinned wide. "Have a nice night, Mr. Nick."

"That's the plan."

But he'd already forgotten about James as he squinted through the day's accumulation of haze hanging upon the dim lighting. Her back was to him. All he could see was the long length of her crossed legs adorned in sheer stockings and wispy heels. There was no chance he'd confuse her with anyone else. He approached with the now familiar breathlessness.

"Hey."

She glanced up, her expression immediately softening from wariness to welcome. Through the miracle of make-up, the bruise on her cheek was invisible in the low light, leaving a flawless surface. "Hi, Nick. What's this all about?"

He lingered at the side of her chair, his fingers buried deep in his pockets to stay their need to touch her. Every curve, every stray strand of her hair encouraged that sensory starvation.

And he was handing her over to Kaz Zanlos who would

hand her over to an endless parade of other men.

"It's not exactly a typing job."

He tried to smile, but the gesture twisted tightly upon his lips, as stiff and unnatural as the sound of his voice. Rae lowered her brows, picking up on his tension.

"What exactly is it?"

"It is very good money for the right kind of lady," came another voice. "Good evening, Nick. I hope you don't mind that I'm early."

Careful to keep his true answer from his eyes, Nick turned to Zanlos with a casual shrug. "Not at all. Rae, this is my boss, Kazmir Zanlos. Kaz, Rae Borden."

The second he said her last name, Nick realized his mistake. Her gaze flashed up to his in surprise and, more damningly, accusation. But she unwound her long legs to stand and extended her hand.

"Mr. Zanlos, perhaps you can explain more about this mysterious job Nick's been hinting about."

Kaz carried her hand to his lips in courtly fashion, but his probing gaze never left hers. "I will leave the job description to my partner. She is the one who will make the final decision, after all. But you needn't worry. She will love you. How right you were, Nick. She is exquisite."

It took all Rae's control to keep her hand malleable within Zanlos's cool grasp. She wanted to crush his fingers, to slap the smugness off his face. Her jaw ached with the effort of holding her smile.

And then, over Zanlos's shoulder, where she hadn't noticed him before, she saw Gabriel McGraw leaning against the bar, one hand wrapped around a beer, the other around the thigh of a slender brunette. And though he was talking and laughing with the woman, his focus was on her.

Watching her back. She felt relief instead of the expected annoyance. This close to Zanlos, she needed all the stabilizing support she could get and, unfortunately, Nick stood beside her, withdrawn and wooden, no help at all. Disappointment in him cut clear to the bone. But that was what she'd wanted, wasn't it? This introduction. This invitation to the inner circle, to the beginning of Zanlos's end? Nick wasn't necessary to her success any more.

The sooner he was safely away from the whole mess, the better.

She touched his arm, and his rather vague attention snapped to her. She smiled up at him. "Thank you, Nick. You've been a true friend. I'm sure you have more important matters requiring your time this evening."

He blinked at her blunt dismissal. His expressive dark eyes filled with confusion and protest.

Don't make a scene, Nick. Please just go away.

His eyes narrowed slightly as he read her meaning. But contrarily, he scooped her arm through his and said almost fiercely, "What kind of friend would I be if I didn't see to your best interests? We're ready, Kaz. Where are we meeting your partner?"

"At the *Noir*. My car is outside."

He led the way, she and Nick following. A parting glance toward the bar showed an empty stool where Gabriel had been and the pretty brunette accepting a drink from a businessman.

Zanlos's long, sleek limo sat at the curb, its door open. Again, Rae felt the tug of Nick's reluctance, pulling her back, slowing her down to give her time to consider the step she was about to take. The step he was letting her take.

"Ms. Borden, after you."

She hated that Kaz Zanlos knew her name. It made her feel more vulnerable than she cared to be. She'd just have to work faster before her cover was blown. She slid into the vehicle, Nick edging in beside her, a little too close for personal comfort. It would have been so much easier to do what she needed to do without him here as witness.

Not that it should matter to her what Nick Flynn thought.

Once the car door closed, the spacious interior went dark. The tinted windows muted the effect of the lights outside. Nick was warm and close beside her, and Zanlos sat opposite, now an unknown in the impenetrable void. She didn't like not being able to keep her eye on him. It was like having something poisonous wending about in a room without knowing its location.

The car pulled smoothly away from the curb. Anticipation and alarm volleyed for prominence.

A scratch of sound and a bite of sulfur preceded a flare of light. The match illuminated, not Zanlos's hawkish features but those of a woman seated beside him. Rae hadn't realized anyone else was in the car. Nick flinched beside her, equally startled.

"Nick, Ms. Borden, may I present my partner in all things, Anna Murray."

Her beauty was flawless, breathtakingly so. Or at least Nick had trouble inhaling. Rae regarded the other woman while fighting the urge to bury her elbow in Nick's ribs as a sort of Heimlich kick start. Anna Murray had the ageless quality of the best fashion models—smooth, fair skin, natural blonde hair styled into a sophisticated roll, a trim yet still voluptuous figure that only a blind man could resist. Yet for all her creamy loveliness, there was something not quite so attractive in the steady focus of her dark eyes. Those unblinking, penetrating eyes seemed to find a dark amusement in what she saw as she extended a slender hand to Rae.

"Ms. Borden, how do you do." A strange voice that was both melodious and at the same time toneless, without accent or depth. Her fingers were surprisingly cold on the steamy night. Perhaps the air conditioning in the big car.

"I'm happy to meet you, Ms. Murray."

And she was dismissed the second those piercing black eyes touched on the man beside her.

"And Nick." The rumble of a big cat with a particularly tasty morsel between her paws. "A pleasure to meet you at last. Kaz has had only good things to say about you. Welcome to the firm."

He held her hand in his, staring until Rae's elbow was cocked and ready, blurting out at last, "You're the Murray in Meeker, Murray & Zanlos?"

"Surprised?"

"Pleasantly so. You're not what I expected."

"I never am." And she smiled, baring even white teeth. "And if your star continues to rise, you might start getting use to the sound of Murray, Zanlos & Flynn."

"Really, darling, don't tease Nick," Kaz chastised as if he, too, enjoyed some inner amusement. "We can't have him measuring Marvin's office for furniture before the poor man is ready to retire, now can we?"

Anna squeezed his hand and leaned close to confide, "Do it discreetly, dear." There was nothing discreet about the way her pale silk blouse fell away from her bosom, giving Nick a long, leisurely look all the way to her navel. Nick blinked, apparently dazed by both temptations.

And they reminded Rae of two pretty, mean-spirited children waving a treat above the head of a hungry stray just for the fun of making him jump. Would Nick jump? How high?

He released Anna's hand and settled back into the seat next to her. His wry smile said he knew he was being toyed with but didn't mind it...too much.

"I'm in no hurry to crowd Marv out. I've got more than I ever thought possible already."

"Then you think too small, Nick dear," Anna chided. "I like a man with rabid ambition, don't I, Kaz?"

"Yes, darling. You'll like Nick. He's not shy about going after what he wants. Are you, Nick?"

"If it's worth having, it's worth your best effort."

"Is that right, dear?" Anna looked straight at Rae. "How good is his best effort?"

"I don't know. He had me with his first smile."

Their gazes locked in a moment of female challenge. Kaz broke it with his husky chuckle.

"Our Nick has a way with women. They love him, but fortunately, our Nick loves his work more."

"And do you like your work, dear?" Anna's question had Rae on a mounting pin like a specimen ready for closer study.

"Like Nick said, anything worth doing is worth doing well."

The glib response apparently satisfied her, for Anna laughed and relaxed her combative pose. And as she turned her elegant head to stare out the tinted windows, Rae caught an odd glint in her eyes, that same almost phosphorescent glow that sparked from Gabriel's and from Marchand LaValois's.

Then the light brush of Nick's fingertips over the back of her hand distracted her from that bizarre coincidence. On the car seat between them, out of sight from the two opposite, Nick began a slow mating ritual with his thumb, making sensuous circles about each joint of each finger until she was shifting restlessly beside him.

She didn't get it. Here he was delivering her into a career of supposed prostitution and at the same time was courting her with these semi-erotic flirtations. If he wanted her so badly, why was he giving her away?

Deliberately, she drew her hand away under the pretense of rummaging through her small handbag. She reapplied her lipstick, using a narrow pocket mirror then, just as she was finished, the car took a quick turn through traffic, jostling her on the seat. The hand holding the mirror angled sharply as she caught herself, catching the reflection of Zanlos in the small rectangle.

And an empty space beside him.

A sudden jarring blow to her wrist from Anna's knee took her equally by surprise. The mirror fell to the floor of the vehicle and, before she could reach down to pick it up, a slender spike heel shattered it into tiny slivers.

"Oh, dear. I am sorry," Anna purred with thick insincerity. "I guess I can look forward to seven years of bad luck."

Nick bent down to pick up the broken mirror. "Ladies as lovely as the two of you don't need to be reassured as to how fabulous they look." He made a small sound of dismay and looked at his thumb where a bright droplet of blood oozed from around a spearing fragment of the glass. As he removed the barb, Rae heard the strangest sound.

A growl, low and throaty, coming from Anna Murray. She covered it quickly, pretending to clear her throat, and Rae was almost convinced she'd been mistaken.

Almost.

Until she noticed the sudden glittering in the stare riveted to the small wound.

"Here." Kaz supplied a linen square for Nick to wrap about his finger. "You don't want to ruin your shirt."

As Nick bound the small puncture, Anna sat back, breathing rather loudly, her gaze slitted and glimmering. A nasty feeling settled upon Rae. Was the woman into strange stuff or just plain strange?

The car pulled up in front of the *Noir de Nuit* and they exited amid a crowd anxious to get a nod from the doorman. The first and only time Rae had been inside, she had snuck in on the arm of some elderly statesman, pretending to be his escort. She'd been an outsider, a threat. But in the company of the two club owners, a path was cleared as if for royalty.

"Good evening, Mr. Zanlos, Ms. Anna," purred a buxom hatcheck girl.

"Hello, Maxine. Good crowd tonight?"

The girl grinned at Kaz. "Big tippers."

"The best kind."

As they walked through the lobby area, the pulsing beat from the dance club below throbbed up the open stairway on a strobe of multi-colored lights. The young D.C. up-and-comers flocked there for a fierce techno rock sound and an elbow-to-elbow mill of fun-seekers. Entrance was for anyone who could afford the exorbitant cover charge, and the group was kept below by several burly bouncers lingering at the top of the steps. The club's exclusive, older patrons were allowed by membership only to the rooms on the first floor, the mix and mingle bar area, the soft sounds dance floor and the private dining nooks.

Their group of four was shown to one of the secluded, curtained-off rooms that looked the way Rae would picture a Turkish bordello. Draped in dark crimson velvets and black satin and fringe, all that was missing were the snake charmer and hash pipe, though she imagined the hash pipe could be found for a price. A semi-circular table faced the outer room, a plush booth curling behind it. The bench seat was backed by dozens of pillows which could be rearranged to give diners ample room for other dessert samplings once the curtains were drawn to seal them into their own isolated haven. They slid into the booth, she and Nick in the back, Anna on the end next to Nick and Kaz beside her. Kaz ordered drinks, and Rae understood that her interview was about to begin.

"Look around, Ms. Borden," Anna began in an almost indifferent tone. "This room is filled with lovely, exciting young women. Tell me why I need you."

She looked and, indeed, the women working the room were to a one gorgeous as they hung on the arms and upon the words of their dates for the evening. But there was also a similarity to all of them that she picked up on at once.

"I'm new here. I don't exude the same *ennui* as your other ladies. Perhaps some of your guests would prefer more of a country mouse to your collection of skilled professionals."

Kaz laughed and draped his arm along the back of the booth behind her. Though there was no actual contact, Rae was very aware of his encircling presence. And uneasy within it.

"My darling, I do believe she is calling your girls jaded."

Anna frowned a bit but upon examining the crowded room, she gave a relenting sigh. "Perhaps she is right. Our ladies will have to work on their enthusiasm. And you are enthusiastic, Ms. Borden?"

"I'm out of money, Ms. Murray. I have nice clothes and nice manners and no place to hang either. I don't want to return to Detroit if I don't have to. I don't have anything of value waiting for me there."

That wasn't a lie. With what she was doing now, she would never be able to return to her previous protect and serve position. This revenge was the only thing left to her, and some of that desperation must have shown through to Anna Murray's dissecting gaze. The woman nodded.

"Plenty is always better than poverty, having lived in both myself." Anna gestured toward the crowded room. "This is just the tip of what we do here at the *Noir.* You understand that, of course."

"Of course."

"My girls are chosen for their poise, their charm, their beauty, of course, and for their ability to make some weary and past-his-prime politician feel young and desirable again. With their families often on another coast, they are lonely and eager for companionship. They come here to form a bond with one of my girls. It starts with drinks and dancing and conversation here in this non-threatening atmosphere. If they like what they see, it becomes more. Once a client decides upon a particular girl, she is his to parade about at public functions as an escort, as a hostess in his home, as a sympathetic listener to all his woes. And she may become more. I leave that up to the girls. Devotion and discretion are what we are known for. None of these gentlemen want to see their current paramour out on the town with another man while he is paying the bills. Do you understand?"

"Like a mistress."

"Exactly, for how ever long the arrangement lasts. Some of the girls don't like that much permanence and choose to date on a night-by-night basis. That's up to them. With all the functions in Washington, we have no shortage of calls for a witty and well-dressed companion. We, Kaz and I, broker out the companions and in return, we receive a percentage dependant upon the experience of the girl and the services required."

"That's what you get, but what do your girls get?"

"Job security. A health plan. We'll even set up a 401K for retirement. There's a housing and clothing allowance up front to get you started. The girls are independent contractors. This is not a family. It's a business, and I run it as such. What you do when you're not on the job is not our concern until your indiscretion forces it to become so. We do not ever embarrass our clients. That is the one inflexible rule."

"An easy rule to work within."

"You think so? Some of the girls have not found it to be so, much to their misfortune."

Threat hung heavy upon that statement. Rae understood. Break the rules, become one of the Murder Capital's statistics.

"I am not foolish or greedy, Ms. Murray."

"What else are you? Nick vouches for you and, according to Kazmir, that says much, but a pretty face alone makes us no money. We require a girl with initiative and imagination, one who is not afraid to be bold. But discreet."

Here was her test, a gauntlet thrown down. How she picked it up would determine whether she left the *Noir* employed or on a plane back to the Motor City.

The curtains to their booth area were still open, and they were the focus of much attention from the others in the room. Discretion and initiative. Okay, she could do this. If she could pull it off, she'd be on the inside where she could do measurable damage to the smug Kaz Zanlos.

The drinks arrived, and as they were passed about, Rae dropped her napkin to the floor. Murmuring a polite, "Excuse me," she ducked down beneath the table.

***

Things were going well for Rae, Nick thought somewhat sullenly as he nursed his drink. She was everything Kaz and Anna were looking for—clever, lovely and, as she pointed out, different from the other sharp-edged women who worked the *Noir.* Clients would snap at her like fresh bait in a stocked trout pond.

And he hated it. Hated knowing that once she began work here, under the terms of her employment, there could be no socializing between them.

But they hadn't hired her yet. Perhaps she would make some glaring error, or offend them, or worse, bore them. Then he could enroll her in a good typing class and . . .

She slipped beneath the table after her purse or napkin, or something she'd dropped. He figured the initial press of her palm over his thigh was an innocent touch, especially after the way she had pulled away from him in the car. He understood. This was business, and he was to keep an impersonal distance. But then her other palm joined the first on his opposite leg, and they ran in tandem up to where he was the least prepared for her attention. A purposeful squeeze had him nearly clearing the seat.

"Nick, is something the matter?" Kaz asked out of

misplaced concern.

"Fine," he assured him in a voice that wasn't half as unsteady as the hand he used to reach for his water glass.

She was at his zipper.

Though he was in full view of the crowd at the bar and his companions, the drape of the table cloth disguised her intentions beneath it. That voyeuristic effect was as alarming as it was unbelievably, intensely, erotically pleasure-charged. He tried to drink from his water as her clever fingers found him through his opened fly. His teeth clattered upon the edge of the glass as he gulped and nearly choked. The feel of her incredibly soft lips on his hot skin sent him into a coughing fit.

"Goodness, man. Are you all right?" Kaz demanded, leaning over to vigorously pat him on the back. And about that time, Rae rose up from beneath the table linens to slide back into her seat. Her gaze was at a sultry half-mast, and when the tip of her tongue slipped appreciatively along her lower lip, no one had any doubt of what she'd retrieved while out of sight.

Kaz cleared his throat, amused by Nick's sudden flush of color. And Anna Murray leaned back with a smile, impressed by the discreet display of ingenuity.

"When can you begin work, Ms. Borden?"

"Any time it's convenient."

"Tomorrow would be fine." Anna fished in her tiny bag and drew out a card. Upon it was a single, gold-embossed number. "That's how you can reach me or my service. Stop by Kaz's office around noon. He'll give you an advance to see to your wardrobe and whatever else you might need. Then be here at ten sharp tomorrow evening to be introduced around. Kaz, we should go now. We have some other business to attend. The two of you, have another drink and a meal if you like. The car is at your disposal."

Then she slid out from behind the table and, as Kaz joined her, he pulled the curtain shut, veiling the two of them in privacy.

Rae looked at Nick. "I start tomorrow." Her eyes glowed

with a feverish excitement that was somehow too intense for the moment. "Thank you, Nick."

Well, now would she tell him to hit the road or find a more fitting way to thank him? An unworthy thought from a jealous soul. She had her fine job, now she didn't need him to protect or amuse her. He'd never had anyone in his life to care for, and he'd hoped...What a fool he was.

Twice the fool for harboring those notions for even an instant.

She leaned into him, her arms winding about his neck. And he forgot his perplexity and his doubts and everything else except the feel of her against him.

Their kiss was long and wet.

"The rest of the evening is ours," she murmured against his mouth. "What would you like to do?"

"We could order dinner."

She frowned prettily. "Not hungry for what's on the menu."

"How 'bout you finish what you started?" he suggested with a nibble of her lower lip. His hands cupped her bottom, lifting to help her step one leg over his, so she could settle on his lap where his attention was so painfully focused. Just the tease of her wiggling above him was nearly enough to undo his control.

It took all of about two seconds for him to forget their surroundings.

She arched against him, all liquid heat and urgency. She held his gaze for a long, seeking moment, letting those mysterious green depths convey her passion, her gratitude, her...affection? Was that what he saw there burning like a slow, emerald fire?

Did she care for him, or was this as far as their relationship would go now that he had seen to his promise?

Why did he want more with such a desperation?

His fingertips tunneled beneath the hem of her short black dress. He followed upward until he came to the end of smooth nylon. She was wearing stockings. He reached higher. And nothing else.

His breathing shuddered.

He combed through the already moist curls, two fingers following the slick passage leading into the ready heat of her. He pushed in, lifting her so that her lush bosom pressed over his face. He breathed in her warm fragrance and licked along the upper swells of her breasts as she squirmed restlessly upon his imbedded fingers. Sensing her soundless need, he sought the source of her distress with the pad of his thumb, pressing until she moaned, rotating until her hips ground down over his hand.

And just when her hot, deliciously damp and clutching flesh began to clamp down and quiver about him, he thought he heard his name whispered in urgency. It wasn't Rae's voice. She was busy panting into the throes of her pleasure. Odd...His gaze happened to skim over her shoulder up into the corner of their booth. And he went still all over.

Smile. You're on Candid Camera.

ELEVEN

Rae gasped in surprise as Nick snatched her back from the pinnacle of her release to deposit her on the impersonal seat beside him.

"Time to go," he told her in a terse voice, looking beyond her instead of at her.

"What's wrong?" she asked with a quiet intensity.

"This isn't the right place."

She laughed a bit recklessly. "Of course it is."

"Not for us," he argued, pulling her from the booth as she smoothed down her rumpled skirt. Then he was towing her toward the door.

What had happened? What had yanked him back from the pleasure they had both sought so eagerly?

Something. Something had happened. She could see it in the taut set of his jaw, in the fierce, shallow breaths he was taking. Something huge to distract him so completely from their involvement in each other.

And damned if he wasn't going to tell her what it was!

"Nick!" She dug in her heels as they burst into the lobby. "What's going on?"

"Nothing. Something came up."

"I know, and I was about to take care of that before you so rudely interrupted."

He was in no mood for humor, and that alarmed her more than his strange preoccupation.

And then she was distracted. For going down the wide steps into the basement disco was a spiked-haired Gabriel McGraw leading a pretty and unexpectedly innocent looking girl. Two things struck Rae—the girl didn't seem at all his type, and he was so enamored of her, he had eyes for nothing else. Not even his job. He rounded the landing and was out of sight without ever seeing her.

Then Nick was hustling her toward the front door. The gleaming silver limo was there waiting. He opened the door so she could slip inside then, to her surprise and dismay, he didn't follow.

"Have the driver take you home. I have some things to take care of here."

"Nick."

She said his name softly. Perhaps he didn't understand. This was good-bye.

He hesitated, one hand on the door, the other on her shoulder, obviously torn by which direction to take.

"Nick," she said again. She took hold of his arm and coaxed him down to her, where she kissed him, deeply, thoroughly, with all the confused desire percolating inside her. Never had she wanted and feared the same man so greatly, the latter because of the former. And because he had her so off balance and she needed her wits about her now, she had to let go.

It was so difficult.

Even after releasing the sweetness of his mouth, she couldn't relinquish his dark, desire-drenched stare. She touched his face, holding it between both hands while she probed his gaze for some clue as to his feelings for her and, at the same time, afraid she'd find them.

"Thank you, Nick."

"I will see you again."

A firmly spoken vow.

One she'd have to make him break.

She sat back, and he closed the door between them. Before she could think better of it, the limo glided away from the curb, carrying her from the one man she might have loved.

***

"Forget something, Mr. Flynn?" The tone of the manager's voice said he'd thought Nick had everything a man could want when he left the first time.

And he would have been right.

"Has Mr. Zanlos left already?"

"Just before you did."

"Damn!"

"Can I help you with something, Mr. Flynn?"

Nick gave him a speculative glance. "Maybe you can, Barry. I need the tape from our booth." He noted Barry's surprise and quick objection and hurried on. "I was going to ask Kaz, but since he's gone, maybe you...I don't want you to get in trouble or anything. There was just a little something on it between me and my girl that I thought might set the mood for later on this evening, if you know what I mean?" He grinned disarmingly.

Barry grinned, too, showing a row of perfect, capped teeth. "I saw your lady friend and could only hope to imagine. But I don't know, Mr. Flynn."

Sensing that he was losing him, Nick tried another tact. "If you're not allowed to, I understand. I mean if he keeps careful track of them or something. I don't suppose he does, does he?"

"A new one for every diner, Mr. Flynn. You know the boss, everything labeled and filed properly."

Nick sighed. "Oh yeah. Well, hell. That shoots down a perfectly good idea." Then he lowered his voice to a husky locker room intimacy. "Hey, Barry, I don't suppose you'd let me borrow it just long enough to make a copy, for my own personal use, of course. I could have it right back to you, and he'd never know it was missing."

"I don't know, Mr. Flynn." But he was looking around to see who was observing their conversation.

"You'd be doing a guy a favor." And he smoothly pressed a folded bill into Barry's hand.

Barry glanced at the denomination. "Oh, what the hell. Who am I to stand in the way of true love."

"You are a prince, Barry. I'll remember you at Christmas."

The manager was gone only for a minute, returning with a small bag of what others might have thought was take-out. Some take-out.

"Go. Go quickly."

"What?"

Barry blinked at him. "What?"

"What did you say?"

"I said I need that back," Barry cautioned.

But that wasn't what he'd heard whispered with a sudden, propelling intensity. Obviously, he was mistaken. Still, anxiety shivered through him, prompting haste. "No problem. We'll just keep this between us. Good night."

He called a cab out front.

"Where to, bud?"

For a minute, he considered giving him the Grovers' address, but it was too late for that, at least tonight. He gave his hotel's name and sat back for the ride, weighing the damning tape in his hand.

Blackmail. So that was what the *Noir* was about, and it explained Zanlos's interest. An influential man doing indiscreet things on tape with a lovely lady not his wife. Possibilities abounded.

So what was he going to do about it?

And later, as he replayed the tape alone, his fingertips traced over the image of Rae Borden's face.

What was he going to do about this? About her? About the way his chest tightened up with heart attack intensity just watching her on the small screen?

And he'd just handed her over into the middle of something as illegal as it was immoral. And, unless he missed his guess, dangerous as well. How was he going to get her out of it?

How was he going to get both of them out?

***

The ninety-degree vista of windows overlooked a city alive with intrigue and opportunity. That's why Kaz loved it, for the same reasons he might have loved the woman silhouetted against the glass...if either of them had had a heart.

It used to bother him that she didn't cast a reflection in the window. He'd gotten over it. He'd gotten over a lot of disturbing little details about her since they'd chanced to meet in his home of South Africa all those years before. Details weren't important. One concentrated on the end result. That's why he was so successful.

And that's why Bianca Du Maurier let him live.

"Do you think he knows?"

"Knows what, darling?"

Bianca gave him an impatient look. Any time the topic turned to Nick Flynn, she grew edgy and fierce. He didn't like it, but it was another of those insignificant details.

"Does he know who Rae Borden is? Or rather what she is?"

"I think not. The question is, now that we know, what will we do about it? It could be dangerous having her this close."

"Keep your friends close and your enemies closer. She could prove useful in dealing with Flynn."

Poor Nick. Kaz had taken a true liking to his naked ambition. Under the proper tutelage, he could have developed into a fine partner. But watching his unnatural partner pace like a wild thing before the windows, he knew that wasn't in the cards for Nick Flynn. "What have you got planned for him, Bianca?"

"There is no need for you to know my plans."

She looked down her haughty nose as if he were something too inferior to understand. At times like this, he truly despised her...enough to rid himself of the threat of her...if only he didn't fear her power and lust for it with an equal abandon. It wouldn't do to underestimate her tolerance. He had to be careful, or he would find himself a slave to her will. Their partnership was hardly a balanced one. Each knew the other's weaknesses and secrets that wouldn't bear the light of day. But she didn't need him quite as much as he needed her indulgence.

"Suffice it to say, you won't need to put his name up on Marvin's door." She chuckled softly. The hairs quivered on Kaz's arms.

"He's a good attorney."

"There are lots of good attorneys. Find another one." The sharp crack of her voice left no room for argument, so Kaz didn't pose one. Then her humor returned upon another dark chuckle. "Poor fool. He has no clue as to what's going on around him or why. He doesn't know that none of us are what we seem to be, himself included. He's in for a harsh education."

The way she said it made Kaz very glad he had been a quick learner. Things could have been much worse than partnering up with a demon.

He looked into the bank of windows, seeing just his own reflection there.

Much worse.

"And what if Nick chooses not to cooperate with your plans, darling?"

Bianca turned toward him. On rare occasions, she allowed him to see what she really was behind the facade of exquisite beauty. The image flickered, faltered and then faded into a juxtaposed shape. The shape of an evil without time or place or rules. An evil so horrendous, so ugly, he had to avert his eyes.

"He will cooperate. Or he will be dead."

Hadn't she offered him that same ultimatum years ago?

Nick was a smart boy. He'd make the same choice.

***

Fog.

Where had all the damned fog come from?

He'd left a clear, starry night behind in New Orleans to begin his long drive back along I-10 to Baton Rouge. The window was down to catch the cooling air in hopes that it would blow off some of the mental fog settling thick and numbing about his senses.

He hadn't meant to drink so much and now, halfway between home and going back, he wished he'd taken his host's offer of a room. He could have been sleeping off the celebration with that pretty girl catering the party instead of fighting against the pull of bourbon-soaked weariness to keep his car between the lines.

Where had the lines gone?

His headlights bounced back off the impenetrable mists blanketing the two a.m. world surrounding his vehicle. If he hadn't taken this road so many times before in a similar condition, he would have thought he'd made a wrong turn into the Twilight Zone.

The stretch of highway was eerie during the daytime, its divided ribbon of concrete suspended on pilings above a swamp. The only thing on either side of the road was a forest of rotted-out tree stumps trying to lift out of the murky water upon spidery roots. He'd always thought it would be a nightmare of a place to have a breakdown. As the sun set behind those ghostly sentinels, the creep factor escalated to the nth degree. Splintered stumps went from sharp silhouette to indistinguishable shadows standing watch in the darkness. Miles of nothing but those spooky shapes wading in treacherous waters.

And now he couldn't see the damned road past the hood of his car.

He turned the lights to low beam to combat the glare, and that was a little bit better. Only twenty more minutes to go before he'd be back in civilization. He should have stayed the night in New Orleans.

The temperature dropped to a clammy chill as threads of damp mists seeped into the car and into his bones. He blinked, struggling to focus through the opaque haze. Maybe some tunes would wake up his brain a bit. He reached for the radio but, after twisting the knob from low to high digits, could find no good reception out in this nowhere land. He fumbled on the passenger seat through a scattering of cassettes, selecting one at random and popping it in to play. Muddy Waters. Appropriate. He nodded in time to the soulful ballad. Yeah, man, he could relate to the woeful lyrics.

He drove on into the abyss of mists to the sound of mournful guitar riffs and the hum of his tires. When the tape ended, the silence woke him from his dozing behind the wheel. He straightened in alarm and scrubbed at his blurry eyes. This was no place to let the attention span wane. If his car went over the side and into those unforgiving waters, it might be days before they found him.

Wake up. Almost home.

He groped for another tape and plugged in B.B. King.

Yeah, the King of the Blues. And he was the king of the world coming back from a meeting that would change his life forever. No more cold canned spaghetti while watching the news on one of the two channels his old television set received. It would be take-out and imported beer kicked back in front of a big screen picking and choosing through a hundred sports selections off the satellite. Instead of trying to find loopholes in landlord tenant leases for nickels and dimes, he'd be working with the big oil boys to the tune of millions and billions for a hefty percentage of the prize. Ah, life was going to be good. And he deserved it. He'd worked hard for it.

And he'd make his daddy proud.

He'd never have to see that anxious, disappointed expression haunt his father's face again. He'd never be another cause for worry in the life of a man who'd known little else. He could give his daddy the rewards he deserved for putting up with the bull and foolishness of his only child's hard partying years. And Stephen Flynn would at last be assured that his only son had settled down into an honorable respectability. Yeah. That notion pleased Nick almost as much as that fat paycheck to come. Maybe more.

Suddenly too dry of mouth to swallow, he reached for the bottle of water he never left home without. It evaded his fingertips, rolling off the edge of the seat and onto the floor. As he dipped down for it, his attention left the road for an instant. Just an instant. And when he sat back up and looked ahead, there she was.

Nick sat up in bed, the sound of his own hoarse cry fading in his head. Breath laboring and bare chest drenched in an icy sweat of dread, he dragged himself to the bathroom to splash cold water on his face. The ashen features staring back at him in the mirror belonged to a man haunted by his past. He switched off the light, not wanting to recognize him.

On wobbly legs, he went into the living room, knowing that sleep was now restless hours away. Adrenaline pumped through him, sped onward by the frantic pulse of his fear and remembered horror. Collapsing onto the couch, he fought off the desire for a drink and let the shivering run its course.

Wouldn't his daddy be proud of him now?

Unable to share the next few hours with his own thoughts, he picked up the remote and rewound the tape from the *Noir.* He pushed play, and the sound of Rae's husky laughter soothed through him with 100-proof potency. He let his head drop back into the cushions and curled his feet up under him, a small smile curving his mouth as he watched the screen. Damn, she was beautiful.

Maybe it was the uneasy residuals from his dream that caused a disturbing queasiness to settle as he watched the tape. Something was out of place, missing from his own recall of the evening. He sat up and pressed rewind once more. What was it? He let the tape play again, studying it with a 'what's wrong with this picture' intensity. There he was stupidly swilling his drink and pretending he wasn't so distressed by the situation that his fillings ached. And Kaz, smooth, charming, like a sleek anaconda wrapping up his victim for just a little squeeze. And Rae, gorgeous, glorious Rae, so vibrant and alive, it made his lungs hurt to inhale.

He blinked, astounded then alarmed.

Where was Anna Murray?

It was the camera angle. It must have been.

But she'd been sitting right beside him. There was no way she could have been left out of the shot, on purpose or by accident.

She'd been sitting right there in that glaringly obvious empty space where on the tape he was laughing and talking to nothing, nobody.

How had the camera managed to catch the three of them to the exclusion of the icy blonde?

TWELVE

"May I help you?"

Rae stared at the obscenely perky young woman behind the desk, wondering why she looked so familiar. "I'm here to see Mr. Zanloz. Rae Borden."

"I'll tell him you're here, Ms. Borden."

The young woman smiled, and it hit Rae with the stunning force of walking into a glass door. Numbness vibrated through her followed by humiliation and pain.

This was the girl with Gabriel McGraw at the *Noir.* The one he'd been so wrapped up in, he hadn't seen fit to do his job—which was to protect her. Gabriel was tripping the light's fantastic with Kaz Zanlos's personal secretary.

But was that all he was doing?

Rae took a seat and began to thumb through a stack of eclectic magazines while sizing up Ms. Perky. Young, pretty with a cheerful energy...that reminded her, suddenly and unfairly, of Ginny. Had Gabriel been dazzled by that sweet smile and zestful innocence? Had he been lured astray, into telling tales out of school that would taint the investigation of Ms. Perky's boss?

Someone was tipping off Zanlos, Marchand LaValois had said. Someone with information about the lawful investigation into his unlawful activities. Someone leaking information that kept the clever lawyer one step ahead of their plans.

Was that someone Gabriel McGraw?

"Hello, Rae."

Just the sound of his voice startled a Snap, Crackle, Pop of awareness. She cast a guarded glance up along the exquisitely tailored suit, stopping with a cowardly hesitation at the burgundy power tie. Then she forced her gaze to meet his. She took a long, slow breath so he wouldn't notice how his very appearance sucked the oxygen from her lungs.

"Good morning, Nick."

He looked spectacular against this backdrop of Fortune 500 success. He would have looked equally spectacular pumping gas. She bet when he was a teen, the girls would line the sidewalk just to sigh as he walked past. As she wished she could sigh looking up at him now.

"Looking for me?"

She dashed his casually tendered hope with a single blunt sentence. "I'm here for Mr. Zanlos."

"Oh."

He lingered, shifting his weight from foot to foot like an awkward teen as he searched for the right thing to say. "I'm sorry about last night. That wasn't the ending I'd planned."

"You know what they say about the best laid plans."

Or the best plans to get laid. He smiled wryly at her play on words and at the insinuation that he'd done everything he'd done for her just for the anticipated reward. Rae knew that wasn't true, but it was better if he believed it. Now was the time to disassociate herself from Nick Flynn. He'd taken her where she'd wanted to go, and the rest of the journey was meant for her alone. He was a complication she couldn't afford—not to her job, not to her absurdly vulnerable emotions. He was no knight in shining armor. Beneath his designer suit lived a tarnished soul. But if he wasn't completely innocent of all Zanlos's scheming, why the zealous need to protect him from the harm of association? She hadn't made Nick Flynn's choices for him. He was here because he couldn't resist the money. And she would do what she could to keep him out of Zanlos's backwash because she just plain couldn't resist him.

That's why distance was imperative.

"It was good to see you, Nick." There was no mistaking the cut-off-at-the-knees dismissal in her tone. *Get lost, pal. You've got nothing I want any more.*

If only that were true.

But Nick had no intention of leaving gracefully. "How

about lunch after your meeting?"

Did she have to chase him off like a stray by pelting him with stones?

"I don't think that would be a good idea, Nick. We had some laughs, and you did a very good thing for me, but I said thank you. Let's not make it more than that, okay?"

He blinked as if she'd suddenly smacked him in the face with a shovel. But she'd say one thing for Nick Flynn, he was quick to regain his footing.

"Not okay, but I'll let it go for now. Just for now."

"Ms. Borden. Right on time."

She stood in response to Zanlos's fluidly accented voice. Everything tensed inside her in preparation for battle. She brushed Nick away with an off-handed, "Have a nice day, Nick."

Nick watched her follow Kaz into his office, trying not to feel as if she was carrying off part of him as a trophy. He knew what part. It ached as if she'd just kicked him there.

"Will this help?"

He glanced over at Naomi Bright. She held a Band-Aid.

"Not big enough for that gaping wound in your heart, eh?"

Was he that obvious? He grinned sheepishly.

"Actually, I think the wound in question was a bit lower, but thanks for the sympathy."

"No problem."

He took a longer look at Zanlos's secretary, as if seeing her for the first time. "I find myself embarrassingly without a lunch date. Think you could get away for a minute to help me soothe my ego?"

"Oh, if it's for a health emergency, how could I say no?"

Why hadn't he ever noticed the tart wit behind the pleasant smile? Naomi would be a nice distraction. And perhaps a fount of information as well.

As they were leaving the elevator on the main floor, an unfamiliar voice hailed Nick.

"Mr. Flynn!"

He turned to greet the beaming face of a new security guard.

"Yes?"

"Mr. Flynn, it's Teddy Kroeze." When the name didn't lessen his perplexity, the guard explained a bit uncomfortably. "You got me this job, remember? You gave me your card."

Nick's brows soared. The homeless man. Of course. From street beggar to this man of proud bearing. Wonder of wonders. He put out his hand.

"Ted, you cleaned up good."

"In a lot of areas, Mr. Flynn. Thanks to you and your friend. If there's ever anything I can do for you, I'm here from eleven to seven and an occasional evening. And the rest of the time, I'm with my family."

"Good man."

"No. You're the good man. I owe you, Mr. Flynn and I won't forget."

Uneasy with that assessment, he simply nodded. "Do a good job. Make me look good."

"Count on it, Mr. Flynn."

Walking a little bit taller, he escorted Naomi to the revolving exit doors.

"Who was that?"

"Just someone who needed a chance and was smart enough to take it."

They escaped the building, finding a small atrium café a few doors down that served a decent field greens salad and melt-in-your-mouth rolls.

"She's pretty."

Nick glanced at his companion. He could have played dumb but decided life was too short. "Yes, she is."

"Is she a friend of Mr. Zanlos's?"

"No. Mine. She's going to be working for him."

Her delicate brows furrowed. "At the office?"

"No. At the club."

"Oh." She drew hastily on her ice tea straw. Her awkward embarrassment goaded Nick to a brusquely given defense.

"Don't tell me you've never done anything you were ashamed of just to get by."

She met his slightly combative stare with one of unblinking

candor. "No, Mr. Flynn, I haven't. I haven't done much of anything."

"Then what makes you such an expert on romance and career choices?"

She blushed. "Did I say that?"

"You did just now. Who is this fellow who's going to make you break my heart?"

Her color deepened as she laughed. "His name is Gabriel."

"And this is a strictly plutonic relationship, right?"

She averted her gaze. "So far. I don't know why I'm telling you all this."

"Because you like me. You can't help yourself." His rakish grin relaxed her into a smile of her own.

"Yes, I do like you. What are you doing at MM&Z? I mean, I thought you were like them at first. But now, I don't think so."

Nick's attention sharpened. "Like them in what way?"

She glanced about, then leaned in conspiratorially. "You know, unscrupulous."

His gave a derisive snort. "I've cast off my share of scruples."

"But it bothers you. I could tell after that business with the Grovers. It doesn't bother the rest of them."

"And why is that, do you think?"

"Because they don't care about the people involved. They really don't ever see them, you know. I've been working there for six years, and you're the first person whose ever acknowledged that I actually have a life separate from my desk chair and computer screen. And have you met Anna Murray? Burr."

"Then why do you stay?"

Her pretty blushes cooled into an ashen intensity. "I don't think Mr. Zanlos would let me leave."

"What?"

She wet her lips nervously. "Because of what I know about what he does, I don't think he'd just let me walk away."

She was serious. He could tell by the shadows in her gaze, by the slight trembling of her lips. She was serious and she was afraid.

"But he's a lawyer, not a mobster."

"Really? Mr. Flynn, open your eyes. You've worked at MM&Z long enough to be spooked by the way things happen. Coincidence, accidents, luck—call them what you want, but nothing happens by chance. Nothing. That's all I'm going to say. I'd appreciate it if you'd forget we had this conversation."

"What conversation?"

She smiled faintly, but uneasiness still marked her movements. Could he trust her? Casually, almost as if it had nothing to do with what they'd just discussed, he asked, "Naomi, could you get me all there is to know about the Grover deal?"

"I–I suppose I could."

"I mean everything. I think it's time I had a little eye opener."

***

Since beginning her masquerade, Rae had never felt like a prostitute until leaving Kaz Zanlos's office with his cash in her hand. She resisted the impulse to stuff it into the cigarette can at the elevator. Without the front money she might have gotten from vice to set up a sting operation, she'd need it to set up the expected lifestyle, and she told herself that the need to get started was what had her hurrying.

But it was the fear of running into Nick again that had her practically jogging out of the building.

She didn't need to confront the distraction he created within her usually focused life. Nick was more than a distraction—he was a course-altering event, like a tide, a meteor, an emotional hurricane. And she wasn't ready to let an outside force have that kind of influence on her direction again. Not yet. Maybe never. Nick, bless him, had gotten her where she needed to be. Now she had to keep him out of the line of fire, even if that meant wounding him to keep him down and alive.

When she entered the Grover home, she heard Bette humming a lighthearted tune. The doors to Tom's study were open for the first time since his death and Bette was inside.

Rae headed there, knowing it wasn't going to be easy saying good-bye and leave the grieving woman on her own.

Only Bette Grover wasn't grieving.

She was packing the shared mementos of Tom and Ginny's past away.

The sight stunned Rae into a long stillness until Bette noticed her at the door. The older woman at first looked guilty then defiant. She started to explain her actions then thought better of it. Ginny's diploma and high school softball trophy went into a big storage box, followed by Tom's medals of valor. The glass in the case behind Tom's desk had been replaced, and the shelves already stood empty. A sense of panic and alarm sent a mortal chill through Rae.

"What are you doing?"

Bette's chin went up a notch. Resentment for the question shown plainly in her stare. "I'm turning this into a music room. It's a shame to waste the space. Such a nice view of the pool and gardens." Her tone weakened as she saw Rae's stony gaze take in the empty shelves. "I'm going to put my collection of porcelains in here to brighten up the room. Kaz said . . ." She hesitated as Rae went rigid. Then she concluded with unnecessary force. "Kaz said it was time I moved forward with my life."

Forward? Rae wanted to scream at her. *Your husband still has suits at the cleaners and here you are, boxing him and his daughter up like nostalgic reminders that had lost their sentimental appeal.* She phrased herself carefully.

"You can do whatever you want, Bette. It is your life."

"I wasn't asking your permission, Rae." And she began filling the box again.

Rae's heart seized up at the sight of an old 8 x 10 of her and Ginny in their prom dresses with Tom standing proudly between them, an arm about each of their shoulders. She'd loved the solid permanence of that arm. The picture went into the box and all its memories with it.

"You don't need to do this now, Bette," she said softly, thinking her abrupt denial might be in reaction to the trauma. But Bette didn't seem traumatized. She seemed hard.

"Yes, I do. I loved Thomas, and Ginny, as if she were my own daughter. But they're gone and I'm here. And I have no intention of living the rest of my life in their shadows. You should understand how destructive that can be."

Surely she hadn't meant for that to be as cruel as it sounded.

"I'm not strong like you, Rae. I can't live alone and by my own devices. I need a man in my life to take care of and to take care of me."

Cold with horror, Rae asked, "And you think Zanlos is that man?"

"Why not? He's been here for me. He's been sensitive to my needs—my needs, Rae—not to the memory of those who can't be helped any more."

"He doesn't care about you, Bette. The only thing he wants are Tom's contracts. Once he gets them, he'll be gone."

"So what? He's got them, and he's still here."

Rae tried to look beyond the belligerence to the woman who'd stepped in to raise Ginny, but couldn't find her. "What do you mean, he has them?"

"I gave him power of attorney for all Tom's business. I never cared anything for it, anyway. What do I know about port duties and import taxes? Why should I care about new warehouses in New Orleans? I just want to feel alive again. And I'm sorry if you don't approve."

"It's not what you're doing, Bette, it's who you're doing it with. Zanlos is up to his five o'clock shadow in illegal business dealings. Why do you think Tom wouldn't sign a contract with him until after Ginny died? Can you seriously be so naive that you think that was a coincidence?"

Bette flushed hot at the accusation, and Rae realized that she had pushed too far.

"You're blaming Kaz for Ginny's death?"

"She was dating him, Bette. He used her to get to Tom, just like he's using you now to grab up the rest of Tom's business assets."

"You just can't stand it, can you?"

Taken aback by the quiet accusation, Rae approached with caution. Bette Grover was cornered and could easily come out snapping.

"You couldn't stand the thought of Ginny being happy, not then and not now. Who's being naive, Rae? Can't you see the pattern? You attack anything that threatens your place in this family."

Rae gaped at her. "That's not true."

"Of course it is. You don't want me listening to Kaz because that lessens your influence. Well, Tom and Ginny are gone, and I don't have to listen any more."

"Bette—"

But she wasn't finished with her increasingly ugly summations. "You want someone to blame for Ginny's death? Blame yourself. That's right. You didn't think any man was good enough for her. You did your best to sabotage every relationship she ever had. I don't think she ever recovered from the way you drove David away."

"He had a criminal record."

"He did his time. He had counseling. The only one who couldn't forgive him was you."

"He beat his former girlfriend nearly to death!"

"She was a drug addict. She came at him with a knife."

"There's no excuse. He would have done it again."

"Rae, not every man is your father."

Rae reared back as that statement slapped her.

"One week before the wedding, Rae. You just couldn't leave it alone."

"He hit Ginny."

"It was an accident. She told you that herself. But you wouldn't believe her because you didn't want to believe her. You filed charges and made sure his parole was revoked. They took him away in handcuffs right in front of Ginny. She was devastated."

"I did it to protect her."

"You did it to keep her for yourself. You couldn't stand the thought of her loving anyone else. It was your suspicions and jealous selfishness that pushed her over the edge. She was in therapy for two years, did you know that? And then, just when she's starting to get her life back together, you send her a note criticizing her affection for Kaz."

"What? I did no such thing."

"Don't lie to me."

"Who told you that? Ginny? Did Ginny tell you that?"

"No. Kaz did. Just a few days ago. He didn't want to mention it before because he didn't want me to think badly of you or to believe Ginny's death was a suicide instead of an accident."

"He's the liar, Bette. I never sent Ginny a note of any kind."

"She just couldn't face your disapproval or the thought of your insecurities ruining everything for her all over again."

"I am not responsible for what happened to Ginny!"

"Just like you're not responsible for what happened to your parents. Face it, Rae, you have no tolerance for people who don't live up to your standards. You won't let people have failings or weaknesses, even if they've accepted them. Who are you to dictate how everyone else should run their lives? Look what your meddling cost you. Look at the damage you've done to those you've claimed to care about."

Breathless and struggling against the tidal pain of those words, Rae insisted, "Zanlos had Ginny killed."

"Get out of my house."

Once that phrase was coldly spoken, they both knew there was no going back.

"Stay away from me and my family's business," Bette concluded with an unexpected ferocity. "I won't allow you to interfere in my happiness out of some sick, desperate need you have to control others. Control isn't love, Rae. You don't know what love is. And don't worry. Your secret is still safe. I haven't said anything to Kaz about your job. But consider that job finished, or I will tell him everything."

And with that, Bette turned back to her packing and her back on her daughter's best friend. There was nothing left for Rae to do but go.

Bette was just finishing up with the last of the souvenirs to a life she'd had no part in when the telephone rang. She answered with a wavery hello.

"My darling, what's wrong?"

At that sound of tender concern, she poured out all the details of what had transpired, glad to release the pent-up guilt over the words she'd said and conclusions she'd drawn. But she needn't have worried. Kaz Zanlos knew just what to say.

"Darling, don't be troubled. I'll speak to Ms. Borden."

"Thank you, Kaz," she gushed in a grateful relief.

"No problem. I'll see she gives you no more cause for worry."

THIRTEEN

Usually a walk along the Wall put Rae's problems into perspective. All those names recording sacrifices far beyond what she'd ever been called upon to make. Among those names were the friends and comrades who'd stood beside her father and Thomas Grover to fight on foreign soil for a cause not all of them believed in but for a country they'd been ready to die for. These men never left the war. Neither had Frederick Borden. He'd brought the horrors and stresses home to his young wife, and they'd created shadows of violence behind the life they made together.

On the stone walk ahead, a family knelt together while the oldest member did a chalk rubbing onto a piece of construction paper and his wife explained to the two young children the significance of what they were doing. This was like grandpa's tombstone, and they were bringing part of it home so they wouldn't miss him so much. The children didn't understand, but Rae did. She thought of this overwhelming monument as her father's burial marker. In Viet Nam, he'd been a hero, decorated for bravery and dedication to duty. It was what he had become when he returned that she tried to forget.

She continued to walk along the Wall as tears burned in the back of her throat, for these young men and woman who would never come home, and for Captain Frederick Borden who'd never left the violence behind. Twilight was thickening along the path making it hard to discern the inscriptions. A man in a Grateful Dead tee shirt was reading off the names under the year 1969 to his wheelchair-bound friend who listened and nodded with tracks of remembrance streaking down his poignant features. Respectfully, Rae skirted around them.

"I was a hero."

She turned to the man in the wheelchair. "Excuse me?"

For one crazy moment, it was her father's face she looked upon.

"I was a hero, and how did you repay me?"

She sucked a loud breath and stumbled back on the uneven stones while the man at the Wall straightened to ask if she was all right.

All right? The man in the chair had just spoken to her with her father's drink-roughened voice and looked up at her through her father's angry-at-the-world glare.

Rubbing her temples, she turned away to walk quickly through the concentration of tourists who were starting toward the beginning of the Wall. Their conversations lapped over her, but under them all she heard was the whisper of a dreaded rhyme chasing after her the way it had at school.

Lizzie Borden took an axe and gave her mother forty whacks and when she'd seen what she had done, she gave her father forty-one.

Then the laughter, the taunting ugly laughter.

She raced blindly from the shaded paths.

Vendors lined one side of the walk, hawking everything from flags and sixties memorabilia to hat pins and company insignias from their makeshift booths. Many of them wore their uniforms and disabilities proudly. Others were simply out to make a buck off a painful moment in history they'd taken no part in.

"Buy a flag to fly this Veteran's Day?"

She thought of the neatly folded flag handed to her after a double funeral and shook her head. She tried to hurry past the way most tourists did, pretending not to see the man or remember the war, but the vendor reached out and caught her arm in a surprisingly firm grip. Startled, she glanced at the man and choked back her scream.

Daddy!

He pulled her up close, so close she could smell the heavy

fumes of stale liquor on his breath. So close she could see the spidery red vessels that seemed to throb in the whites of his eyes.

"Thought you could betray me and get away with it, did you, girl? See what you've made me do."

She refused to lower her gaze, afraid she would see the big survival knife in his hand and the blood still soaking into his khakis.

This isn't real. This isn't happening.

"See what happens to betrayers? See what happens when naughty little girls don't keep their mouths shut? You haven't learned anything, have you, Rae? Not a thing."

With a mewling cry, she jerked back and, as breaths panted from her, stared uncomprehendingly at the equally startled Vet, who resembled Elmer Fudd more than he did her hawkishly handsome father.

"Ma'am, are you okay? I thought you were going to faint. Do you want me to call someone?"

Yeah, Ghostbusters.

"I'm fine. I just need to sit down. I thought I saw-"

What? What did she think she'd seen? The past brought back by Bette Grover's harsh conclusions?

She stumbled from the vendor's area, wobbling across the wide street to the foot of the majestic Lincoln Memorial. She staggered up the steps, not to visit the expectantly seated former president where he waited like Santa Claus to hear the country's wishes, but to get a higher perspective on what was happening to her. Halfway up the broad marble stairs, her shivering knees gave way. She sank to the traffic-worn white step and let the tremors engulf her as she hugged shaking knees to her chest.

It was the ugliness of Bette's words that brought him back. Those horribly wrong accusations that she'd somehow been to blame. It hadn't been her fault. She'd done the right thing. She'd been trying to protect, not provoke. How could she have known the tragic turn things would take? How could she have known?

"Let go, Rae. Let us go."

Never in a million years could she mistake that voice. Never did she not believe that she wouldn't see Ginny Grover standing on the steps behind her, looking beautiful and benevolent against the glowing backdrop of white stone.

"Ginny?"

It wasn't a cry of denial but rather a plea that it be true.

But of course it couldn't be. Ginny was dead.

A mistake. Had it been an awful mistake? Had some other unfortunate been killed upon the tracks and wrongfully identified as her best friend because of the belongings scattered nearby?

Her mind told her no, but her stubborn heart wanted to hang on desperately to the notion.

"It's too late for you to make amends, Rae. You've got your own life to live. You had your chance to make it up to me. Four years, Rae."

"But I never had a chance to say I was sorry," she cried in her own defense. "I never had a chance to tell you I was wrong."

"You just did. Go home. Let us rest."

"I can't, Ginny. Not until I know what happened to you."

"What difference does it make now?" came a sadly spoken truth. "You can't change what's happened. But if you don't leave things alone, you'll join us. Is that what you want? To be like us? Is that the price you want to pay for the mistakes you've made?"

"No."

Even as she said the word, Ginny's beloved features began to dissolve into the horrifying remains of a track accident. As she spoke, the flesh fell away from the crushed side of her face, leaving an unrecognizable mess of shattered bone.

"Don't make us come after you, Rae. Mind your own business. Your pride and guilt are denying us the peace we deserve."

"Let us rest," came another agonizingly familiar voice, one Rae hadn't heard for decades...except in restless dreams. Her mother—wearing the same polka-dot spring dress she'd had on when Rae had found her lying on the kitchen floor with blood splatters playing connect the dot—stood, impossibly, next to the mangled corpse of Ginny Grover. "Haven't you done enough? Haven't you ruined enough lives with your meddling?"

The shock Rae felt was numbed by remembrance. Wasn't that what Bette Grover had said?

"Listen to them, Rae." Thomas Grover's demand, always the voice of reason. He joined the pair on the steps, the fact that the side of his head was blown out like a smashed melon didn't lessen the compassion in his gaze. "If you'd only listened, none of us would be here. This isn't about you. Let it go."

"She won't listen. She never listens to anybody."

Rae staggered to her feet at the sound of her father's condemning tone.

Sporting a self-inflicted wound that mimicked the one destroying the symmetry of his best friend's skull, Frederick Borden started down the steps. Blood, brain and bone rained down onto the pristine white stairs behind him. His lips drew back from impact-shattered teeth in a frightening smile.

"You can't tell my girl anything. She only learns through example. Hands on, right, Rae? Is that what you need? A little hands on?"

"Mama?"

Rae looked past the threatening advance to the figure of her mother. But now, as then, Anita Borden remained passively out of the way, looking at her through sad, dead eyes, smiling serenely as if to say she must resign to her fate.

"No. No!"

She wasn't Anita Borden, waiting complaisantly for the escalating violence to claim her life. She wasn't Ginny Grover who cast off caution in spite of consequence. She was a survivor. That's what had saved her sanity, and now would save her life.

She bolted down the steps, away from the menacing apparition and the mournful trio behind him. She didn't look back. With the setting of the sun, humidity settled in, heavy and thick. Her skin was wet with it. Her lungs labored with the effort of wringing air out of each breath. Tour buses were loading their final call along the side street. She pushed her way through the lines, muttering apologies but never slowing down. She had to get away. She had to think.

They rose out of the darkness ahead of her, heroically over-sized, determinedly focused on their goal beneath the glow of the moon. Nineteen poncho-clad ghosts from another past war intent upon their final advance. Rae dodged between the eerie figures left to their eternal patrol in a distant Korean rice paddy. Finding herself among the gleaming specters gave Rae a chill of foreboding. But none of them moved. None of them were real. Not as real as the memories pursuing her.

Panting, she collapsed on the edge of the wishing pool. She could see her own reflection in the still water upon the scattering of coins littering the bottom. She looked disheveled and terrified, like one of the silent soldiers frozen in time. Over her shoulder, at any moment, she expected to see other faces tragically altered by less heroic events. But she was alone. With the tourists called back to their buses, the monument area grew quiet. A tranquil silence, not an unsettling one. Gradually, Rae's racing pulse slowed.

With a shaking hand, she dipped water from the pool to cool the fires blazing in her face and neck. The horror she's experienced took on manageable proportions.

Of course the ghosts from her past were crying out to her. But not for rest—for justice. But in order to mete that justice out, she'd have to deal with these long-denied memories and question her motives to be certain that they were pure. Only then could she affect a satisfactory retribution. Only then could she move on.

To what? What did she have awaiting her? A crappy apartment in Detroit. A job that frustrated her. Loneliness that stretched out achingly through the months and years ahead. She didn't want to go back and, because of what she was doing here, probably couldn't go back. So what did that leave her besides the here and now? What was there to consume her beyond this quest for truth?

Nick Flynn.

Thoughts of him whispered through her mind like a warming breeze. Strange, because she'd never allowed herself to equate happiness or success to a relationship with a man. She'd never had any thoughts on the subject at all, until Nick Flynn with his devilish smile and soulful dark eyes she could drown in. The thought of being with him now, of curling up with him for the night, was an addicting dream. But that's all it was. She'd pushed those longings aside to pursue her goal and, by the time she attained it, she wasn't fool enough to think Nick would be waiting.

She had nothing waiting and nothing to lose. Except her momentum if she remained where she was, paralyzed by the past.

She had a job to do and it started tonight at the *Noir.*

She'd reached her rental car and was unlocking the door when another call assailed her.

"Detective Borden?"

She whirled around, her hand instinctively diving for the gun that wasn't there. Upon recognizing the speaker, she released her breath savagely. "Good God, Palmer, you should know better than that. If I'd been carrying, you could be fitted for a navel ring about now."

"A little testy, aren't you, Detective? Something got you jumping at shadows?"

"No, just at careless policemen who've forgotten how to make a safe approach. What do you want, Palmer?"

"I want my partner back, but he seems obsessed with that accident/suicide case of yours."

"It's not my case, and I'm not McGraw's keeper."

"Maybe not your case but it certainly is your crusade. I don't want the kid pulled into something he can't get out of."

"McGraw can take care of himself. I didn't get the impression that he was stupid."

"Well, he's doing some stupid things, like not checking in, like not letting his partner know what's going on." Palmer sounded more irritated than concerned at being kept out of the loop.

"Well, I don't know what's going on with him, either. Maybe it's a conflict of interest with his girlfriend at Meeker,

Murray & Zanlos."

Palmer's brows angled up like a drawbridge, and Rae instantly regretted her words. She was tired and shaky, but that was no excuse for being indiscreet with her suspicions. She opened her car door and gave the other detective an impatient look.

"Do you have some information for me? Otherwise, I'd like to get the hell out of here."

"Don't do anything stupid on your own, Borden. You're not officially on this, so don't expect official courtesy if you get yourself in trouble."

"I wasn't aware you could be courteous." She dropped down onto the sticky seat and cranked the engine. Hot air steamed out of the vents. She glanced up at Palmer who was leaning on the car door. "Thanks for your concern but I can handle myself, too."

"Sure thing, Lizzie." He shut the door and stepped back before she could react to the name he'd called her.

The air came on, jetting a cold blast from the dash, but that wasn't what had Rae shivering.

Lizzie.

She started to react the way she always did to the unfortuante coincidence of name that brought such a mocking pain to her past tragedy from the cruel taunts of fellow classmates to the unfounded rumors whispered at the academy. She stiffened, frozen in gut-twisting denial.

It isn't my fault! It isn't my fault that they're dead!

From the sly smugness of the other officer's expression, she knew that was the reason he'd flung that old insinuation into her face. To put her on the defnesive, to knock her off balance by using her own demons against her.

Not this time.

Her tone was as cold as the air conditioning seeping out of the partially opened window. "My father used a knife, not an ax, and he closed the case himself with his own .357. And that's what it is, Palmer, Case Closed. Old news. I'd have expected something a little more original from you."

And Palmer leapt back as she trod down hard on the gas

pedal, leaving him and his ugly inuendo behind in a cloud of exhaust.

***

Rae's evening at the *Noir* was anticlimactic. Neither Anna nor Zanlos put in an appearance. Nor did Nick, though she refused to admit she'd been looking for him. Under the guidance of an icy blonde aptly named Crystal, she was introduced around as the new girl to both fellow employees and potential clients. She danced, she laughed at bad jokes and ignored some heavy-handed groping. The customers were horny and her fellow employees treated her with a remote mixture of curiosity and competition. Both she found unsettling and disagreeable to her mood.

She'd worked vice for long enough to see what was going on. It was more than an escort service, but how much more and how to get the illegal doings tied to Zanlos in a direct hangman's noose was the challenge. Since she didn't intend to take her undercover work under the covers, she had to act fast and efficiently. The procuress, Anna Murray, of whom all the girls were afraid, wouldn't let her work the room as eye candy alone for very long, especially since she'd already entertained some startlingly large offers for extracurriculars.

Then there was the overshadowing threat of Bette Grover. How long could she be trusted to say nothing to her dangerous new lover?

She'd promised LaValois she'd get inside, and here she was. He'd been as good as his word and had erased the trail back to her real job in Detroit. She didn't ask how, but apparently her new background had survived some serious scrutiny. The only ones who knew her true identity were Gabriel, his rather disagreeable partner and Bette Grover. How long Bette would keep that news to herself, especially now that their relationship was strained, wasn't something she wanted to bet her life on.

So she had to make the most of what time she had.

The girls were no help. They weren't much for conversation. Her overtures about Anna and Zanlos were greeted with blank looks or lightly veiled hostility. The answers she did get were all maddeningly similar—the pay was great, Anna Murray was a generous but ruthless employer who didn't appreciate questions, and Kaz Zanlos was one delicious trick they'd all love to turn. But apparently, he never played in his own back yard. Not even with his glamorous partner. Rae wondered why.

While the action below in the dance club intensified, the activity at the *Noir* slowed as dawn approached. Most patrons had found what they were looking for and had paired off, either in the surrounding booths or off-premises. A few die-hard revelers continued to drink and gamble and sample from the girls remaining– the on-call call girls, Rae supposed they'd be titled, the ones who worked the room for the entire evening. Taking advantage of the quiet, Rae slipped from the thinning crowd to do some exploring on her own.

The first floor held no mysteries—main room, private party areas and gambling nooks, and the girls' dressing room in the back. And a locked door at the rear of the building in the stairwell where Gabriel had dragged her out that first night. Behind it, she guessed the stairs went up. And that's where she would go.

She withdrew her lock pick from her carefully coifed hairdo where it had been serving double duty holding the elaborate twists in place. After casting a cautious look around, she went to work on the lock. Tricky but not invincible. Stairs leading up. She took them as fast as her hooker shoes would carry her. She'd just reached the first landing when a low purring voice stopped her cold.

"Where you going, sugar?"

Rae turned to see the sleek and icy Crystal three steps below her. Finding her that close without her knowledge sent a shock of alarm through her system. How the woman had managed a stealthy climb in her five-inch stilettos was one of the great mysteries of the universe. Apparently, the woman hadn't been as distracted below as Rae assumed and took her shepherding position seriously. As serious as a heart attack.

"You scared me," Rae stated rather breathlessly to explain away any residue of guilt that might have crept into her expression. "I didn't know anyone else was here."

"What are *you* doing here?"

There was nothing in the chill blue stare that hinted at a sympathetic or easily fooled listener. Rae sized her up covertly, wondering if she could take the Nordic queen out quietly and make good an escape. If she ran, leaving Crystal behind without a good story to tell, the masquerade was over.

"I was looking for Anna. She told me I could come to her in the office with any questions."

"No, she didn't."

Well, hell this wasn't getting her anywhere.

Taking the offense instead of the defense, Rae squared out defiantly. "Are you calling me a liar?"

"No one is allowed up here. What would you call it?"

"A misunderstanding, I guess." She let all the hostility drain away to adopt a silly-ole-me attitude. "I must have heard her wrong. One of the other girls told me I'd find her up here. I didn't mean any harm. It's not like I was going to steal anything. Like, why would I want any trouble on my first night here, right? Unless you make it into trouble." Rae opened her eyes wide and smiled, playing up the sisters-got-to-stick-together ploy.

"How did you get past the locked door?"

"It was open."

"It's never open."

Rae sighed. "There you go calling me liar again. We're not getting off to a very good start here if we're going to be friends."

"We're not."

Something changed in the other woman's stare, a glitter of dangerous intent warning Rae that becoming bosom pals was out of the question. Time to bluff and run.

"Well, if Anna's not up here, I'm going back to the party. It's been fun getting to know you better."

And she started down the stairs. There was silence except for the sound of her heels and the stir of the hair rising up on the back of her neck. She tensed, ready for an attack from behind...that never came.

At the bottom of the steps, she risked a look behind her.

The stairs were empty.

Puzzled, yet counting her blessings, Rae returned to the main room. She ordered a club soda at the bar and watched the doorway for signs that the jig was up.

"Hey, girlfriend, you look like you've seen a ghost."

Rae smiled at the ebony-skinned beauty beside her who seemed to find great hilarity in that stock phrase. "Just a little spooked by Crystal. Is she always that intense?"

"Everything around here is intense, Snow White." And she grinned, displaying perfect white teeth. "You're not in the inner circle yet. That's where the excitement is."

Rae's questions stalled when she noticed several bright spots of color on the other woman's beaded halter top. She followed Rae's stare and chuckled, wiping at the shiny droplets.

"Must have gotten a little too enthusiastic with my date," she murmured, then sucked the blood off her fingertips. Her eyes drooped with a lazy pleasure, as if she'd just snorted up a healthy line of coke. Rae took an uncomfortable step back as the other mused dreamily, "Just one of the perks of the job, baby. You'll know what I mean soon enough."

And her throaty laugh sent a cold shiver to Rae's soul.

***

Watching the bold little liar start down the stairs ahead of her stirred a fierceness within Crystal Faye Johnson—or at least that was the name on her bus pass when she'd headed for a new future of political intrigue from the flat, far-reaching fields of her home town in Nebraska to an internship in Washington. She'd never made it to that exciting new career, and her name was Crystal Delite now. She'd gotten sidetracked in that darkened bus station on her first night in town, a distraction that led to an entirely different future for the political science major who'd once held to such liberal views.

The only view she was interested in at the moment was that of the silky throat of the woman in front of her.

Just one little taste. No one would know. And then she'd have the truth from the sneaking little bitch.

She glided closer, opening her whetted mouth, anticipating the sweet, hot delight to come. A sudden jerk from behind had her sharp teeth snapping together on air as she was whisked into the upper hallway.

"Sorry, sweetheart. She's not on the menu," goaded an unfamiliar male voice.

The instant he released her, she spun to furiously attack whomever had been foolish enough to interrupt her plans for dinner.

***

At dawn, surprised and relieved that Crystal had never put in an appearance, Rae went home alone to the new apartment she'd just rented in the hilly neighborhood of sprawling old homes...within walking distance of Nick's hotel.

She'd told herself the price was right and the hilltop view was worth far more. She'd noted the advantages of a short walk to the subway, high ceilings and eclectic neighbors who tended to live and let live.

But truth be told, she could look out her bedroom window and see the majestic silhouette of Nick Flynn's rooftop, and if that was as close as she could get to him, she'd take it at any price.

A sad state of affairs in the love life department.

She'd gotten out of the cab on the sharply angled street, looking forward to slipping out of her heels and into some heavy duty REM slumber. Until she glimpsed a chunky black convertible parked on the other side of the street a block down. Foot freedom would have to wait.

She paid the driver and, instead of going up her own short walk, crossed the narrow street. There was no mistake. It was Gabriel's boat of a vehicle. As she circled it, she paused at the trunk. A scrap of flashy silk protruded from beneath the lip of the closed lid. Just the sort of gaudy fabric Gabriel would wear for one of his shirts. Okay, he carried his laundry in his trunk. No big deal.

Until she saw a spattering of rust-colored specks on the bumper.

Not rust. Not on McGraw's baby.

Uttering a soft curse, she pulled up on the trunk. Locked. Having dropped her favorite tool for the job on the stairs at the *Noir* when she'd thought she'd been discovered, she fumbled in her inadequately supplied purse and came up with a slender-bladed pocketknife. She carried it 'just in case.' This was one of those cases, if someone had dumped Gabriel McGraw's body in the trunk of his own vehicle.

After a frustrating minute of jimmying, she managed to pop the lock. As much as she didn't want to see what was in the trunk, she knew she had to look. But the moment she started to lift the massive lid, it was yanked down with surprising force. From inside.

"No!"

"Gabriel?"

"Don't open the trunk."

His voice sounded strained by alarm, and all her warning bells and whistles went off.

"Gabriel, are you all right?"

"I won't be if you pull up this lid."

"Are you hurt?"

"I'll be dead if you don't close the trunk. Now!" Then quickly, breathlessly, he urged, "Do it, Rae. Trust me like I'm trusting you to do what I tell you. I'll explain later. Please."

There was just enough raw anxiety in that last word. She slammed the trunk lid down, but it was a long minute before she could walk away.

What the hell was a wounded cop doing hiding out in the trunk of his car?

She could wonder, but she wouldn't act against his wishes.

Gabriel McGraw had some serious explaining to do, and she had the feeling that she wasn't going to like it in the least.

And that feeling just got bigger. Because after she'd showered and was preparing to draw the blinds in her bedroom to get some much-needed sleep, she glanced down onto the street in time to see a woman slip behind the wheel of the big Mercury and drive away.

That woman was Naomi Bright.

FOURTEEN

Trust me. I'll explain everything.

Yeah, right.

After an hour of restless tossing, Rae gave up on the idea of sleep. Lying on her back in the artificially darkened room, she stared at the ceiling and tried to make sense of things.

Gabriel McGraw was in collusion with the woman in Kaz Zanlos's office. Had he been tipping her enemy off right from the start? Had he attached himself to her with his offer of help just to see how close she managed to get before they pulled the rug out from under her?

She was very close, dangling above the open maw of her own certain death on a literal limb. There would be no help for her should that branch break. Palmer had made that crystal clear. She'd abandoned official sanctions the moment she acted on her own without going through proper channels with the D.C. police. Whom could she trust? Someone was in league with Zanlos. Was it Gabriel? And what did she really know about the mysterious Marchand LaValois and his shadow ops organization? She'd burnt her bridges with Bette Grover by speaking out prematurely. So who did that leave her to turn to?

That left Nick Flynn.

And that left her with nothing at all.

She'd needed to trust Gabriel. The sting of his betrayal carried a near-fatal venom. She'd needed him for a backup, for a safety net, for a guide to keep her from going too far off course. She'd needed to trust Gabriel...but she longed to trust Nick.

She'd opened her heart and soul to a stingy few: her parents long ago and to the Grovers—and see where that had left them. Their losses cut away the tendrils of trust reaching out for a hopeful connection. Without them, she was alone. There had been no relationships, no loves, either minor or earth-shattering, no close friendships in the interim. The tragedy of her past taught her to keep others at bay. It taught her that love and dependence didn't hold the storybook promise of happily-ever-after. Love meant vulnerability. Dependence led to weakness and poor judgment. Both things were better kept at arm's length. And that had been her credo. She hadn't let others get close, discouraging those who would try with the cut of her defensive indifference that was so well-pretended, they thought she really preferred to be left alone.

But though a solitary existence guaranteed safety from hurt, it was sorely lacking in the companionship department.

She'd enjoyed Gabriel's banter. Something good might have developed from their friendship, until worms of suspicion had wriggled in to contaminate that prospect. Now he was to be watched and guarded against, like a potential enemy.

And that left Nick.

Her need for Nick Flynn went far beyond the want of friendship. The feelings she held for him stirred with the promise of life and expectancy, two things missing from her day-to-day pattern. He excited her. He scared her because of it. She had never intended to want a man—to want his company, his attention, his touch—his love. She wanted Nick Flynn so badly, she ached inside, for all the right reasons that were somehow still all wrong.

He was a good man with bad connections.

He was a great lover with a zero percent in the commitment department.

He made her bubble up with hope of what might be while well knowing it could never happen.

There was no future with Nick because everything she was actively doing to bring down Zanlos would topple him as well.

Unless he chose to sever the association now before the damage was done. Or was it too late already? Nick had made his choices. Whether he agreed with Zanlos's policies or not, he was still in his employment. That implied a complicity strong enough to damn him and destroy his career. And any hope of them ever being together.

No, it was best she put thoughts and dreams of Nick Flynn aside as unrequited. Happily-ever-after wasn't a page to be written in her life story. She was alone with her hard lessons in life to guide her and only her own instincts to trust.

But could she trust them?

Closing her eyes, she could see the apparitions that haunted her at twilight. Her father, her mother, Ginny and Thomas Grover. All dead through tragedy. All whispering to her from beyond the grave.

Of course, she hadn't really seen them. That was impossible. She knew that. She *knew* that. She believed that because she had to. The alternative was insanity. Had Bette Grover's accusations pushed her beyond that line? That same line her father had crossed, where reality no longer had the same appeal as his fantasy world of alcohol and paranoia?

Logic gave only three solutions to what she'd seen the night before: they were stress-induced figments of a guilt-ridden imagination, she was crazy...or she was in very serious trouble.

***

Going to work had lost its appeal since his eyes had been opened to the truth about Meeker, Murray & Zanlos.

Rubbing those tired eyes, Nick let the elevator carry him upward as his mood sank proportionately lower. He'd been up most of the night pouring over the documents Naomi had smuggled to him. Documents so damning he could no longer hide from the truth. He was up to his eyebrows in trouble—illegal and dangerous trouble. By the time he'd fallen into an exhausted sleep on his sofa with all the facts spread out on his coffee table before him, he knew what he had to do. He had to get the hell out of Dodge before the law came gunning for him.

And he fully intended to take Rae with him.

He hadn't gotten very far on that plan yet. Not beyond the

notion of bursting into the *Noir* to carry her out over his shoulder. That had a basic, caveman quality about it that appealed to him. But would Rae see it more as a kidnap than as a rescue?

What if she didn't want to be rescued? That was his biggest worry. What if even after he laid out the facts as he'd discovered them, she didn't want to leave? He couldn't force her to choose an uncertain future with him over the seductive allure of Anna Murray's world of dazzling clothes, exhilarating political circles and cash in hand. Lots and lots of cash. Would she care where it came from if she cared so little about how it was earned? He hated himself for thinking that. He was no angel and had no right to cast judgment upon what she did to earn a living. But the fact remained, he wanted her to care. If he was going to toss everything aside to take a stab at decency, he wanted to take that step with her at his side. They could walk away from their pasts and start over fresh like the D.C. streets each morning, scrubbed down and free of grime and litter. That's what he wanted. But could he make her want it, too?

The elevator door slid soundlessly open upon the world he'd once craved like an addiction. And like a recovering addict, the sight of it still gave him the yearnings and the shakes. Power. The scent and sight of it exuded from all he observed. How he'd wanted it. Still desired it. But not at the cost attached.

Naomi Bright sat at her desk staring listlessly at the colorful aquarium fish swimming across her monitor's screen saver. Even as self-absorbed as he was in his own predicament, Nick noticed her unusual demeanor. She was like a champagne gone flat.

"Good morning, Naomi."

Her gaze lifted slowly, and only after she'd stared at him for a long moment did recognition spark then just as quickly extinguish. A dull opaqueness shuttered her gaze.

"Good morning, Mr. Flynn." Her tone was as lifeless as her demeanor.

"Naomi, are you all right? You don't seem yourself this

morning."

Her hand rose unconsciously to clutch at the collar of her blouse. The movement drew his attention to the flesh-colored bandage that stood out against the unnatural pallor of her throat.

"I'm fine, Mr. Flynn. Just a touch of a bug, I guess, so don't get too close."

She tried to smile, and that made her appearance all the more artificial. Nick's alarm mounted.

"Maybe you should go home or to a doctor. You don't look well."

Objection infused a brief animation, but it quickly faded away. "I can't do that, Mr. Flynn. Not today."

"Why not today?" He glanced at Kaz's closed door. "Is something going on?"

"You haven't heard."

The back of his neck prickled. "Heard what?"

"About Mrs. Grover. She was in a car accident last night. She's in critical condition."

Nick's first thought was of Rae. How was she going to handle this latest tragedy? Then his mind moved inevitably, awfully to the connotations of what he'd just heard.

Bette Grover was in the hospital.

And Kaz Zanlos had power of attorney.

Coincidence? Not a chance in fiery hell.

"Naomi, I need a favor."

Her glassy eyes never blinked.

"I need you to find me an address for Rae Borden."

Naomi's well-manicured hands tapped over her keyboard. Nick watched them and wondered how difficult it could be to learn to type with proficiency. After finding the right contact file, Naomi jotted the address down on one of her pastel Post-It notes.

"I'll be back later this afternoon if anyone asks."

As Nick started to turn, Naomi's lackluster response stopped him.

"He's already asked. He wants to see you right away."

Nick glanced at the door again. There was no comparison

between what Kaz Zanlos wanted and what Rae Borden might need when it came to his time and attention.

"He'll have to wait until I get back."

"Mr. Flynn, he's asked for the Grover files. What do I tell him?" Only a minimal distress touched that monumental question.

"Tell him I asked you for them. Tell him I took them home with me to do the research he asked me to do. That's the truth, isn't it? Don't try to lie, Naomi. I don't want you to get into any trouble."

Too late. That was what was wrong with Naomi Bright. She was already in trouble, and consequence had sucked the effervescence from her.

He put his hand over the back of one of hers to give a supportive squeeze.

How cold she was!

"Naomi, I'll take care of things when I get back. Tell him I went to get the files. You were just doing what your were told to do. I'll make things right for you."

She stared up at him, never blinking. "All right, Mr. Flynn."

As disturbed as he was by her odd behavior, he couldn't spend any more time on it now.

"I'll be back, and I'll take care of everything."

She just stared. The eyes of a condemned soul.

***

The last person Rae expected to see after shuffling like a zombie to answer her bell was Nick Flynn. She pulled the overlap of her robe together as if that would contain the leaping of her heart.

"Nick? What are you doing here?"

Something in his face, some sympathetic softening, alerted her to bad news.

"What is it?"

"There's been an accident. Bette Grover is in the hospital. Get dressed. I'll take you."

What followed was a blur. She got dressed but didn't remember what she put on. She took a moment for some rudimentary grooming, then was out the door with Nick's stabilizing hand at her elbow. He didn't speak beyond telling her what little he knew. A car accident. Critical condition. She sat stiffly on the passenger side of his rental car, taking small, shallow breaths because if she tried to breathe deeply, she feared it would become a sob.

Though she had no reason to jump to that conclusion, Rae knew she was to blame. Somehow. Bette Grover was in the hospital because she'd failed to protect her. She'd failed...again.

Nick was wonderful, she realized in a numb periphery. He got them quickly to the hospital and handled the details for her. He told the wary nurse that Rae was a relative and then led her along the antiseptic hall to Room 801.

The sight of Bette Grover stunned her. Nick's arm went about her waist as her knees gave slightly. The always immaculate second Mrs. Grover lay within the white sheets, bruised, untidy and looking well beyond her age. Contusions darkened her brow and jaw as if she'd taken a beating. Miles of IV and monitor lines were strung from her chest and motionless arms. Rae looked away, needing to find some scrap of composure.

And that's when she saw Detective Palmer.

"What happened?" she asked weakly, not caring why he was there as long as he had that answer.

"As far as we know, it was a single car accident. She was driving at a high rate of speed and lost control of her vehicle. It flipped over and landed in a culvert. It was a couple of hours before anyone noticed the car."

Rae shuddered, imagining the other woman trapped in the car, perhaps conscious and frantic with pain and fear while minutes ticked into hours.

"What do the doctors say?"

"I'll be lucky if I get a statement. She's been in a coma since they brought her in this morning. Massive chest trauma and internal injuries. She wasn't wearing a seat belt."

"She didn't like the way they wrinkled her clothes," Rae explained, as if the drape of her designer garb justified the price Bette Grover might ultimately pay for her vanity.

The doctor came in then to check the unconscious woman's vitals. He ignored Palmer's petition that he be allowed to stay. A badge meant next to nothing with a life hanging in the balance. After Palmer left begrudgingly, Rae touched the doctor's arm.

"Was she in any pain?"

When he saw the anguish in her expression, the doctor's attitude softened. "I don't think she knew what hit her. A smart-looking lady like that." He shook his head sadly. "You'd think she'd have enough sense not to mix alcohol and prescription drugs."

"Alcohol? She'd been drinking?"

"The car reeked of it from what the reports said. I haven't gotten the toxicology reports back."

Rae's tone was suddenly stone cold sober. "I'd like to see them when you do."

"I don't know if I can–"

She took the prescription pad from his coat pocket and made a quick note on it. "There's my number. Call when you have news."

The doctor glanced at the digits and at the brief sentence scrawled beneath it. *I'm a cop.* He folded the paper and put it into his trouser pocket.

"I'll call."

"Thank you."

It wasn't until they had taken the large stainless steel elevator down to the first floor that Rae began to feel the events of the morning catching up to her. Instead of heading toward the garage exit, she noticed a sign that offered more in the way of comfort.

The chapel was empty yet still welcoming with its scent of oil soap and candle wax. Nick followed her to the second pew from the front, genuflecting slightly before sliding in beside her. She didn't bow her head or appear to pray, but he thought it best to leave her to her private grieving. And when she finally spoke, her words astonished.

"It's my fault."

"Rae, how could it be?" he argued gently.

"We had words when I moved out the other day. She said some things to me that I didn't want to accept. She'd just lost two members of her family. I should have been more understanding."

"You can't seriously think an argument you had a day ago forced her off the road and into a hospital bed."

Rae didn't look at him. Instead, she focused on some spot in space. "She never drank, Nick. Never. It was one thing we had it common. Alcohol made her deathly ill, even a small glass of table wine. She must have been more upset than I realized to do something so uncharacteristic and harmful."

If she had done it at all.

He considered speaking out, if only to lessen Rae's self-flagellation. But what good would voicing unsubstantiated theories do? He had to come to her with the whole truth. The truth that his boss, Kaz Zanlos, was behind the ruin of the family she'd loved like her own. And that he'd known it from the very beginning.

And once she knew, would she allow him close enough to comfort her? Would she allow him anywhere near her if she knew the entire truth, that the Grover incident merely scratched the surface of his sins?

He was kidding himself if he thought she'd find him to be a good enough risk to walk away from what she had.

Would she even want to know that the man who'd hired her, who'd brought her off the streets into a posh existence, was behind her many miseries? Was he being naive to think she'd be grateful?

She sighed heavily and stood. "There's nothing more I can do for her here. Would you take me home, Nick?"

He almost asked to his home or hers, but he knew the answer. Hadn't she made herself clear on more than one occasion?

He was crazy to think she'd listen to his talk about caring for her when her stock in trade was bartering affections. Perhaps a ride home was all he could offer.

She was equally incommunicative on the way back, her

thoughts miles away and upon things that didn't concern him, so he stayed silent, too. What could he say to her when he still was on Zanlos' payroll, when he still hadn't found the courage to come forward with what he knew? His continued silence regarding his role in Grover's death made him a participant in her unhappiness. To console her would add insult to that injury.

He would drop her off and go straight to Zanlos. Or should he go directly to the police with the evidence in his possession? First, he needed to get Naomi to safety. Then, for once, he'd do the right thing for someone other than himself.

He pulled over on the sharply angled street outside her house and set the parking brake. Rae didn't move, so he got out and came around to open her door for her. She let him lift her out. The firm warmth of her kindled a reluctance to carry through his plan. How could he sacrifice the pleasure of being with her, near her, touching her? What made him think a man like him could topple the empire Zanlos had erected? A party boy from a small town, small-timer with selfish dreams who had never done a single thing right in his whole life? Would he prove to be any more of an annoyance than a bug flying into the windshield of Zanlos's influence?

He could be throwing it all away for nothing, his job, his feelings for Rae, his future, perhaps even his life.

And for what? A taste of highly over-rated self-respect?

Where had decency ever gotten his father?

He walked Rae up the short sidewalk and then up the carpeted stairs to her rooms on the second floor. He waited while she fit her key and opened the door. And then she turned to him with all that he'd ever desired shimmering in her gaze. And he panicked.

"I'd better go."

He'd taken two steps down when Rae caught his sleeve. He'd barely completed his revolution before she was on his lips with a kiss of pure invitation. He returned the pressure and the sweet strokes of her tongue. And then he leaned back to let her tell him her intentions.

And they led him into a private hell.

"Come in, Nick."

FIFTEEN

He hesitated there on her steps long enough for Rae to wonder if she'd made a dreadful mistake. She was the one who'd put up the barriers between them. She'd insisted upon the distance. Now she was coaxing him to break the rules she'd laid down. No wonder he looked cautious. But not reluctant. His reaction to her kiss told her that more plainly than any words.

"Are you sure?" he asked at last, with enough inflection in his voice to betray his anticipation.

"I don't want to be alone."

"Oh."

It was the wrong thing to say. It implied that any warm body would do, and nothing could be farther from the truth. She wanted him, Nick Flynn, no other. But if she spelled it out, how much more difficult would things become between them? She didn't want to give him false hope.

And then she heard herself saying, "I want you to stay with me, Nick."

So much for keeping emotion at bay. Oh hell, what did it matter if he knew how much his mere presence meant to her? As long as he stayed.

He came in and stood just inside the threshold to have a look around.

"I like what you've done with the place."

Boxes lined the wall, things she'd purchased and hadn't had a chance to put up or away. There was an overstuffed striped couch still in delivery plastic. A big Boston fern stretched out on the hardwood floor as the room's only decoration. Sparse and uninhabited, but since Nick had come inside, it no longer felt empty.

"A true reflection of my personal taste," she replied with a faint smile.

"Ah. A minimalist, I see."

"I've always been one for understatement."

Then he did what would always be the one thing she would remember that broke the dam of her reserve. He opened his arms to her and said, simply, "Come here."

Stepping into the circle of his embrace held the indescribable feeling of coming home. Warmth, care, security, all enfolded about her for a timeless moment she never wished would end. He held her close but not crushingly, letting her direct the intensity. She hugged tight about his middle, burying her face in the crisp white cotton of his shirt. He'd left his jacket in the car. There was something so permanent about a man in shirtsleeves. A coat implied a willingness to leave at any moment, but shirtsleeves were meant to be rolled up for a longer stay. And she wanted him to stay.

"I'm sorry for what happened."

She nodded into the comforting curve of his shoulder then sighed to expel the emotion she'd bottled up all morning. "You have no idea how much I needed this...needed you."

She felt his lips move against her hair. "Happy to help."

She could have stood there all day, just breathing in the warm scent of sandalwood and laundry service, but the temptation of him beneath the conservative line of his business shirt teased her from that simple pleasure to ones less innocent in nature. She rubbed her palms from the wide span of his shoulders down to the taper of his waist. He felt good, firm, strong, capable. Male. Earthier needs began to stir.

"I can't seem to resist you," was her mild attempt at protest.

His chuckle vibrated beneath her cheek. "Don't expect me to complain about my good fortune."

"I expect you to take advantage of it."

"Whatever the lady wants."

His palm scooped beneath her chin, tipping her head back so he could sample long and leisurely from the willing part of her lips. When he lifted up, she made a purring sound, her eyes still closed.

"You make me weak in the knees," she told him truthfully.

"You make me weak in the head."

She suspected he meant to say heart but caught himself at the last moment. That was okay. It was a lot for the both of them to get used to, this sudden companionable intimacy for two die-hard, commitment-shy loners.

"I like your hair down," he murmured, his fingers playing through the locks that swung several inches past her shoulders. When he brought the dark, coppery strands to brush across his mouth, her resolve collapsed beneath the weight of a sudden urgency.

"Do you want to see how I've decorated my bedroom?"

"Not in plastic slip covers, I hope."

"A little more cozy than that."

He rocked against her, his pelvis doing a seductive roll. "Couldn't get much more cozy than this."

"Oh, yes it could."

And she unthreaded his tie, giving it a toss. He responded by unbuttoning the tiny pearl buttons of her skinny knit sweater. Then she was at the placket of his shirt, hurrying down the even row to part crisp fabric and tug it free from his trousers and slip it from the broad rack of his shoulders. The snug A-shirt underneath nicely delineated his torso, scooping low enough to display a healthy mat of dark chest hair. She combed the fingers of one hand through it while the other traced the whorls of muscle in his upper arm.

"Pretty cut for a lawyer-type," she murmured. "What did you do down there in the swamps to develop such an impressive resume?"

He was unfastening her jeans. "My daddy's brother runs a charter boat service down in Louisiana. I spent the spring building him a new dry dock." Drying out, was what he didn't tell her. He'd been a mess at the time, barely able to hold a hammer without smashing a thumbnail for the first weeks. But the heat and the work had steamed the alcohol poisons from his system. It had been work or drown in it. He chose the work, making light of it now while it had been a matter of life or death then. "You know, hammer, nail, sweaty physical labor."

"Ummm. That's the kind I like. Let's get down to some, shall we?"

Gripping a handful of undershirt, she towed him toward her bedroom. She'd had just enough time to settle into this one room, and the result was obvious and personal. No fluffy feminine touches amid the subtle slate greys and ivory pearl silks and sheers. The big bed sat in a frame of gracefully curved pewter-toned bent metal covered by a simple checkerboard pattern of black and silver. On the wall, she'd hung a metal sculpture of a horn-playing musician riding a sweeping curve of notes. Seeing it, Nick smiled.

"New Orleans?"

"Motown."

"Jazz or blues?"

"Both."

"Compatible musical taste is almost as important as which way you hang the toilet paper." And with that pronouncement, he went to thumb through her CD collection, nodding in appreciation. "I think I'm in love," he murmured, summarizing her selection.

Seeing him standing there in her bedroom in his undershirt, dark head bent over her favorite tunes, she had to agree with the sentiment.

Settling on the Drifters for common ground, he slid in the disk. The mellow sound of "Up on the Roof" crooned from her stacked music center. Humming along, Nick stepped in close to take her up in his arms...for a dance. He had a slow, sultry rhythm that was easy for her to follow as he moved them about the room. Glancing out her window, he noted the upper floor of his hotel and grinned.

"Nice view."

"I like it." Her gaze was riveted to the darkly handsome lines of his face. His grin settled into a sassy smile. Then he pulled her in tight and let the suggestive sway of his body speak for him as he continued to slow dance her about the bed. Her eyes closed, her cheek pillowed on his shoulder, Rae let the music and Nick Flynn move her.

Then the next song began, the prophetic "Let's Get it On."

As his hips ground in tight, Nick looked down into her smoky eyes and murmured, "Shall we?"

"Let's shall."

And as the sexy rumble of the song spun on invitingly, Nick bent to kiss her mouth, her jaw, her neck, her collarbone— all the while shifting seductively to the tempo of both the music and the rising passion. With thumb and forefinger he plucked open the last button on her top then skinned it off her. His hand went to one cup of her lacy bra, form-fitting for a leisurely moment, then teasing out a tempting melody with the roll of those same two talented fingers. His other hand soothed up the curve of her back to deftly unhook that taunting scrap of hot pink. She sighed as he slid the straps down her arms.

He fast-stepped her through a quick combination then dipped her low over his arm. His mouth fastened hot and wet upon the center of her breastbone where he made a loud, smooching sound.

Rae laughed. She couldn't help herself. She took such delight in his company, in his playfulness, in the suave charm so sweetly balanced by his compassion. Clutching the back of his head, she let her own drop back so that her hair swept the floor.

Then with her bowed over his arm in an inviting arch, his mouth followed a scorching trail down her taut belly to the open snap of her jeans. Everything inside her quivered as he created a light suction on the soft flesh just above her panty line.

He stood her up so fast her head spun. But then he'd had her spinning out of control since their first meeting. Covering her lips with a soul-snatching kiss, he tucked one arm under her bottom and the other about her waist and carried her to the bed. After laying her down, he shucked her out of her jeans and took a long look at her stretched out in unashamed nakedness awaiting him.

"You look so good, I could eat you up."

Her tongue slipped with a nervous naughtiness along her

upper lip. "Please do."

Too much of a gentleman to refuse a lady's special request, he sank between her bent knees to do just that, using his mouth and the stiff feathering of his tongue to pursue her to a fast, bed frame-rattling climax. He allowed her a dazed and breathless respite while he stripped his remaining clothes down to white cotton boxers. He sucked in a breath as her fingertips traced down the erection straining behind the thin fabric.

"Are your legal briefs more prepared this time?" she asked. Her voice was low and husky with the rough purr of good, satisfying sex.

"My briefs are packing, ma'am," he assured her.

Her rubbing grew more insistent. "I can see that."

He fumbled for a condom and sat on the edge of the bed. With the warm nudity of Rae Borden spooned about his backside, he wondered how the hell he was going to hang on long enough to get the damn rubber snapped safely around him.

"Allow me," Rae offered, forcing him to do some deep breathing exercises as she rolled the gloving rubber down, obviously taking her time to enjoy the urgent pulse of him beneath her attentive care. She gave it a final tug. "There you go."

"Mama always told me to wear my rubbers when I went out to play."

"Smart lady, your mama."

"From what I remember."

But he hadn't followed her advice that first time, had he?

Then he turned to roll over her, and she forgot about mothers and rubbers to concentrate on some serious play.

He claimed her emotions with a deep, open-mouthed kiss, reaching down until a moan of need shuddered in her throat. Then, with one slow, measured movement, he claimed her body and soul. As damp as she was already, there was no friction, just a delicious, stretching sense of fullness as he pressed inside to stay for a long reacquainting moment. When his subtle strokes picked up the tempo of the song, Rae felt the music sing along her nerve endings. All the while he finessed her mouth with his tongue, he teased her passions with those controlled pulses until she writhed with impatience and anticipation. Her hands hooked on the backs of his thighs, directing a more forceful beat, one that got the bed rocking and her heart knocking and her breath pumping in time to the surging thrusts that crowded all the way to her womb. *God, he is great.*

With that thought warbling harmony to her panting breaths, a hot, fierce crescendo built, shivering along her legs, tightening through her hips, clamping down around the insistent thickness of him to provoke a roaring finish, the type with cannon fire and cymbals crashing and the entire string section sawing like mad. His explosive groan provided a punctuating grand finale, then all was trembling stillness.

And the Drifters crooned, "Save the last dance for me." Oh, yeah.

He stirred at last, spreading nibbling kisses along her neck and shoulders before gradually leaving her body. His absence left her all weak and weepy, and not wanting him to witness that vulnerability, she turned her head away. He wouldn't allow her that privacy. His fingertips grazed her flushed cheek, tipping her back so their gazes could meet and meld.

"What is it, *cher*? This is no time for regrets."

She burrowed into his shoulder as long restrained sobs quivered though her. He held her close, absorbing the tremors, soothing them with a slow caress and tender kisses.

"Talk to me, Rae," he whispered into the tousle of her hair. "Let me help you."

The combination of fatigue and the exquisite way their coupling had stripped her emotions raw proved too much.

"I killed them, Nick."

"Who, *cher*? The Grovers? No."

"The Grovers, my parents—everyone I've ever loved." Her head came up, her incredibly green gaze fixed on his with a fierce intensity. "Leave, Nick. Run far, far away. I don't want to be responsible for you, too."

For a moment, he missed the big picture as heart and mind seized on what she didn't say.

Was she saying that she loved him?

That would explain the hot/cold emotions, the way she pushed him from her life as if trading in an old car and yet still couldn't resist enjoying the ride whenever possible. He'd had a car like that. He loved that car, the gas-guzzling, oil-burning old wreck.

The way Rae Borden loved him.

Wonder and elation spread through him like a warm sunrise.

But of course, now wasn't the time to call for a less cryptic declaration. She was hurting and scared, and dammit, he wanted to make those bad things go away.

How could he, when he was one of those bad things?

That he could change. Hugging her close, he vowed that he would change.

So he held her, so whipped up inside with the unknowns of desire and devotion it was all he could do to listen to her when she finally began to talk. Until he heard what she was saying. Then he forgot all else.

"My father came back from Viet Nam with Thomas Grover and that policeman we met in the hospital Palmer. Dad was a hero, with ribbons and commendations and my mom as his biggest cheerleader. She read me his letters as bedtime stories. At first, they were so romantic. She would never read the ones from his second tour. She never said so, but I suspect that was when he started to change."

He stroked her hair back from her brow and placed a light kiss there. "Men don't go to war and come back unchanged. Seeing that much horror strips away all the innocence from life."

"It stripped away more where my father was concerned. It stripped away the man who'd written those first letters, until he only lived in my mom's memories. That was the man I grew up admiring, the one who never came home. I sometimes wish he'd never come home. The memories would have been easier to live with."

She fell silent and Nick didn't push. He figured it needed to be expressed gradually, like poisons from a long-festering wound.

"He drank," she said at last. "A lot. And when he drank, he got angry—at his boss, at the government, at life, at the boy who delivered our paper a few minutes late on Sunday. But mostly, he got mad at my mom for still loving the man he wasn't anymore. And when he drank and got mad, he'd hit her."

She said it so matter-of-factly, the shock value increased tenfold.

"And you? Did he hit you, too?" He couldn't keep the timbre of his own anger from shaking through his voice.

"No. He never put a hand on me. He didn't need to. I felt every slap, every kick he gave my mom. When I was old enough to understand what was going on, I begged my mom to get him into some kind of program, but he was too proud to ask for help, she told me. Too proud to admit he had a problem, but not too proud to expect his wife and daughter to lie at the emergency room about her falling down some stairs. It was our family secret."

She closed her eyes, and he could imagine the nightmare of it playing out within the privacy of her mind. And he hated that he couldn't take that horror away.

"She wouldn't leave him, Nick. When I asked her why, she said it was because he needed her. That's when I got angry and decided if I didn't do something he was going to kill her."

"So," he asked softly, "what did you do?"

"I went to the police and I filed a report. I was thirteen but, bless those guys, they took me seriously. They came out to our house, and what do you think they found? The picture of domestic bliss and tranquility. My dad told them that I was a troubled teen and that they were getting me into therapy. My mom stood there right beside him and backed every word he said. What could the officers do? They knew my parents were lying. I could see it in their faces that they believed me. But they couldn't do anything if my mom didn't press charges or even admit that there was abuse. When those officers left, her last chance to escape went with them. And she yelled at me, and she slapped me for trying to ruin everything. Do you believe it?" Her voice caught on a sob, and Nick tucked her in tighter.

"She loved him more than she was afraid of him," he intuited. "She probably never gave up the hope that she could make him back into the man he'd once been."

"She was a fool."

The harshness of her claim stunned him but not so much as the rest of her story.

"I came home from school the next day to find them in the kitchen. My mom was so proud of her new ceramic tile floor. Dad had laid it for her. She pretended not to notice how uneven the rows got the more he drank. I found her on the middle of those uneven rows. He'd taken his commando knife and butchered her there in the kitchen and then sat down at the table with a cold one to wait for me to come home from the bus. Do you know what he said to me?"

"No." No, he didn't know. No, he didn't want to know.

"He said, 'Look what you made me do.' And then he shot himself, the coward. He was afraid to stick around and let anyone tell him he was at fault."

"Son of a bitch," was the only comment he could think to make regarding the story and the man. In a final act of meanness and control, he'd left his daughter behind to suffer the weight of blame, ruining her life just as surely as if he'd killed her, too.

"That's when the Grovers came in. Ginny was my best friend the way Tom had once been my father's. He'd been trying to get my dad to get help since they'd gotten back, but Dad wouldn't listen to him. Because he couldn't help my dad and my mother refused to help herself, they took me in as often as they could just to get me out of the house. And after my parents were...gone, they took me in permanently."

"He was a good man, Tom Grover." As he said it, Nick could see Kaz Zanlos signing that good man's name with his dead hand.

"So, for a while, I got to live with a real family. It was wonderful, Nick. You can't imagine."

No, he couldn't. But he smiled, grateful that she'd had

that opportunity.

"Ginny and I had a falling out over her fiancé. I didn't trust him. He was too smooth, too polite. But Ginny wouldn't listen. She was in love, and she told me I was just jealous. So when she showed up with a swollen lip and a story about them horsing around, I decided to prove that I was right. I dug into Mr. Too-Good-To-Be-True's past and found out that he had a criminal record for assault and battery. He had a temper that got him into trouble with the law and an ex-girlfriend who swore out a warrant when he nearly broke her jaw. I didn't tell Ginny privately. I knew she wouldn't want to hear the truth, just like my mother would never admit to it. So I announced it to everyone at her engagement party to prove that Mr. Right was Mr. Dead Wrong. And Ginny never forgave me for it. She told me he'd confessed everything to her when they started dating, that he'd had counseling and anger management, that he wanted to start over with a clean slate, and she gave him the benefit of the doubt. But I couldn't, Nick. I couldn't risk him hitting her. I got my way, though. He was so humiliated for both himself and for Ginny, that we never heard from him again. And Ginny never spoke to me again. I got a job out of state, moved away and pretended that she'd thank me for it someday. That someday never came."

"And what happened to Mr. Wrong?"

"He married someone else, and they had the three kids Ginny always wanted. He's a bank vice-president and funds an abuse center. I really pegged him, didn't I?"

"You thought you were doing the right thing. You did it out of love for your friend."

"But I never once thought about what was best for Ginny. I never gave her credit for making her own choices."

"Are you saying she killed herself over some unrequited love how many years ago?"

"No. I'm saying I never should have walked away from those people who were like my family. I let my pride force me to leave rather than admit that I was wrong. Kind of a family pattern, don't you see?"

"No, Rae. I don't see it that way at all." He hesitated a

moment but had to ask. "Is that why you do what you do?"

"What?" She stared at him blankly for a long beat.

"Because you're afraid to make the wrong choice again? Because you still think all men are pigs who beat the women who love them if they get the chance?"

"No," she said too quickly. "I don't think that."

"And that's why you picked a profession that glorifies a stable relationship, right?"

Her genuine confusion finally lifted. Her expression closed down, and he knew he'd said the wrong thing.

"A little Psychology 101, Mr. Flynn?"

"Am I wrong?"

"Probably not, but that doesn't mean I have to like hearing it."

"Rae, you're not responsible for the choices those other people made for their own reasons, right or wrong."

"But I could have stopped them, Nick."

"How, *cher*?"

"By listening to them, by trying to understand what they needed instead being so sure I knew what was best for them. If I had been here for Ginny, she wouldn't have died."

"It was an accident, Rae." He said that with all the conviction he could muster.

"No, it wasn't. No more than Tom and Bette were accidents." She stared up at him unflinchingly to demand, "And you know it, don't you, Nick?"

SIXTEEN

"Don't you, Nick?"

He didn't dare move, afraid if he did she would see every guilty sin parade across his face in damning Technicolor. This was his opportunity, his chance to come clean with everything, to expunge the lies and the culpability and beg to start over.

But he didn't. He'd been a creature driven by self-preservation for too long. He couldn't trust her to accept the truth and him with it. Not yet. Not when his promises were backed by empty deeds. Not when talk was cheap, and she was used to cash in advance.

"I don't know, Rae." He picked his words carefully. "I didn't know Ginny or Bette Grover, and I only met Tom that one time at the house."

"But you know there's something wrong with the way they died, don't you?"

"There's nothing right about it. They were your friends, your family."

"I've seen them, Nick."

She said it so quietly he was sure he must be mistaken. "What do you mean? In dreams?"

"Last night. At the war memorials. They spoke to me, warned me away."

He betrayed none of his alarm at what he was hearing. "It was your subconscious, Rae, telling you what you know to be true."

"My subconscious wasn't wearing a dress covered in my mother's blood!"

She was startled by the vehemence of her own claim, and it took her aback. She rubbed an unsteady hand across her eyes. "I know it sounds crazy. I don't expect you to believe me. I know it's not every day that you have dead people speaking to you, even if the movies have made it politically correct to see them. I'm not crazy, Nick."

"I know. I've seen things, heard things myself that others would say . . ." He shook his head as if he could scatter those remembrances. "Never mind. But I'm the last one to call you crazy. Be careful, Rae. Where I come from, the dead, they don't rest easy." His gaze softened as he stroked back her hair. "But you need to, at least for this morning."

When she looked as though she might protest, he kissed her lightly, fighting the want to linger there on her warm lips. He held her close until he felt the tension ebb from her limbs and her breathing quiet. Until he knew it was safe to leave her alone.

"Go to sleep. I have some errands to run, then I'll be back. Do you mind if I grab a shower here?"

"Help yourself, Nick. To anything."

That last was murmured as her eyes were closing but the connotation was hard to walk away from. *Anything.* He smiled to himself, his gaze adoring the lines of her face as they relaxed into a pose of irresistible innocence...and fatigue. That gave him the strength of will to ease from her bed, to gather his scattered clothing then close the blinds so that the morning light would be kinder to her exhausted state. Then, because he couldn't resist the sight of her curled upon the rumpled sheets, her hair a wild tangle across the pillows they had yet to share in a night's slumber, he bent and touched his lips to her brow, whispering words he knew she was too far gone to hear.

"I love you, cher."

Rae struggled to open her eyes. Had he really said that? She wanted to ask. But the pull of sleep overcame the need to know. At least for the moment. On a vague and far-distant periphery, she heard the water running. Nick in her shower. A smile bowed her mouth as she nestled deeper into a healing slumber.

I love you, cher.

She hadn't believed those words would ever hold the power to move her so. Or that she'd ever feel compelled to respond in kind. But just as she eased over the edge of dreamless rest, she answered.

"I love you, too, Nick Flynn."

He stopped long enough on his return to work to make a complete copy of all the documents pertaining to Thomas Grover. He had the copies notarized as genuine duplications then bought a post office box at that same copy center and stuffed his evidence inside. He did all this with a single driving purpose, keeping his thoughts narrowed to the task at hand. Nothing else could matter now except the new future he saw for himself—the future he'd share with Rae Borden.

Naomi wasn't at her desk. Her computer was off, and the lights on her phone system blinked unattended. Perhaps she'd taken his advice and gone home sick.

At least he hoped that was the reason for her absence. A chill swept through him as he recalled her somber words. *He won't let me go.*

Determinedly, he marched past her empty desk and straight into Kaz Zanlos's office. His employer looked up from the spread of documents, not at all surprised by the intrusion.

"Nick, I've been waiting for you. Come in. Close the door."

Without complying, Nick strode directly to his desk to demand, "Did you have Bette Grover run off the road? Was that before or after you choked the booze and pills down her to make it look like an accident?"

Zanlos leaned back in his chair with his flat, humorless smile. "Why, Nick, I'm shocked at your suggestion. What you describe would be-"

"Business as usual, I'm finding out." He slapped the files down on the immaculate desktop. Zanlos never gave them a glance.

"You've been a busy boy, Nick."

"I'm not your boy, Zanlos, and I don't like what you do here. I haven't liked myself much since I let myself become a part of it."

"And what kind of business is it that you object to so strongly, Nick?"

"Extortion, smuggling, fraud—my guess is drug running and probably murder."

Zanlos shrugged eloquently. "Nobody's perfect, Nick, and that's why we picked you. Did you ever ask yourself why a firm like ours would be interested in a small town, small time ambulance chaser like you? Yes? No? It's not because you'd be a brilliant asset. It's because you're not perfect, either, are you, Nick? You and I are alike in that we'll deal with the devil to get what we want, and what we want are these nice clothes, these expensive offices and the power to make annoying legalities go away."

"We're not alike, Zanlos. I don't set people up for blackmail then bleed them dry for cash and favors like you and your partner, Anna Murray."

He didn't even try to deny it. "A brilliant scheme, really. I can't take the credit. Anna came up with it. It's not exactly original, but it's worked quite nicely."

"What about Grover? Couldn't coax him into your little den of thieves?"

"Grover was a fool."

"So you killed his daughter and now you'll murder his wife as well."

"No, Nick. That would be wasteful. I don't need her dead, just incapacitated until I make certain arrangements for import licensing into New Orleans."

"Importing what? Coke, guns, illegal aliens?"

"Aliens. That's an amusing way to put it." He laughed softly at his own joke, well knowing that Nick missed the punchline. "The truth is, I don't care as long as the money's good, and neither should you, my friend."

"But I do."

"Since when?"

Since Rae, was the answer he wouldn't give the other man, but he saw it in Nick's face anyway.

"Ah, for the woman. Nick, Nick, Nick. My foolish friend. You try to do the decent thing for once in your life to impress a woman. And you think she'll thank you when the tape of the four of us in the *Noir* is released to the press. You think she'll give up her career and reputation as quickly and easily as you seem to be? You think she'll be grateful that you ruined her?"

The fact that he had the tape in his possession was one Nick didn't care to share. But all the same, Zanlos's statement puzzled him. Something was askew with his logic, and it wasn't like Zanlos to make such a miscalculation.

"How could the release of a sex tape ruin the reputation of a prostitute?"

Zanlos's laugh was filled with dark amusement. "Because, my friend, your lover isn't a prostitute. She's a policewoman."

The news hit like a twelve-gauge pattern to the chest. Nick reeled back from the unexpected impact.

"Now, dear boy, if you want to survive this with your career intact, you'll want to rethink your loyalties. Just as my previously faithful secretary will be rethinking hers after passing information to her cop boyfriend. What is it with the two of you? Can't you see you're being used? I like you, Nick, so I'll give you time to reflect on your foolishness. I haven't decided if Miss Bright will have the same opportunity. The two of you have hurt my feelings, and now you will apologize or be punished."

Nick was only half listening. *A policewoman!* His thoughts scrambled to assimilate that information, seeking a reason to deny...finding none.

Damn. She was a cop.

"I'm sorry to put a damper on your little romance, Nick, but think how your girlfriend would receive this tidbit of information."

Zanlos set a small newspaper photo down on the desk, turning it so Nick could read the caption. He didn't have to read it. He recognized the face as the one that haunted his nightmare. The face of the woman in the fog. A cold brick of dread and dismay sank in his belly as he read the fine print.

Young Baton Rouge mother killed in hit-and-run.

"So you see, Nick, we aren't so different after all. And you'll find me much more forgiving than Detective Borden regarding this little indiscretion. Think about it, Nick. You weren't willing to risk your future over that woman you didn't know. Why would you do so now for the sake of a woman who will betray you? You're a smart boy, Nick. Figure the odds. You're no longer an acceptable risk to Ms. Borden, but you're just the sort of man I need. Men like us don't let people like this get in our way." His fingers spread over the news photo then crumpled it upon closing into a fist. He tossed the tiny ball. It bounced off Nick's shirt front before he caught it instinctively.

"Don't disappoint me, Nick. Be smart."

***

He didn't come back as promised, nor did he call.

Rae paced her apartment as the daylight waned, and she grew tired of waiting. What kind of man said "I love you" then didn't come back? Her experience with men was a little too jaded for a logical answer.

If she told him the truth, she'd have to trust him with it. Could she do that? He might hold a non-threatening passion for a prostitute, but would he be similarly enthralled with a police detective? One who'd deceived him and used him and manipulated his emotions to an unfair degree? Would he walk away from everything he struggled for, or would he dig in his heels and go down with Zanlos rather than lose his prestigious position? Or worse, would he turn her over to his employer so that she could become another statistic like the Grovers?

She'd given Nick a chance to choose, and he hadn't taken it. He could have confessed everything to her that morning, and she wouldn't now be faced with this dilemma. But he hadn't. He'd hedged around his knowledge of Zanlos's wrongdoings, and in doing so was equally guilty for covering them up.

How could she do her job without embroiling the man she loved in the middle of it?

The man she loved.

The idea was still so new it surprised her. But would it also cripple her investigation? Only if she allowed it to.

The hour grew later still and no call, no show from Nick

Flynn. She opened her closet to select an appropriate costume for the evening. Something short and black and simple, she decided. Almost like funeral garb.

Kaz Zanlos's funeral, she hoped and not her own.

***

He sat at his desk, numb from the heart up as the hours lengthened into late afternoon.

A cop.

The news threw him hard, just as Zanlos had intended. How long his boss had known of this particular deceit didn't matter. Long enough to have a good laugh at his expense, to give him just enough heart string to hang himself.

A cop.

While part of him rejoiced that she wasn't a woman of the night who made her money off men, another coldly assessed the facts. She'd played the role to perfection with him. She'd slept with him and taken his money.

But hadn't kept it.

What game was she playing, and where did he fit into the rather loosely-woven rules? He didn't like the answer he received. A pawn. Unimportant except for the nature of the piece. An insignificant man meant to be sacrificed to advance the aggressive plan of the queen. And she had, hadn't she? She'd used him to get close to Zanlos, to Anna Murray to avenge the death of her friend and her father figure. And now, she was leaving him out to dry, with the tatters of his career flapping in the merciless breeze.

He glanced down at the news photo he'd meticulously smoothed out on the desktop before him. The woman's cheerful smile beamed back at him. An innocent like Naomi Bright, who had no business being a part of his tangled quest for fame and glory. He'd never meant to make that climb over the bodies of the blameless.

How had Zanlos known about this particularly ugly secret? No one knew. Not the police, not his father. Only him.

How had he found out?

The truth was, it didn't matter how he knew, only that he knew, and what he would be able to do with that information.

He closed his eyes, shutting out the sight of that pretty face, of those clear and clueless eyes looking toward a future he'd snatched away. And then he'd run away. He could see her now as he had then, just a brief frozen image appearing out of the fog. And then the sound, that awful hollow thump of impact that obliterated that face from view. Again, he felt the clawing horror tearing within his chest as his mind fought what his heart knew immediately. He experienced that same breathless agony as he'd sat in the restlessly idling car with the weight of his conscience dragging down the shooting star of his future. The celebratory alcohol from his partying in the city in honor of his soon to be secured success curled like acid in his belly, rising up in his throat to sear and choke off all the sweet times that lay ahead. He knew the instant he heard that fateful thump that his life was over.

No. It doesn't have to be.

That denying whisper snaked about the burn of regret and responsibility and squeezed slowly, relentlessly, until it cut off the natural progression from guilt to accountability. He'd glanced in the rearview to the empty roadway bathed in the red of his brakelights. No broken body caressed by the cold ribbons of mist. Could he have been hallucinating? Had the woman been induced by drink and a self-destructive need to sabotage his good fortune?

What was a woman doing out on a lonely highway at this time of night?

He checked his sideviews. Nothing. His rearview again. Only empty road leading back to where he'd already been.

Drive away. Just drive away.

His hand clutched, wet and shaky, at the four-on-the-floor, but the muscles in his arm refused to comply.

His breath shuddered up past the sickness of fear and culpability bringing a flash of clarity to the goading panic that cried, *Run. Get away. Who'll know?*

He'd gotten out of the car on legs nearly too weak to hold him. Clinging to the car for support and direction, he stumbled back to that pooling of red upon pavement marked with the frantic streak of his remorse. Too late. Too late to take it back.

The drinking, the arrogant pleasure, the flush of accomplishment. All crushed beneath that smear of rubber on the road.

So where was she? He'd wobbled through the wisps of fog, searching for the evidence of his careless deed. No body. No blood on the bumper of his car.

Could he have imagined it? Hope seeped through the paralyzing anguish clogging his airways.

Or had the glancing impact thrown her over the side and into the murky bayou waters below? He leaned over the guardrail but could see nothing in the void of darkness below. Could hear no cries for help or moans of pain. Only the fractured cadence of his own breathing.

He wasn't aware of slipping back behind the wheel. He wasn't fully cognizant of the drive that took twenty minutes to get to the nearest chance for assistance. He dialed beneath the revealing glow of the phone booth, careful to keep his head down and his features obscure as he reported a possible accident on Highway 10 then quickly hung up as they asked for his name.

Help would come. He'd done everything he could.

Not everything, his wretched conscience cried as he sped away from the booth after meticulously wiping off the receiver. He hadn't stayed to admit responsibility for what he'd done in a moment of inexcusable carelessness. And consequently, because of an anguished sense of accountability he'd never known he had, he'd never gone back over that lonesome stretch of road to claim the brass ring of success. He hadn't been able to take it, knowing what he'd done to earn it. Instead, he'd allowed himself to try to forget in a guilty haze of alcohol and self-abuse.

Until Meeker, Murray & Zanlos jerked him from that wallow of blame and self-pity...and, ironically, saved his life.

How desperately he'd wanted to leave his sins behind. That was impossible now. His fingertips traced the shape of the unfortunate woman's face. His secret was exposed for all its shameful cowardice.

And if he couldn't forgive himself, how could he expect

that miracle of absolution from Rae Borden? Rae Borden who had coldly and cleverly included him in her plot to exact revenge. Was it more than he deserved?

What inevitable irony that he should lose all in such a fashion.

How he accepted that loss would distinguish him from Kaz Zanlos.

He picked up the phone and dialed.

SEVENTEEN

The fresh-faced Naomi Bright was the last person Rae expected to see as she approached the entrance to the *Noir.* A girl like Miss Bright seemed more the library than the lap dance type. But there was no mistaking the identity of the young woman shivering in the sudden D.C. downpour.

"Miss Borden? Please...can I talk to you?"

Struggling with the collapsible umbrella that threatened to invert itself with each gust of cloying wind, Rae glanced from the pathetic waif to the beckoning shelter of the club. "Come inside then."

Naomi shrank further back into the shadows, her big eyes rounding with dismay. "No, I can't go in there."

"Not twenty-one, or just below your moral standards?" She couldn't help the wry remark. The girl's condescending attitude irked her because she was so right to hold it.

Naomi shook her head. Strands of wet blonde hair stuck to her cheek, her brow, the corner of her mouth. She didn't brush them away. All her focus was on Rae. "It's below everyone's moral standards," she whispered with an odd emphasis that was more fear than judgment. "Over here. Please, for just a minute."

Taking pity on the trembling creature, Rae angled her umbrella into the force of the rain and stepped around the corner to confront the girl in the narrow alley running between the buildings. She started when Naomi seized her hand. Her grip was cold and desperate.

"Have you seen Gabriel?"

Ah, a lover's quarrel. Rae really didn't have time for it and impatiently was looking back toward the sidewalk. Her

tone reflected her mild irritation with both the delay and with
her absent partner. "I thought he was with you, sharing secrets."

"I have to find him. You don't understand, Detective
Borden."

That brought Rae's wandering attention to heel with a
sharp yank of the leash. "What did you call me?"

"I know who you are. I know that Gabriel is working with
you. I won't tell anyone. I have no loyalty to Mr. Zanlos. In
fact, I've been helping Mr.–" She broke off, sensing that she'd
said too much. "I've got to find Gabriel."

Rae took a long, hard look at the young woman and didn't
like what she saw. Behind the shaking and the wide, pleading
eyes, there was an aura of fright, of something beyond fear. It
clung to her, a palpable perfume on the dank, darkening night.
Panic. Terror. But those things couldn't explain the sudden
swirling lack of orientation that wafted over her as she swayed
as if buffeted by a brutal gale. Rae gripped her elbows to steady
her, but for a long moment, Naomi seemed beyond reach. Her
eyes rolled back, her head lolled ragdoll limp upon the slender
column of her neck. She had an angry mark on the side of her
throat, a savage sort of bite that made Rae wonder if the girl
and her partner were into some kind of kinky sex. The notion
shouldn't have surprised her, but somehow it did. And more
than that, it made her uneasy deep down to her soul, as if that
mark was indicative of a greater disease. Drugs, perhaps. She
didn't know. But there was something wrong with Naomi
Bright, and she didn't have time to address it now.

"Naomi, I haven't seen him since . . ." Since he was hiding
in the trunk of his car. "Since this morning."

That news sapped the girl's strength like a sudden purge.
Rae held tight as her knees buckled and she fell forward into
a semi-swoon. Her body was as cold as death. Alarmed, Rae
started pulling her toward the front of the *Noir.* "Let's get out
of this weather. I'll make some calls. I'll find him for you."

Naomi's energy returned like a bolt of lightning. She
surged back, out of Rae's grip and backed into the alley. She
shook her head, the dazed look compounding with abject
horror. "I can't go in there. You don't understand. He knows.

I had no choice but to tell."

"Who knows? What did you tell, Naomi?"

The harder she tried to speak, the more the words eluded the increasingly confused girl. She was panting, shivering like an addict hours beyond the need for a fix. Rae no longer thought it was a drug problem. But exactly what kind of problem was eating away at the lovely young secretary?

"I've got to get away from here before they find me. Before they call me. There's more I haven't said. More I daren't say. I need to hide. I need to rest. I need Gabriel."

Impulsively, Rae pressed her apartment key into the curl of the girl's cold fingers. "Here. You'll be safe at my place. Get a cab, lock yourself in, and I'll bring Gabriel to you as soon as I can."

Tears of relief and resignation quickened in the other's gaze, but Rae didn't want her gratitude. She wanted to know what the hell was going on, and Gabriel had those answers.

"I'm going to go inside first, then you flag down a cab and get yourself away from here. Do you understand? Can you do that?"

Naomi nodded but in her disoriented state, Rae began to have her doubts. If Naomi had crossed Zanlos, she couldn't afford to be linked to the girl, lest her own cover be blown. And she was too close, had made too many compromises both personal and emotional, to back down now. She needed to get Naomi under wraps so she could get behind the truth of the girl's babblings. Tonight might be her last night at the *Noir*, her last chance to peg Zanlos and Company with their misdeeds. She would look for answers in the club then she would see what secrets her partner had been holding from her. With Naomi safely tucked away at her place, she could continue to do her job. Perhaps for the last time.

She gestured down the alley. "Go through here to the next block. Don't let them see you. Do you know my address?" How else had she appeared to pick up Gabriel? At the girl's bobbing nod, she braced her with a slight shake. "Be careful, Naomi. I'll find Gabriel. Okay?"

The girl supplied a wan smile. It beamed of hope and trust,

and Rae prayed she wouldn't fail either.

"Go."

She gave Naomi a directing push and waited until she was wobbling away into the cloaking darkness before she herself returned to the front of the building. Tonight, she would find Gabriel and she would demand to know everything. Damn his secrets when they could very well get her killed.

The peppering sting of rain against her stockinged calves prompted Rae to get out of the weather and back to work. There were answers here at the *Noir,* and she had the hours until dawn to find them.

From the crowded lobby, with the pumping beat of the night wending its way from the club below, Rae found a secluded corner to shake out her umbrella and slip out her cell phone. She punched in Gabriel's number and gave a frustrated sigh at the sound of his recorded message.

"Gabriel, I'm at the *Noir.* Naomi's under my wing. You've got some explaining to do, my friend."

After disconnecting, she decided to double her chances of reaching him by dialing the station. Palmer's gruff tone responded to the call.

"Gabe? Haven't seen him yet tonight. He should be checking in any time now. Can I give him a message?"

"Just let him know I'm holding him to his promise. He'll know what I mean."

A pause, then Palmer's almost earnest appeal. "If you're in some kind of trouble, Borden, maybe I can help."

"No trouble...but thanks."

Maybe Palmer was human after all.

She tucked her phone away and took a deep breath as she watched the power suits pass by on their way to the delights Anna Murray offered. Tonight she would find a way to get into the offices upstairs to find out what else the enigmatic Ms. Murray offered besides sex for sale. If Naomi Bright had spilled the beans on her boyfriend's association with the police, her own chances were dwindling. She didn't want to be caught in this place of pleasure, pants down. Figuratively or literally.

"Hey, Rae," called one of the ladies of the *Noir.* Suzanne, a strapping redhead who topped nearly six feet of curvy café au lait temptation, waved to her in passing. "Congressman Genelli has been asking for you." She winked. "I think you've got a date. Better hurry. That bitch Wanda's been after his treats forever, and I'd love to see you slip in and steal him out from under her...thumb. It's time you got yourself some sugar, baby. We're short-handed tonight. Crystal never came in and never called. Ms. Anna's gonna have her tucked and toned butt for breakfast. Yours, too, if you don't start shaking that money maker."

Congressional sugar was the last thing on her mind as Rae nodded her thanks. "Be in in just a minute. Tell him I'm fixing myself up for him."

"Oh, I can hear his motor running, doll. Don't let him idle too long, or I might just have a spin myself."

Suzanne smiled and Rae was taken aback by the feral intensity of her grin. She hadn't had much of an opportunity to bond with the women of the *Noir*. Most of them were hard-edged freelancers who didn't appreciate competition or invite confidences. Suzanne typified their aggressive attitude. Rae's intuition whispered that it was more than the money they were hungry for. The power, perhaps, or the prestige of claiming an influential lover. Still, that didn't capture the motivational drive of Suzanne and her nighttime sisterhood.

A sisterhood she had no intention of joining. Congressman Genelli would have to get used to the disappointment.

One more chance at that office upstairs. At least she wouldn't have Crystal to worry about this time.

She was plotting her attack upon the secrets of the *Noir* when a distracting commotion at the front door snagged her attention. With sinking dismay, she recognized the bedraggled Naomi Bright under the forceful escort of two pierced and tattooed street punks. The girl wasn't fighting them. She looked close to catatonia. Had they drugged her? They must have, to have gotten her to walk like a docile lamb into this place she'd sought to avoid like a slaughterhouse.

She had seconds to decide as they marched her through the lobby. Go on with her plans or step into it here and now.

She uttered a soft expletive.

"There you are, honey. About time."

The two punks looked up in surprise at her frontal assault. With a bump of her rump, she knocked one of them aside to assume his position on Naomi's right. Up close, the girl looked like a member of a Timothy Leary field trip. Her glazed eyes rolled under her fluttering lids, and her delicate jaw hung slackly. What had they given her?

"Thanks, boys. I'll take her from here. I've got about ten minutes to get her cleaned up and ready to work."

It wasn't a great bluff but a good one. For a moment, as they stared at her and at each other, Rae thought their indecision might outweigh any orders they'd been told to carry in their rather limited brain pans.

It almost worked.

Rae saw the objection form in their bovine stares, and she didn't wait around to hear it. She cinched her arm about Naomi's waist and hauled with all her might, jerking the puppetlike girl out of the other's grasp. In a quick sweep for her options, she noted the burly pair at the front door stepping into a unified barrier to block her exit. The doors to the inner *Noir* swung open to reveal a for once, nonplussed Kaz Zanlos. As Rae met his wide stare, she understood her alternatives in one agonizing second. In order to continue her ruse, she would have to turn Naomi over to him, relinquishing her to whatever fate he had planned. But in doing so, she would turn her back on every tenet of decency she'd ever followed. *To Protect and Serve.* On the "serve" end, she'd been rather shaky of late but as to the "protect" portion, she'd meant that. To the limit of her life. And that's what it might cost her to get Naomi Bright out alive.

She had one choice, one chance, and she took it in a bold move.

Stepping toward Zanlos as if she meant to capitulate gave her one scant moment of relaxed aggression from the others. They'd expected her to give up and were ready to accept her surrender with a smug nod toward inevitability.

They didn't know her very well.

As soon as she saw their guards lower, Rae acted. Hugging Naomi's limp form in tight against her side, she dodged for the stairs leading down into the mosh pit below, hoping she could lose them in the confusion of black light and hammering volume. She dragged Naomi down those wide, crowded steps and out onto the teaming dance floor where the press of bodies provided both camouflage and containment. She struggled to hold Naomi up and push forward at the same time as the strobe of light revealed opportunity then opposition with each pulsing beat.

Zanlos's thugs stood at the edge of the dance floor, speaking to several others as they gestured toward the squirming dancers. Quickly, the increasing pack of aggressors fanned out to block any attempt to escape. With frightening precision, they began pulling startled couples off the dance floor, silencing their objections with the flash of eyes that glowed red in the unnatural light.

As the surrounding cover diminished, Rae realized it was fight then flight time. Not exactly what her thigh-hugging dress and three inch heels were designed for. She kicked out of one shoe and snatched up the other, turning the stiletto spike into a weapon just as one of the thugs rushed her. The heel of her shoe nailed him neatly in the forehead. He went down without a sound, taking her imbedded shoe with him.

A rough hand gripped her by the arm. Rae spun without hesitation, her elbow flying up to take her assailant in the nose. Cartilege pulped at the impact but instead of dropping the man, it only made him angry. Lips curled back from bloodstained teeth. And as Rae watched, those teeth began to elongate, becoming fangs in a horrible snarl. Even as the impossibility of what she saw registered in her mind, she was striking again and again, battering with her elbow like a blunt instrument until the hold on her arm lessened. Then she jerked free of whatever it was that held her and, with Naomi's burden dragging at her side, pushed through the remaining dancers, seeking concealment until the chance for escape presented itself.

The music pounded, attacking the eardrums and provoking

a quivering response in the internal organs. Swirling lights and laser darts in various colors created a confusing pattern upon the crowd. Smoke rose up from the lighted panels of the dance floor, forming a momentary haze in answer to Rae's prayers. She ducked low, wending through the gyrating figures in a purposeful path toward the rear fire exit. Until a huge form blocked her advance.

In the dazzle of lights and wreathing fog, she saw a monster before her with red eyes and wicked fangs. Gasping in shock and alarm, she spun away, only to find that avenue barricaded by a similar unearthly creature. She turned and there was another. Hugging Naomi's nearly boneless body closer, Rae faced the improbably and admitted the inevitable. She wasn't going to get away.

Then, out of the fog, salvation appeared in the shape of Gabriel McGraw.

Rae's relief was short-lived, for this was not the Gabriel who teased her with his grin and easy manner. This was the unnatural being she'd glimpsed so briefly outside the door when they'd gone to see Marchand LaValois, and she didn't know if she was greeting friend or foe...or even a man.

Against the psychedelic flashes that put every movement into jerky frame-by-frame progression, Gabriel swung at the nearest target, not with his fist but with his open hand. But not with a normal hand. His fingers had twisted into talon-like claws that tore through the man's throat in a crimson geyser before the threat disappeared down into the blanket of mist. Then with a speed Rae had only guessed at before, he rounded on the next man, clamping his hand atop the man's skull and, with one vicious turn, wrenched it backwards.

"Head for the stairs," Gabriel shouted over the escalating music. Rae paused only long enough to see his fist smash through an attacker's chest. Then she was running, not taking the time to process what she'd seen. Flight was foremost in her mind as she hauled Naomi toward the stairs. As she mounted the bottom steps, a glance upward revealed Kaz Zanlos flanked by three other goons rapidly approaching. She might have plowed through them if not encumbered with the stuporous girl.

Gabriel's arm cinched about her waist, pulling both her and Naomi tight against him. Then in a feat that hadn't amazed her since witnessing Superman's first ascension on film, Rae found herself airborne.

They rose straight up, past a cursing Zanlos, continuing to rise until Gabriel's feet touched down on the stair rail on the main floor. Then, as Zanlos's thugs turned and scrambled back up, Gabriel whisked them with unbelievable speed out the front door to where his big boat of a car was waiting. He deposited Rae and Naomi in the passenger seat on his way to the driver's side. The engine roared to life, and they hauled away from the curb through a scattering of patrons.

Once they'd reached the open road and pursuit didn't appear imminent, Rae stared agog at the driver who now appeared to be the Gabriel she recognized . . .except for the gore extending all the way to his elbow from perforating his victim's body.

Gabriel glanced her way, noting her reaction before assessing the young woman slumped motionlessly beside her.

"Is she all right?"

As he looked back up for an answer, the streetlights glittered a luminescent silver in his eyes.

"What are you?" she demanded in a tight voice.

Gabriel responded with a wry smile and an amazing question of his own.

"What do you know about vampires?"

***

Kaz Zanlos was in no mood for his partner's attitude. He'd spent the last few hours laying down damage control, convincing the hysterical clientele that what they'd witnessed was a carefully staged production for their entertainment. Having the characters they'd seen savagely murdered appear and shake their hands went a long way toward calming their fears. No police would be called. Disaster had been averted. But now Bianca Du Maurier, in her guise as Anna Murray, was in his face demanding an accounting. And she didn't like what she heard as they spoke privately in her office.

"You let them get away?"

"For the moment. What harm can they do?"

"Harm? I'd say significant considering what they've managed already."

"The policeman was a surprise."

"He shouldn't have been."

"Then why didn't one of your people pick up on what he was? I thought you had some sort of radar built in when it comes to sensing one of your own."

"He managed to slip by us somehow." Her eyes narrowed thoughtfully, becoming gleaming slits in her not so beautiful face. Anger changed that surface loveliness into something closer to her primal form, something rather monstrous that Zanlos preferred not to see if at all possible. When she was in this kind of mood, his throat always felt horribly exposed. And Bianca's kiss was something he'd managed, through cunning and threat, to avoid during their long association. Best to turn her annoyance to some other target lest she forget herself and their tenuous bargain.

"I think it's time to end this game," Kaz pronounced, gratified when his preternatural partner didn't argue. "We've got to start our little discrediting campaign before Ms. Borden starts talking." He stabbed at the intercom button. "Barry, come in here."

The manager appeared, looking uneasy after all the evening's excitement. He never asked, but he knew better than to believe what Zanlos told their patrons. Nothing was as it seemed at the *Noir,* but he'd developed a blind eye in order to keep his extremely well-paying position. He looked to Zanlos. The man was a harsh boss, but he was better than the woman, Anna Murray. She made his family jewels shrivel.

"Barry, bring me the tape on Nick Flynn from the other night."

A dreading silence.

Zanlos glared at him impatiently. "Is there a problem?"

"I didn't think so, sir. But I guess, maybe there is."

"Speak plainly, man."

So he did, reluctantly, fatefully. "Mr. Flynn has the tape.

He asked for it the other night, and I didn't think..."

"You didn't think?" Zanlos roared.

Barry shrank back, seeing his future in counter work at the local burger franchise. "He said you wouldn't mind."

"He was wrong. You gave him the only copy?"

"There wasn't time to make another. He said he'd return it right away, and I guess I forgot about it. It was my mistake, Mr. Zanlos."

"Your last."

And as Kaz Zanlos turned his back, the quaking manager looked to Anna Murray to make a final petition for his job. He found no sympathy there and quickly realized there was more at stake than his career. Baring her sharp teeth, the ghoul Anna Murray had suddenly become lunged for his throat to deliver his termination notice.

EIGHTEEN

"What has he told you?"

Rae studied Marchand LaValois with a calm she was far from feeling. Disbelief was still a buffer to the wilder emotions careening through her. An analytical curiosity also kept her fears at bay.

"Not much beyond the fact that you're the good guys. If he can be believed."

From the sumptuous luxury of his Federal-style Leesburg, Virginia estate, Marchand responded to her wry comment with an indulgent smile. In this setting, it was hard to cast him in the role of late night movie monster, especially with his beautiful and obviously doting wife sitting at his side. Nicole LaValois was all that was elegant and well bred. She'd opened her doors without question in the middle of the night, ushering Gabriel, his arms filled with a motionless Naomi Bright, up into the silent recesses of the house then moments later, returned to politely offer her tea.

Rae didn't want tea. She wanted answers. And she wasn't quite as polite as Nicole LaValois when she demanded them.

"I could not tell you our origin," Marchand continued, "only that it goes back to the dawn of man. We have co-existed with humankind for centuries, hiding in the shadows, living off them in secret, like a curse to be feared and ashamed of. Within our numbers, just as within mankind's, we have those who would abuse their powers with a reckless and selfish disregard. Your laws cannot control them. That's why our *Corps du Justice* was formed."

"And here I thought you were black ops for the government. Silly me."

"We are not without government support. Our influence reaches into places that would surprise you."

"Not much would surprise me at the moment." She looked to her sleek hostess. "Do you have anything stronger than tea?"

"Of course."

Rae watched her move to the sideboard, a study in grace and fluid strength. She looked...normal. An illusion? Rae remembered the creatures at the club. She took the brandy offered with a wary nod of thanks.

"I apologize for my ignorance, but are the myths about your kind true?"

"Some yes, some no. Some are created by Hollywood, and some are perpetuated by our own kind to maintain an aura of awe and fear. Sunlight is our enemy. Silver is toxic to us."

"And you feed on blood."

He regarded her somberly. "We have and we do. Unfortunately, it is necessary to our survival. But we do not kill except in extraordinary circumstance, and we do not turn the unsuspecting into one of our kind without their knowledge and consent. Those are the laws we now live by. Or at least, most of us do. Those who refuse to conform are more a danger to us than to you."

"So where does Kaz Zanlos fit into this? He's not a vampire...is he?"

"No, not in the traditional sense. Though he is a parasite who sucks off others for his survival. It's the woman you know as Anna Murray. She is one of our oldest and most deadly creatures. She has no regard for the laws of man or those of her own kind. She is evil incarnate, a blemish on our name that has gone on long enough. We did not know where she was hiding. That's why we needed you to draw her out."

Anna Murray, who cast no reflection in her mirror. The truth of it shuddered through Rae.

"Then why haven't you destroyed her?"

"We need to know what she and Zanlos are involved in."

"Murder, for one."

"Yes. But there is more, and that more keeps us from punishing them as they deserve. We cannot afford to let any of their evil continue beyond them."

"So my friend and her father go unavenged? You promised me that that wouldn't happen."

"Oh, they will pay for the Grovers as well as for the centuries of souls before them. And we are close. Ms. Bright has been working with us through Gabriel. She's provided enough for us to know we are on the right track. But there is more we must discover before we act."

"And I haven't gotten you anywhere."

He warded off her bitterness with a dismissing hand. "On the contrary. You have gotten us closer than we believed possible."

There was more he wasn't saying, so Rae prompted him to finish. "How?"

"You brought us Nicholas Flynn."

Rae froze up inside. "I used Nick Flynn, and I am not proud of that. But it didn't get me anywhere. He won't help us."

"He must, Rae. For his own sake as well as for our cause. He doesn't understand what is at stake, and it's vital that when he learns the truth, he be our ally."

"Why? He's a lawyer from a small town trying to make it big in the city. He's turned his back on what his boss is doing. What makes you think you can trust him?"

"Do you trust him, Rae?"

I love you, cher.

"I don't know."

"Bianca DuMaurier, or Anna Murray, brought him here for a purpose. She is a creature of predictable desires. Power is one, vengeance is the other."

"Which of those could Nick possibly give her?"

"Both, Rae. Both without him ever knowing why. It's not who he is as much as where he comes from."

"Baton Rouge?"

"Italy, during the Renaissance, when a monster named Bianca converted two friends to darkness for her own twisted amusement. One of them was Nicole's father. The other is tied to Nick Flynn through marriage and the intermingling of blood. Both escaped her influence, and she would stop at nothing to punish them through those they love. She tried once to manipulate Nicole to hurt her father. And now–"

"Now she's after Nick."

"Yes."

A bristle of protective anger rose up at the thought. "So, how do we stop her?"

"Does he trust you? Enough to walk away without question? Enough to listen to what I have to say with an open mind? Is he a man of character and conviction? Or would he be easy to seduce with the darkness of what we are?"

"I don't know."

She could have said more, that Nick Flynn was on the wire doing a difficult balancing act between ambition and ambivalence. She knew how desperately he sought success. Desperately enough to look the other way at Meeker, Murray & Zanlos. Desperate enough to look the other way when murder was done. What leverage would tip that scale to convince him to surrender all that he sought?

She was that leverage.

He might not do it for decency or the good of mankind. He might not relent to an appeal to his conscience. But he might do it for her. If she asked him.

Before she could voice those hopes, Gabriel returned to their company. He looked weary and anxious enough for Nicole to approach with the offer of an embrace. He sank into it gratefully.

"How is she?"

He stepped back from the comfort his hostess provided to uneasily regard his host. "She's been initiated. She's weak and will have to be watched carefully once she awakens. She'll be their eyes and ears now in spite of her wishes."

"Initiated?" Rae's thoughts spun toward summer camp and fraternity hazing. This had to be much worse to bring such a bruising of worry to circle Gabriel's eyes.

"With a bite," he told her bluntly. "Once one of our kind

drinks from a mortal, a psychic bond forms between them, one that cannot be broken until the death of the vampire in question. Or until the mortal is brought over by another of our kind." Seeing she didn't understand, he clarified. "Until the mortal dies in their human form and is reborn as one of us."

Rae didn't want to know the particulars there. She had enough to grapple with already. "So what do we do now?"

"Bring Flynn here to us. Gabriel will go with you."

She could see protest form in his expression, but Nicole intercepted it.

"We will take care of your lady."

"And if he won't come with me?"

"As our friend or as our enemy, his choice."

***

With the top down in the big Mercury and the feel of the wind in her hair to restore the sense of normalcy, Rae fixed an accusing stare upon the driver.

"What?"

"You could have told me."

"You weren't prepared to hear the truth." He'd changed from the blood-soaked shirt into a dark pullover belonging to Marchand. Against his shaggy blond hair and dramatic facial planes, he looked noble and a bit poetic. Not at all like a ghoul who fed off live blood to survive.

"So what's your story?"

"It's a long one."

Her steady gaze said she had time.

"I was a bold and rather arrogant knight who let pride keep me from holding onto happiness when I was lucky enough to have found it."

"Knight as in Round Table."

"As in Crusades. My need for the quest left those who depended upon me vulnerable. It cost me the only woman I ever loved. I accepted my fate in order to search for her through the centuries."

The catch in his voice told her more than his words.

"Naomi."

"She is my soul mate reborn, and I will not lose her again."

The passion, the promise in his tone—to have a man hold a woman up with such reverence amazed her. This was love, she realized. Not the possessive, warped web her father used to trap and ultimately destroy her mother. Could what she felt for Nick evolve into such unselfish devotion? The idea frightened as much as it tantalized. To strip her emotions bare before another, she couldn't imagine a more naked, more vulnerable position. And if that love wasn't returned, what then?

She studied the angles of Gabriel's face, the tautness of his jaw, the pucker of his brows, the tightness about his mouth. He was in pain and suffering for the sake of love. Is that what she wished for herself?

She laughed, drawing Gabriel's questioning glance. She shook her head to say it was nothing. Here she was being chauffeured by a vampire, about to do battle with unnatural forces for the soul of the man she loved. Life couldn't get more melodramatic than that without offering the requisite happy ending. She wanted that happy ending with Nick Flynn, whatever the risk.

But would he come with her?

"Where to?" Gabriel asked when they entered the traffic flow.

"My place, so I can change. My wardrobe needs a major makeover now that I'm no longer employed. I don't want to see another pair of stiletto heels for as long as I live."

"I don't know, Sugar Rae. They came in pretty handy at the club."

She grimaced. "Thanks for the reminder. You came in pretty handy, yourself. Thanks."

"You broke your cover for Naomi. I'm the one who needs to thank you."

"Before we start singing "Kumbiya" and holding hands, we need a plan."

"You sweet talk Flynn, and if that doesn't work, I stuff him in the trunk."

"That's your plan?"

He shrugged.

"I like it."

"You're all right, Borden."

"So are you, Sir Gabriel."

He grinned, the tension relaxing in his expression. It was hard to picture him as anything other than a cocky policeman with punk shirts. Vampire was just part of the package. She could see again the way he'd waded into the men at the bar. Having a vampire as a partner might not be such a bad thing. As long as he was well fed.

"Naomi...have you ever . . .?"

He shot her a disdainful look. "Never. I've never touched her. We do have some self-control."

"Unlike most red-blooded males."

"She doesn't know what I am. It would be unfair to take advantage of her ignorance of the truth."

Gabriel's prickly dignity made her writhe in shame. Isn't that what she'd done with Nick? She'd encouraged his affections while hiding the truth. The truth that she, like Gabriel, was not what she seemed.

Gabriel eased the big car over to the curb. "Go on up. I'm going to circle around and check out the area."

She slid out without question and had the keys she'd recovered from Naomi in hand before he pulled away. In her stocking feet, she padded up the stairs to her apartment, her mind spinning with possible scenarios concerning Nick. All started with telling him everything. His reaction was the only variable she couldn't count on.

In the darkness of her front room, the strobing light on her answering machine was a beacon. As she went toward it, a voice spoke from the room's shadows.

"That would be from me."

She whirled, heart in her throat, to see a figure seated on her couch. The plastic had been peeled off and was folded on the floor beside it.

"Jeez, Nick. You nearly gave me a coronary. How'd you get in here?"

Silence, then the soft drawl of his reply told her everything. "You think cops are the only ones who know how to jimmy a lock? Just one of the perks they teach you at lawyer school."

He knew.

"Glad to see you made yourself at home."

"Home is where the heart is. Right, Officer Borden?"

"If you say so. Give me a minute to change. We've got a lot to say to each other."

No reply. Not good.

She quickly shed what she'd deemed her hooker clothes and pulled on her usual comfort attire consisting of bike shorts and an oversized tee shirt. She gathered her hair into a pony tail high at the back of her head then returned bare-footed to the living room where Nick had yet to turn on the light. Why prolong the inevitable?

"I'm a cop from Detroit. I got into it after working with battered women, teaching them self-defense. I wanted to make a difference, to make up for things that I'd done wrong."

"And did you?" His tone rang flat and neutral. No encouragement there.

"I like to think so. I wanted to mend my friendship with Ginny and didn't know how. I thought that would be a good start. And then I got the word that Ginny was dead, that it was too late to make amends. It made me mad as hell that the chance was taken away from me."

"So you came here and offered your services to the D.C. police."

"Not officially. I'm working with another group, one that can actually do some good. I needed to get close to Anna Murray."

"And I provided the introduction." No bitterness, no accusation, just that same tonelessness that told her nothing of what he was feeling. So she didn't insult him by prettying up her actions.

"Yes, you did. There was an attraction between us. I felt it after the funeral the first time I saw you. And I used that spark to play on your sympathies. It was an expedient way to get me where I needed to be."

"Waste not want not. I admire your brevity of tactics." He didn't sound like it. "They worked like a charm."

"Nick—"

"Don't you dare apologize to me." Finally a flash of raw emotion ripped through his voice. To defuse it, she kept her own calm and professional.

"I wasn't going to, Nick. My friend and her father were dead, and I needed to know why. The means didn't matter at that point."

He didn't respond to her blunt claim right away. When he did, he was in control once more. "And now they do, is that what you're trying to tell me?"

"The only thing I can focus on right now is making sure Zanlos and Murray pay for what they've done. I can't let my feelings become an issue."

"How very conscientious of you."

"I have to be, Nick. These are some bad, bad people. Ginny and her dad were all the family I had, and I owed them to do whatever it took to see them avenged."

"Well, lady, I'll give you this, you're more than willing to pay to play. You certainly had me fooled, fool that I am."

"Game's over now. I blew my cover tonight."

"Hanging up your fuck-me pumps?"

She blinked at the fiercely rendered crudity. "I've never heard it put that way before. But yes, gladly."

"I'd have thought you'd had it put to you in all sorts of ways by now."

Color burning in her face, she said, "That was a cheap shot, Nick."

"Oh, *cher*, there's nothing cheap about you."

Glad for the darkness hiding the contempt in his expression which dripped from his voice, Rae said softly in her own defense, "I never—"

"Don't forget who you're talking to, Detective. I know exactly what you were willing to sacrifice for the job."

"Am I interrupting something here?"

Mortified that Gabriel had heard the last exchange, Rae concealed her discomfort by shedding light on the situation. Blinking in the soft glow of a table lamp, the three of them regarded one another stoically.

"Don't tell me. Another cop."

"Rae's partner, and if you ever speak to her in that tone again, I'll tear out your throat."

The mild, conversational statement would have had less impact if Rae hadn't witnessed him doing just that earlier in the evening. She put a staying hand on his arm.

"It's all right, Gabriel. He has the right."

"Thank you for that small concession." Then Nick studied Gabriel with renewed interest. "You're the boyfriend. The one Naomi was talking about. I'm worried about her."

"She's safe with us."

"Us, who? Are you in on this covert little venture, too? Don't any of you people do things by the book any more?"

"We're using a different book, Nick, and different rules," Gabriel remarked casually. "Somehow they found out that Naomi was leaking information to me, and now her life is in danger. Would that tattletale be you...*Nick?*" His eyes glittered dangerously.

"I asked her to get certain documents for me, and Zanlos found out about it. If she's in danger now, it is my fault. I should have taken better precautions to see she didn't get pulled into it."

Gabriel backed down at the evidence of his sincerity, his own guilt weighting his words. "We both should have. Now they know who Rae is, and she can't get close enough to get any hard evidence on them."

"They already knew who she was, maybe from the very beginning. They were playing her the same way she was playing me."

Rae winced at his harsh tone but couldn't argue the truth of his claim.

"The thing is, while they were busy watching her, they weren't paying much attention to me."

"What have you got?" Rae demanded.

"Besides a big dose of humiliation? I've got everything. Tapes, records, eyewitness testimony, everything you need to put them away."

Initial elation gave way to caution. Her eyes narrowed

slightly. Had she been totally wrong about seeing good in Nick Flynn? "And what's this information going to cost us?"

He stared straight at her. "A damned good apology when I'm ready to hear it." He broke eye contact and addressed the rest of his speech to Gabriel. "At first I thought it was straight blackmail. All the little nooks and crannies at the *Noir* feature video cameras to catch naughty indiscretions for future extortion. Only they don't ask for money, they require certain favors. A change in lobbying position here, a push for a certain variance there. Amazing what a man will do with his career on the line, especially in a town where public opinion can make or break it. I would imagine they have quite the video library built up. I managed to snag a particular volume for my own personal viewing pleasure." He glanced at Rae so she would catch his meaning and relax. Their escapade wouldn't be popping up on one of the late night cable channels any time soon.

"So we've got them for extortion. What else?" Gabriel wanted to know.

"When that little deal doesn't work, like in the case of Thomas Grover who was so proper he squeaked, they applied more direct pressure. I can't prove that Zanlos had his daughter killed, but he showed up after the funeral that day with one of her personal belongings just before Grover blew his brains out. Zanlos forged those documents right in front of me. He was in a big hurry to get import rights into New Orleans and wasn't about to let something like the man being dead get in his way. He wants to bring something into the country, but I don't know what."

"Or who," Gabriel added in a pensive aside.

"Zanlos thinks I'm still on the fence. Maybe I can find out more—"

"No."

Both men looked at her, startled by the vehemence of her response.

"You're in danger, too, Nick. Not from Zanlos, but from this woman who calls herself Anna Murray."

"What would she want with me?"

"Probably things you don't want to know about. It has

something to do with your family."

"My family? My family are crackers from Louisiana."

"Not if you go back far enough," Gabriel interjected with just enough melodrama to peak his interest.

"I want you in protective custody, Nick," Rae insisted.

He shook his head. "No chance. The only one I can trust at this point is me. That's the way it's always been, the way it always will be."

Rae twinged at the isolating fierceness in his voice, but she was in no position to give assurances or comfort. Not yet. Not until he was ready for that apology.

"It'll be light soon," Gabriel noted. Nick missed the significance, but Rae did not. "He should be safe until nightfall. Then we need to bring him in."

"In where? I told you, I'm not setting myself up in some cop fishbowl."

"That's not what we have in mind, Nick. You'll provide us with what we need to get Zanlos and Murray? Your word you won't try something funny?"

"I have absolutely no sense of humor at the moment. I'm going back to my room. You can find me there when you're ready to start playing the game again. I'd appreciate knowing my part ahead of time though. I'm not in the mood for any more surprises. You get my testimony, but you don't get to play me for the fool anymore. That's a role I'm tired of." He got up and, without a further glance at Rae or Gabriel, went to the door. "You might say you can trust me about as much as I trust you."

The door shut quietly behind him.

"Do you want me to stuff him in the trunk?" Gabriel asked at last, observing more of Rae's shattered psyche than she'd like.

"Let him go, Gabriel. They won't move on him until tomorrow night. By then he'll have gotten over his ego and will be ready to come with us."

Gabriel made a disparaging noise.

Rae didn't quite buy her confident claim, either. For all she knew, Nick could be on the phone now spilling everything to his boss.

But she didn't think so.

Because, though he had no reason to trust her, she'd begun to trust him to do the right thing.

A restless Gabriel glanced about her apartment. "If you're all tucked in here, I'm going to go..."

"Go tuck Naomi in. Go." She waved her hands at him. "No reason both of us should be miserable." At his questioning look, she made another shooing gesture. "Don't ask. Just go."

"Get some sleep. I'll see Flynn gets home safe."

"Good night, Gabriel." She smiled wearily and locked the door after him.

Gabriel was surprised to find Nick Flynn waiting for him on the front step.

"I need a small favor, cop, since I'll be doing such a big one for you."

"Fair enough." Gabriel glanced down at the news clipping Flynn passed to him. "What's this?"

"I need the article that goes with that photo. It's from early March of this year. Can you have it faxed to my hotel?"

"Sure. It shouldn't take too long."

Flynn nodded.

"Anything else?"

"No. That'll do it." But he hesitated, wanting to say more. Finally, Gabriel said it for him.

"She'll be fine. She's one tough cookie."

"Don't I know it."

***

"Dad? Sorry, did I wake you?"

A mumble, then an irrate, "It's four in the morning. Did you think I'd be out jogging?"

"Dad, I need to know some things...about our family. About why Mom left."

A long pause. "Now?"

"No time like the present."

The time was long overdue, and they both knew it. The elder Flynn's reluctance dragged out into a lengthy silence, then his sigh carried along the line.

"Why now, Nick? What's the urgency?"

"I'm in trouble, Daddy. I need to come clean with some things I've done. I've got enough bad things hanging over my head. I don't need any more surprises. I've always known there was something you weren't telling me. I've let it slide, but I can't any more. I've got to know the truth."

Another hesitation, then a resigned murmur. "I'll call you later, son. There's something I have to do first, and it can't wait until daybreak."

***

Stephen Flynn found himself where he never expected to be, at the front door of a huge mansion in the lush Garden District of New Orleans. He'd always known the address. He'd even driven by it a time of two just to have a look see. But this was the first time since learning the truth that he'd been motivated to make contact.

The sound of his knocking echoed inside. After a long beat, he'd almost convinced himself that no one was home, that he'd made a mistake, that it wasn't too late to run back for the safety of the old Volvo he'd parked out front.

But for his son's sake, he stood his ground, waiting until the big front door opened.

"Yes?"

"Do you know who I am?"

"I know you. To what do I owe this singular pleasure?"

"My son...your heir...he needs to learn the truth. He's in some kind of trouble. Will you help?"

Silence, then a soft, "You only had to ask."

NINETEEN

What the hell am I doing here?

He couldn't come up with an answer until the door cracked open for a peek then swung wide.

She was standing there in the oversized tee shirt and bulky socks, her hair in a tangle and her eyes groggy from lack of sleep.

And she looked so damned beautiful his heart dropped right to his insteps.

"Just wondering if you were doing anything for breakfast."

She squinted at her watch. "It's two in the afternoon."

"Seemed like breakfast time to me."

"I've got some coffee I can put on."

"Sounds good."

She shuffled away from the door, leaving it open for him to follow. He took a slow, deep breath and crossed the threshold into a commitment he'd had no thought of ever making until just this very minute. He locked the door and trailed her into the sunny kitchen where he appreciated the way her shirt swayed against the back of her thighs with each step.

Call girl...cop. What the hell did it matter to him, anyway? It wasn't the profession he'd fallen for so hard he couldn't seem to pick himself back up. She was the only thing he could think of when he'd woken from the misty nightmare. Hers was the only opinion that mattered when he considered the irreparable damage to come when the truth of it hit the papers. He felt sorrow for what his father would suffer, but it was true terror he experienced when he thought of this woman's rejection.

He'd been alone all his life, scrapping for everything he'd managed to hang onto. He'd thrown it all away once on his insecurities and fondness for a high-living, party-hearty lifestyle. He couldn't let his fear of the truth cost him a greater loss this time.

She was rummaging through the painfully inadequate ice box when he came up behind her.

"I thought I had some eggs in here somewhere."

She straightened when his hands slipped under the hem of her shirt to rest on her hip bones.

"Forget the eggs," he muttered in a voice so low and rough-edged with want he didn't recognize it as his own. "I need to hear you say you love me."

God, had he said that out loud? He felt her stiffen. Slowly, she revolved within the circle of his hands, then simply looked up into his eyes, her own as warm and welcoming as deep green island waters.

"I love you, Nick."

Her fingertips touched to the black stubble of his unshaven jaw, moving lightly to sketch along his lower lip.

"Will that do for an apology?" she asked with the tease of a smile.

"No," he told her gruffly. "But it will do for now."

His arms cinched up around her, enfolding her with a possessive tenderness until they were pressed full length to one another. That simple contact felt more fulfilling than sex with any other woman. They stood toe-to-toe, heartbeat to heartbeat for a long moment, too absorbed in the sensations to move or ask for more. The elemental closeness was enough.

"I want you to stay away from them," he said at last, emotion grating on that demand like coarse gauge sandpaper. "They're dangerous and scary people."

"In my profession I deal with dangerous and scary people all the time."

"Not like them, Rae. I don't how to explain it. There's something wrong there at the *Noir,* with those women, with Anna Murray."

"I know." Her reply was little more than a whisper against the open throat of his shirt.

"I mean really something wrong. When I go in there, my

skin creeps. I've never had that feeling before. And another thing...It'll sound crazy."

"Try me."

"In that tape of the four of us, Anna Murray is missing, as in doesn't photograph. How weird is that?"

"Not in photos, not in mirrors. Not so strange at all...considering."

He leaned back and studied her features warily. "Considering what?"

"What she is, what most of the other women at the *Noir* are."

"Unnatural." That explanation came to him with a sudden clarity. He looked to her for confirmation. "That's it, isn't it? What are they?"

"Vampires."

His hands fell away from her. For a moment, he could only stare. Then he issued a soft laugh and a wry, "I picked a hell of a time to stop drinking."

"Sit down, Nick. I'll make coffee."

As the strong brew filtered down into the pot, Rae watched her guest soak up the news. He slumped on her sofa, his head back, his eyes closed. She almost would have believed him asleep if not for the agitated tapping of his fingertips on his knees. She was familiar with his distress. It had kept her awake until just before he'd arrived.

Vampires. Who would have thought . . .

"Here. Careful, it's hot."

He sat up and took the mug gingerly. "Thanks. Is it just me or do you expect to hear Rod Serling's voice-over at any minute?"

"It's not just you."

She sat on the other end of the couch, facing him with her feet curled under her. He looked a mess. He looked great.

"Are you going to be all right with this?"

He shrugged. "Oh, hell yes. What's the big deal? I'm from the heart of voodoo country, *cher*. My mind is wide open to possibilities. You know, the funny thing is, I'm not all that surprised. Imagine that."

"That's not the worst of it, Nick."

His heavy brows soared. "It gets better?"

"They want you because your family somehow ties into them."

"And here I thought it was because of my dynamic tort feasers." He sipped his coffee and focused on the dark liquid as if he could read his fortune there. "I should have known it was too good to be true. It was more than I deserved."

Sensitive to his brooding, Rae pushed her bare toes up against his blue jeans and crunched them to knead his thigh. His free hand covered them, his thumb lightly massaging the sensitive curve of her instep. Then he glanced at her.

"Tied how?"

She told him everything Marchand had revealed to her, then went on to describe how a fugitive from the French Revolution had assembled and led a supernatural tribunal against rogues of their own kind.

"And didn't this seem a bit out there to you?" he asked when she finished.

"I wanted Zanlos. I was ready to believe anything."

"Even in me?"

"Especially in you."

She climbed up to her knees and took his coffee cup from him, setting it on the floor before straddling his lap. Her fingers laced behind his head as their gazes communed for a long moment.

"I didn't think you were in this line of work anymore," he complained mildly as his thumbs grazed down her ribcage.

"You inspire me to take on new hobbies."

She leaned down to taste his mouth, sampling the richness of Columbian beans and the silkiness of his tongue. Without sitting back, she whispered against his lips, "I want us to survive this. Are we, Nick?"

"That's always been my plan."

They ended up in her bedroom, naked and entwined, touching, kissing, tasting, enjoying as if each experience was all they'd ever get. As well it could be.

She kissed and nibbled and chewed and sucked on his

swarthy skin, at the rough burr of his whiskers, on his earlobes, his shoulder, his flat male nipples—until his husky groan warned he wouldn't take much more of this sweet abuse. Finally, he gave her a toss onto her back so he could pin her to the bed between the brace of his hard thighs and strong arms. Not that she couldn't have escaped if she wanted to...but why the hell would she want to?

He kissed her long and languorously, all but swallowing her tongue until she moaned for a saving breath. Then, up on his elbows, he searched her face, his eyes dark-centered to the point of blackness and so intense she could feel his stare to the soul.

"A cop, huh? I'll be damned. Handcuffs and night stick and everything?"

"Yep. I can get them out some other time, if you'd like. And we can play cops and lawyers."

He chuckled, the deep vibration creating a naughty sensation where the heaviness of his erection prodded her belly. Slowly, the sense of play evolved into a fierce need to give and take satisfaction. A feeling so big it hurt expanded within her chest.

"I want to grow old with you, Nick Flynn."

"That's my plan, too."

And because the hugeness of those emotions scared her, she broke the somber mood by toppling him onto his back once again, pressing his wrists into the mattress while she stretched out full length atop him.

"Umm, cop stuff. I like it when you play rough."

"Then hang on, big boy. Things are about to get bumpy."

***

He came awake suddenly and completely, not sure what had startled him from his lethargic slumber. Rae was curled up, not next to him, but around her pillow on the edge of the bed. She was snoring softly, and he would have found that adorable except for the sense of anxiousness settling on his chest like a VW bus. Panic surged when he couldn't draw a decent breath. Finally, he stopped fighting it and let himself relax, taking shallow pulls of air until the tightness lessened.

He'd suffered from similar attacks of anxiety right after his mother left them. He'd wake up alone and frightened and unable to breathe. He'd cry out silently for his mother's touch and, amazingly, inexplicably, she'd be there, her soft voice whispering for him to close his eyes, the feel of her caress on his rigid face. Even the scent of her perfume lingered, sometimes clinging to the pillowcase and his pajama top until morning.

But of course, she'd never really been there with him. He had been alone and lonely and aching for love so badly he'd created it within his imagination.

But he wasn't imagining it now. It wasn't Rae's light floral scent filling his nose or her urgent voice that reached out to him.

"She's gone."

Rae muttered when he shook her shoulder then she, too, was fully awake in the dark room. The sun had set while they slumbered.

"They've got Naomi."

She didn't question how he knew. "I'll put out some calls."

He started tugging on his clothes. "Meet me at my place. I've got to pick up a safe-deposit key. Then I'm all yours. I'll do whatever you say."

She grabbed him about the neck, kissing him hard enough to cut his inner lips against his teeth. "You be careful. I won't lose you."

"That's a promise."

He ran the blocks to his hotel. The oppressive mood seemed to translate to the atmosphere as storm clouds gathered above the hilltop building, sending out sheets of lightning to dazzle across the heavens. The old building, the threatening clouds scudding behind it—it was a scene right out of *Ghostbusters*. A cold gust of wind blew down the drive as he climbed upward, burning his eyes with grit and increasing his effort to hurry. By the time he reached the entrance, he was gasping. He pulled open the door and stepped inside the crisp climate-controlled back lobby just as the sky tore wide open in a torrent of rain.

From where he stood waiting for his elevator, he had a clear view down the long glass hall leading to the newer portion of the hotel. The glass began to fog from the abrupt temperature change outside. That was understandable. What he couldn't figure was why a thick mist began to rise out of the floral carpet at the far end of the hall. As he stared, mesmerized and bewildered, the fog took on a human shape, that of a woman. Though he'd only seen her once, briefly, hers was a face indelibly imprinted on his soul.

The young mother on I-10 just an instant before his car hit her.

"No, it can't be."

He looked away long enough to stab at the UP button. When he reluctantly glanced back, she was still there, a wraith swaddled in New Orleans mist. There was no mistaking the heavy odor of decay that came only from the swamps. But how could that be in the middle of a posh Washington, D.C. hotel?

And as he watched, as stiff and still as one of those cypress stumps mired and dying in the muck, the figure approached without seeming to move, carried down the slight incline of the hall on a steady avalanche of vapor roiling toward him.

His breath plumed in short, savage bursts as a deathlike cold seeped about him.

The ding of the elevator had him leaping nearly out of his shoes. He jumped inside the empty car and frantically jabbed the Close Door button. He didn't draw a breath until they slid together soundlessly, expecting a skeletal hand to reach between them at the last second to part the way to the horror of his past. With a gentle jolt, the car started upward. He sagged against the far wall, chest shuddering as he watched the numbers climb toward his floor.

Always before, she'd come to him wrapped in dreams. Never like this, as an apparition while he was wide awake. Closing his eyes, he struggled to control his heart rate as its beats seemed to pinball erratically around in his chest. Ghosts couldn't harm him. The harm had been done all those years ago when he'd put his car in gear and burned rubber. The harm had been done when he hadn't said no to those last few glasses or yes to a place to sleep it off. He'd gotten a rare second chance, yet he couldn't make the most of it until he settled his debt with those past mistakes and let the chips fall where they would.

The door opened silently at his floor. He peered out, checking both directions. No inexplicable mists, no hovering threat. Key card in hand, he rushed toward his room. As he entered, the flash of the message light on his phone was the first thing he saw, distracting him from throwing the deadbolt. He pressed the appropriate button and expected to hear from Rae. Or his father. Instead, it was the desk.

"Mr. Flynn, you've received a facsimile. You can pick it up at the front desk at your convenience."

"Is James working the concierge?"

"Yes, he is."

"Ask if he'd bring it up to me, would you please? It's very important, *cher.* "

The girl at the desk must have known who he was because she got all gooey at that drawled endearment. "Of course, Mr. Flynn. It would be my pleasure."

He hung up then reached beneath the shade of the table lamp. He'd screwed the safe-deposit key where the shade attached to the base. He removed the topper and the key, pocketing it before rethreading the brass top. From there he went into the bedroom to replace his rumpled shirt with a plain black tee shirt. With it swaddling his hips, half tucked in, his face dark with a day's growth of beard, a desperado looked back at him in the dressing table mirror. Or a desperate criminal.

He scanned the contents of his room. His designer suits hung neatly in the closet, the appropriate shoes lined up beneath them in orderly single file. Armani, Ricci, Verri, Barbera, Redaelli and Venturi–a whole fricking foreign legion hanging at attention to testify to his success. But how far would the possession of those worldly goods go toward testifying as to his character...with the law, with the children that poor woman left behind...with Rae. His whole life had been a hit-

and-run with him just one step ahead of the piper and his payment due notice. Tonight he stopped running, and he was as much relieved as he was afraid to accept responsibility for what he'd done. At least it would be over. The woman's spirit could finally rest. He'd sell all these fine suits and the sports car he had on order and send the money to the woman's family as soon as he had a name to put to her. He hadn't wanted to know it before because it would make what he'd walked away from that much more personal and less like a drink-induced nightmare. Nothing about it had appeared in the papers. He'd scanned them for weeks afterwards. He must have missed the picture in his haste, the picture of that face he could never forget or outrun.

He shut his closet door and glanced about to see if he'd be leaving anything of value. Chances were, he'd never return to this room again, to these things he'd hoarded to remind him that he'd made it. In the end, that's all they were, just things. And none of them mattered a damn to him. The things that mattered were in Baton Rouge, the few pictures he kept, the postcards to his father he'd fished out of the trash from exotic countries around the globe imprinted with his mother's handwriting. She'd wanted to let his father know where to reach her—just in case he changed his mind. About what, Nick had always wondered.

A knock at the door pulled him from his brooding thoughts. Glancing through the peephole, he saw the young black man in the hall with a sheet of paper in his hand. He opened the door and nodded distractedly at James's chatter. Taking the fax, he passed the young man a $50.00. James looked down at it agog.

"Ah, Mr. Flynn, maybe you meant to give me a five but this . . ."

"Is what I meant to give you. Thanks, James."

"Any time, Mr. Flynn. You the man."

"Yes, I am."

Nick closed the door and steeled himself for the sight of the woman's face smiling out at him from the full article.

Young Baton Rouge mother killed in hit-and-run.

His stomach took a nasty roll. Madeline Rousseau. That was her name. Madeline. She'd been twenty-eight. A dental hygienist going to night school for a degree. Her car had broken down on I-10. As she stepped out to wave down a passing motorist, she'd been hit and killed instantly. The impact had hurled her broken body over the cement and steel guardrails. It was only by a fluke that she was ever found. She was survived by a husband—a man she'd wed right out of high school—and their two daughters. Two daughters growing up without a mother because he'd had to drink to that last toast to his future while irreparably changing theirs. The price of his fancy clothes and fast car wouldn't come close to repaying them. Not even close.

He was blinking away the sting in his eyes when he caught the date almost by accident. Thursday, March 2. Thursday. She'd been killed on Thursday on her way home from class. But he'd been driving down I-10 on Saturday night.

Some mistake. It had to be.

He checked the date at the top of the page. Friday, March 3. The article on her fatal accident was in the paper a full day before he'd taken that last drink and gotten behind the wheel. No wonder he'd never seen it. He hadn't started looking for a report until Sunday.

A soft tap at the door behind him startled him. With relief and trepidation, he saw Rae Borden in the hall. He let her in and wordlessly passed her the fax sheet. Her brows lowered as she read the article. Her eyes were shining when she looked up to him for explanation. He tried to speak, couldn't. He cleared his throat and began again.

"There was a party in New Orleans celebrating my interview. I drank too much then got in my car. Hell, I was invincible that night. Everything I'd always wanted was mine for the taking. Until this woman stepped out of the fog in front of me."

"Oh God, Nick."

Her horror couldn't come close to matching his own. "I left the scene, Rae. I called in the report from a pay phone and went home. I went home, Rae. What kind of a man is so afraid of losing what he has that he just drives off and pretends because he made a call, he's done the right thing? That he's done enough. I weighed my success against that woman's life, and she lost. I let her die out there in the bayou because I didn't want that fancy firm to see my name in the paper attached to vehicular manslaughter."

"It was an accident, Nick." Her voice was strained. She was having as much trouble saying it as he was believing it.

"No. I thought so for a lot of years. But now I know better. Look at the date. Thursday. I left that party on Saturday night, two days after that woman was hit and killed."

The sheet of paper trembled as Rae lowered it. "It wasn't you."

"Then why do I see her face every night when I close my eyes? Don't you see? It doesn't matter if it was me or not. I did what I did. Thursday, Saturday, that doesn't change anything. I'm just as guilty even if I wasn't behind the wheel when it happened. How am I going to make up for that?"

She didn't know how to answer him. She simply stared up through wounded, anguished eyes while her policewoman's mind assessed the facts of it. And he saw her verdict there even though she didn't want to recognize it.

He was guilty of the act if not the commission.

A gust of rain and wind swept through the room as the balcony doors burst open. As Nick went to secure them, he pulled up short in dismay.

For there on the balcony stood the ghostly figure of Madeline Rousseau.

TWENTY

Instead of shrinking back from the apparition, Nick stood his ground with a defiant growl of, "You're not Madeline Rosseau."

Laughter that set crystal shivering on its stems filled the room. Riding the cloud of mist, the figure advanced into the room and while they watched, amazed, the ethereal features began to shift and change.

"You were expecting the Ghost of Christmas Past?"

"Anna Murray...or should I say Bianca Du Maurier?"

"The masquerade is over, I see. Such a pity. I was so enjoying the game." The icy blonde demon regarded them with an amused contempt. "You know who I am, and I know who you are. Now that we are all properly introduced."

"Why did you do it?" Nick demanded. All the anguish he'd suffered since that night on I-10 crowded thickly into his voice. "That was you, wasn't it? You let me think I hit that woman. Why? Why?" That last cracked with barely restrained fury.

"To bring you here, of course. If you'd taken that job in New Orleans, you might not have found our offer that attractive. And besides, it was a test of sorts. We needed to see what you would do. And you passed—or failed, as you will—magnificently. You see a man of character wouldn't have been half as easy to manipulate. You disappoint me, Nick, developing a streak of decency this late in the game. Kaz hoped you would join us, but I have always had my reservations. Treachery runs in your family, if not through your genetics then through your inheritance of blood. Too bad Kaz was mistaken. But if not a partner on Earth, then a servant in hell."

She sprang. With movement so swift it defied time and space, Bianca Du Maurier was on Nick. Before Rae had a chance to draw her pistol or cry out a warning, the creature with her horrible fangs exposed, ripped into Nick's throat, devouring the hot jet of blood with a ravenous purpose.

"No!"

Shaking off the shock that held her momentarily paralyzed as the fiend rode Nick down to the floor, Rae fired her pistol, once, twice, three times, striding forward with each pull of the trigger until the last volley was delivered up against the side of the blonde head.

Then Bianca looked up from her feast, the charred circles marring her body, Nick's blood bright and thick upon her lips and upon the hideous sharp teeth she bared in a snarl.

"Weren't you taught it is impolite to interrupt someone while they are eating?"

Bianca's hand closed over the pistol. With her thumb under the still-smoking barrel, she bent it upward as if it were one of those cartoon guns that could be tied into a knot. She jerked it from Rae's hand and sent it sailing out the open balcony doors. Then, she stood, letting Nick roll off her blood-splattered lap to thump loosely on the carpet. She smiled with a vicious pleasure at the other woman.

"You can have him now, for what he'll be worth to you. You see, live or die, it doesn't matter now. He's mine. I'll have my revenge upon his family. And you, for all your clever tricks and plans, will have nothing at all."

That said, the creature faded, becoming once again a thin smoke that dispersed on the evening air. Only her laughter lingered, ringing pure and malevolent as Rae fell to her knees.

"Nick? Nick! Oh God, God!"

Her mind told her there was no way he could survive such an attack, but her heart goaded her into taking every possible measure. She scrambled to the bathroom, snatching towels to press against the awful wound in hopes of stemming the bleeding. First one, then another became saturated. She wasn't aware that the wrenching sobs she heard were her own.

"Nick, don't you die on me. Don't you leave me."

His eyes opened slowly, as glazed as black marbles, then clearing as he focused on her tear-stained face. He tried to say her name. It gurgled in his savaged throat.

"Don't try to talk. I'm here. I'm here with you. I won't leave you."

"Rae, you have to," came his bubbly whisper. He fumbled in his pants pocket then pressed what he'd retrieved into her hand. She glanced at it. A key? "Box at the Copy Mart. Evidence against Zanlos in it. Go now."

She threw the key away. He turned his head toward the sound of it clattering on the kitchen tiles, obviously distressed. "I don't care about the damned evidence. I have to get you to the hospital."

He put his hand to her damp cheek. The cold of his touch effectively stilled her. "You can't do anything for me now. But if you don't do this, it will all be for nothing. Rae...it's got to count for something."

She covered his hand with her own as her tears flowed over both of them. "I love you, Nick."

"Then help me come out on top this one time. Don't...don't let them beat us. Get the evidence to Gabriel. Find Naomi. I'll call 911."

She hesitated, torn between what she had to do and what she would be leaving behind. Her greatest fear was that once she left his side, she would never see him again. She clutched his chill fingers against her cheek.

Seeing her agony of indecision, Nick managed a faint smile. "If you love me, *cher*, do this for me. Do it now...before they have time to cover their tracks. I'll be all right. You have my promise on that."

"Dammit, Nick, this isn't fair."

"I can't make it fair...but you can make it right. Go now. Make it right."

She stared deeply into his dark eyes, as if she could absorb part of his soul along with the strength of his love. She'd need both to break away from the desperate heartache that held her at his side. Uttering a soft curse, she kissed his palm then placed the phone receiver into it. Before her emotions overruled action, she scrambled into the kitchen to retrieve the key. When she looked back, Nick had dragged himself up to lean back against the sofa and had pulled the phone onto his lap.

"Go," he told her simply.

And she did while she still could.

And as the door closed, a mechanical voice sounded.

"If you wish to make a call, hang up and dial again."

The receiver rolled from Nick's hand to bounce forgotten on the rug.

***

As she rode down in the elevator, Rae caught a glimpse of her reflection in the bronze-toned mirrored wall. Determinedly, she scrubbed the wet streaks from her face with the backs of her hands, stopping when she saw blood on them.

Nick's blood.

He was going to die.

That truth quaked through her with a numbing certainty. There was nothing she could do that the paramedics wouldn't try. All she could do for him was make his life count, to make his last actions matter.

Her hand hovered near the Stop button. How could she leave him to face his eternity alone? Slowly, her hand dropped to her side. He wasn't alone now. Any more than she was alone as long as she was wrapped in the security of his love.

And there was more. Something she hadn't told him because she wasn't sure. Now she might never have the chance to share the miracle of potential life quickening inside her. She placed her palm upon her flat belly as if she might sense some precognitive vibration that would tell her yes or no.

Yes.

The answer formed with unshakable certainty.

Nick Flynn was not going to leave her alone to face her future.

When she exited the elevator, she expected to hear the wail of sirens. Nothing. The rain had stopped outside leaving a world covered with fog and clammy darkness. She paused at the door, glancing back toward the elevator as the door slid silently shut. She should be with Nick. She greedily wanted those last few minutes, hours, decades with him. Regret and remorse burned once more behind her eyes. She could either start weeping or get moving. Which would be a more fitting requiem to her fallen lover?

The air outside slapped around her like a wet, heavy towel. With that weight pressing on her, it was an effort just to breathe, let alone muster up the energy to consider wading through it in a walk several blocks down and over to the Copy Mart which she prayed didn't close its doors at dark. She started to hurry along the sidewalk, past the beds of flowers that appeared to be veiled in thick gauze. Headlights cut across her path. Hoping for a cab, she turned to face an unfamiliar blue sedan. The passenger side window cranked down. If it was some John who still thought she was on the job . . .

"Detective Borden?"

"Palmer?" She approached the car, weak-kneed with relief. Now she wouldn't have to desert Nick. She could pass her investigation on to Palmer who would see to Zanlos's fall. It didn't have to be a personal retribution any more, as long as it was done. The only important personal thing in her life was bleeding to death on the hotel room floor behind her. She reached into her pocket for the safety deposit box key. Palmer could retrieve the evidence and see it properly processed. By morning, warrants would be issued, and Zanlos would be marching across the a.m. news in handcuffs. Seeing that spectacle would satisfy her thirst for revenge for the Grovers.

Then she would go after Bianca Du Maurier for Nick.

"Can I give you a lift?" The detective called out. She opened the passenger side door and leaned down.

"Just who I wanted to see."

"Climb in. I was just on my way to pick up Gabe and his girlfriend. We're setting her up in a safe house. No surprise considering all that ruckus you caused in the club last night."

Rae froze. Every finely honed scrap of instinct cried out, *Liar.* Naomi didn't need a safe house when she was getting the care she needed at the LaValois's...if she was still safe at all. She remembered Nick's intuitive alarm. Naomi and Gabriel weren't waiting for Palmer to offer up a ride. Nor would Gabriel have had time to fill his partner in on what had happened at the *Noir*.

But Palmer seemed incredibly well-informed despite that fact. And he just happened to be sitting outside Nick's hotel hoping she'd emerge so addled and distraught that she wouldn't question his presence there.

He was hardly a godsend. More like demon driven. If she peeled down the top of his tight shirt collar, would she find the telltale marks of possession on his throat? She didn't have to see them to know Palmer was the one working on the inside to scuttle police investigations against Meeker, Murray & Zanlos, the one who had told them that she was a cop. And she was the one with her careless words at the Memorial park that informed on Naomi Bright. He had taken that information to Zanlos and his ghoulish partner. And now he was here at their direction to do what? Lead her astray? Or to her death?

And she needed to lead him away from Nick.

She settled onto the stiff car seat. "Let's go. I've got lots to tell Gabriel."

"He said something about Flynn having evidence against his law firm," Palmer mentioned casually as he gestured for her to buckle up. "You know anything about that?"

She smiled at him. *You sonufabitch!* "All safe and sound and tucked away in Nick's office."

"Shall we go there first and get that stuff safe under lock and key?"

"Good idea, Palmer. Let's do that."

And as they sped toward the downtown area, Rae frowned out the side window. Then she heard it, a wail in the distance. Help on its way to Nick Flynn. She relaxed against the seat and said a silent prayer, as unbeknownst to her the ambulance that had been music to her ears pulled into the drive of an old house three blocks over to pick up an elderly woman struck down by the heat.

***

A strange sound stirred Nick back to awareness, like someone dragging something heavy slowly up the stairs.

Thump-thump. Thump-thump. Thump-thump. The weight must have gotten the best of the unfortunate porter, for the bump-bumps got farther and farther apart.

So tired. It was all he could do to move his hand where it rested upon the unpleasant stickiness of his tee shirt. He felt a weary rhythm pulse beneath his palm. As he focused the wanderings of his attention, he drew a parallel between the thumping sounds and the vibration beneath his hand. His heartbeats. That's what he was hearing, growing slower and fainter by the second as his life gradually and without any dramatic fanfare drained away.

He was supposed to have dialed 911.

Forcing his eyeslids apart, he glimpsed the receiver where it lay on the rug beside him. So far away. So impossibly out of reach. He'd just rest awhile and try to retrieve it later. Rest awhile.

His eyes closed, and with a sudden shock he realized it might be for the last time. But that jolt of realization wasn't severe enough or strong enough to jump start a heart that was running out of fuel to pump.

He was dying. And he knew no miracle he could summon through 911 was going to save him now.

So cold. He shivered, wondering who'd turned the air conditioning up so high. But of course it wasn't the A/C. It was his body going deeper into shock without the warning insulation of blood circulating through it. Even as he contemplated his own death, he was aware of something else nudging against the edge of his consciousness. That breathless sensation of something important growing near, welling up in his chest to clog his throat, to quicken his nearly worn out heart. It was the feeling he'd gotten as a child when he believed he could feel his mother near him.

Help me. Don't let me die.

And as if in answer to his silent mental summons, he heard a softly accented voice speaking close by.

"I've just been waiting for you to ask."

TWENTY-ONE

Nick struggled to focus on the figure bending over him, and then he could not look away. Caught in the dazzling brilliance of the other's gaze, all else faded to unimportance.

"Do you know me?"

Nick started to nod even as he mouthed the word "No." A strange contradiction. Even though he'd never seen this man before, a sense of the familiar overwhelmed.

"I am Gerard Pasquale. I am your...we are related. You are Nick. Your father sent me to watch out for you. I can see I arrived none too soon."

"I'm dying." Once said, it was easier to accept that truth. He was too tired to deny it any longer.

Gerard took him by the chin, gently guiding his head to one side so he could observe the savagery done to his throat. He pursed his lips, and the light in his eyes flared hot and white. "Perhaps. But not in the way you understand it. Who has done this to you?"

Nick shut his eyes, meaning to rest for just a moment so he could find the strength to answer, but the instant he closed out the intensity of the other's stare, he felt himself slipping, effortlessly sliding away.

"Nick. Nick. You must look at me. Look at me."

He forced his eyes to open, and with the connection between their gazes, Nick felt a faint stir of energy return. He understood. Gerard Pasquale and this odd conversation were the only things keeping him alive.

"She said her name was Anna Murray, but it's Bianca Du Maurier."

"Ah, yes." The acknowledgment hissed from him. "*Il*

nemico. I didn't recognize her work. She's grown sloppy in her old age."

Nick fought to concentrate. "It's you she's after. You she's trying to punish."

"Yes. Our disenchantment goes back a long way, my friend, and I am sorry you were drawn into it. I should have been paying closer attention, but I thought you were insulated from her wrath." He sighed regretfully then studied Nick for a long, fateful moment as if making some tremendous decision, a decision he passed on to the dying Nick Flynn.

"You must listen carefully, young friend. Time grows short for you, and you must make a choice."

"A choice," he repeated. His voice sounded hollow, drained of strength. Gerard lifted the hand that lay limp upon his chest and searched for a pulse. His touch was cool and somehow soothing.

"You must choose now how you want to go on."

Nick shook his head. Dizziness had his thoughts floating, scattering like fog in a breeze.

"Nick, listen to me."

"I'm going to die. What choice do I have?"

Gerard chuckled. "Infinite, my friend. But you must tell me now before the choice is taken from you."

"I don't—understand."

"Then listen, Nick. Look at me. Listen. You have been bitten by a powerful creature. She controls you now. If you die, she will still hold you to a parody of life as a *revenant.* It is an ugly, graceless existence, rather like the zombies you Louisianes are so fond of. You will serve her mindlessly until your body rots away. As I said, not a pleasant way to go. If you would have managed to survive, you would have had no will but hers. Again, slavery is a poor substitute for existence."

"I won't be her slave."

"Or, if you choose, I can send you to a peaceful rest."

His breathing quickened into soft, shallow pants as he considered these unappealing options. And disregarded them all. "No. I don't want to die. There has to be some other way." Rae. He couldn't leave Rae. He'd promised.

"There is, *mio amico, mio figlio*."

The luminescent fire in Gerard's gaze blazed higher, hotter, yet with such cold, clear power.

"Tell me."

"I can bring you over to what we are. You can share the eternal night with us and be free of Bianca's control. You will live on in a way that expands and limits what you are capable of."

"But I will live."

"Yes. This is not a simple choice. Do not make it carelessly, but make it quickly." His thumb stroked lightly over the quiet veins in Nick's wrist. "Your time is almost gone."

A vampire. That was what Gerard was talking about. Nick's exhausted mind couldn't grasp the ramifications. But there was one thing he understood and clung to with a fierce certainty. If he did nothing, he would lose Rae forever. If he took this alternative Gerard offered, he wouldn't have to let her go.

"Make me what you are."

"You are sure? You make this choice freely?"

"Yes. I still have things to do."

"*Va bene.*" He leaned in closer, and Nick shrank back instinctively from the instrument of his own end. Gerard smiled, overwhelming that resistence with a touch of vampiric magic, just enough to ease the fear and relax his misgivings. "Don't be afraid. I will not hurt you. Prepare for eternity, young friend."

And as he touched one hand to Nick's cold cheek, he brought Nick's wrist to his mouth with the other. A sudden sting then no pain.

Nick drifted in a pleasant dream, sinking deeper and deeper into a peaceful and forever slumber. He resisted Gerard's insistence that he return.

"Nick. Open your eyes. Look at me."

He fought the suggestion, wanting only to remain on that quiet, blissful plane.

"Nick, you must drink if you want to live."

"Don't drink any more."

"Oh, but you must. A drink like no other leading to an existence without equal. Drink."

Dampness touched his lips, and he swiped it away with his dry and strangely thick tongue. Not cool but warm. The liquid was thick and heated, its taste exotic and all at once forbidden in the way it made him instantly crave more. So he opened his mouth, and he swallowed and let the hot flow of life reenter him from the gash Gerard had torn in his own wrist. He drank. Then he drew with a ferocious urgency until his senses swirled in the thrall of an intoxication far beyond any alcohol buzz.

"Enough."

Nick gasped as the elixir was withdrawn. Then cried out as a sudden violent cramping brought his knees up to his chest.

"You lied," he panted frantically. "You said I wouldn't die."

Again, the soft knowing chuckle. "This is not death, *mio fratello*, this is rebirth. And you will arise from it stronger and more alive than you could ever imagine. But rest now while your body adjusts to the change. Rest. And when you awake, we will discuss what you have become."

***

Rae used the time it took to get downtown to compose her emotions and steady her purpose. By now, Nick had survived or he hadn't. Her presence wouldn't change that. She'd been alone for so much of her life, it surprised her to find a huge cavern opening up inside her. That space Nick Flynn used to fill.

She took a strangled breath. Not 'used to.' She wouldn't give up hope. Not yet.

The gleaming facade of the office building captured the pulse of D.C. nightlife in flickers of passing lights. As they sank into the underground parking structure, tension roiled off Palmer with the failure of his antiperspirant. The musky odor exemplified an animal afraid and cornered. Whatever Palmer was about to do, he didn't like it.

And Rae was sure she wouldn't, either.

"Why are we here, Palmer?"

"I thought we'd stop and pick up the evidence first." How nervous he sounded. He was walking her into a trap. What reward would he get for this betrayal? A pay-off? How much was enough to turn on one's fellow officers? Or maybe there wasn't money involved. Maybe Palmer was motivated by forces beyond his control. And that made him all the more dangerous because he'd be operating without conscience or hesitation. As he parked the vehicle, she pragmatically planned how she would handle the problem of Detective Palmer. No way he was going to march her up and hand her over like a docile lamb to his employers both natural and supernatural.

As they left the steamy garage for the startling chill of the office building, Rae slightly preceded Palmer up the stairs. Did he have a gun on her? Was he prepared for her resistance, or did he think he had her totally buffaloed?

__"Palmer, who was first on the scene to investigate Bette Grover's accident?"

"How should I know?"

"I thought you had your finger on the pulse of D.C. and knew everything." She didn't have to see his features to know her words had them tightening with resentment. Then she added a lie of her own just to see what his response would be. "I saw your name on the report. Why else would you have been at the hospital?"

"I got called in because I was in charge of her husband's investigation. What's so sinister about that?" She could smell his sweat, could hear the strain wearing on his tone.

"Who said anything was sinister? I was just wondering why, if you were on the case, you weren't up at the hospital tonight."

"Why would I be there?"

"You didn't hear? She came out of her coma this afternoon and was going to give a statement. From what I understand, things are pointing away from accident and toward attempted murder. Some news, huh?"

"Yeah. I mean good news for you. She was a friend and all." He sounded as rattled as a diamondback with its sheltering rocks kicked over.

"I've heard she's implicating members of the force. I wouldn't want to be in their shoes when they get tied into Zanlos and his operation. Of course, a smart cop would know the right time to turn state's evidence."

The unmistakable bore of a .38 stabbed her in the kidney.

"So that's what a smart cop would do, eh, Borden? That smart cop who's been trying to put three kids through college on a public servant's salary? What would you know about it, Lizzie? You've never had to worry about anything but that smudge of suspicion on your record. Did she or didn't she waste her father after he'd killed her mother?"

Rae didn't react as he pushed those obvious buttons. Instead, she continued to prod for the decency that may once have resided in the now absent morals of Detective Palmer.

"A smudge? You mean like betraying your department, your partner? They're going to kill Gabriel, you know. He's not going to let them erase Naomi Bright as a bad risk. And how are you going to justify your blood money then?"

"Gabe's a smart kid. He's not going to stop a bullet."

"Unless they ask you to pull the trigger. Would you do that for them, Palmer? Where do you draw the line?"

She winced as the gun barrel jabbed her in the back.

"Shut up. Just shut up and walk."

So much for conscience. He may feel bad about participating, actively or passively, in her and Gabriel's deaths but not so bad that he'd give up the tidy nest egg he was being paid not to care enough to do something.

The door opened to the huge, gleaming lobby. And Rae saw her chance. There at the security desk, stood the beggar turned guard.

As they approached, recognition sparked in the guard's face then puzzlement as he tried to fit what he knew of her into this time and place. With Palmer behind her, she was able to touch her forefinger to her lips, bidding him not to give her away. She read his name plate. Ted Kroeze. That was the name of her rescuer.

"Can I help you folks?"

Palmer pulled out his badge. "Here to see Mr. Zanlos. He's expecting me."

Ted studied the badge, and she could see him calculating what it might mean. The man was a cop, and she was a prostitute. Perhaps her chance had just slipped away.

"He's turned his phones off for the night, so I'll have to take you up myself. Could I get you both to sign in, please?"

Palmer scribbled in the log book then reluctantly handed the pen to Rae. She wrote quickly, and before Palmer could see what she'd put down, Ted picked up the book. He glanced at the page, his expression never altering as he read her plea.

He has a gun. Help me!

"This way, folks."

After unlocking the panel with his key, Ted ushered them into the elevator. Rae went to the back of the car so Palmer couldn't get behind her to use her body for a shield. Ted got in and punched the appropriate floor. His back was to her, so she couldn't tell how he'd reacted to her message. He hadn't said anything to Palmer. But he hadn't made a move to assist her, either. She was asking him to risk his cherished job, his new and trusted position in the community to help someone most people would view as beneath contempt.

But Ted Kroeze wasn't most people.

"Nice night now that the rain's moved off."

Palmer grunted at his comment.

"Makes me glad I've got a job inside out of the weather."

Damn, he wasn't going to help her.

"But I can think of five hundred reasons to be grateful for other things, too."

Yes!

Rae tensed and got ready.

The car stopped.

"Hey, this isn't the right floor."

"This is where you get off, sir."

As the door opened onto the floor below Zanlos's office, Palmer started for the panel, meaning to shove the obviously moronic guard out of his way. His hand was buried deep in his rain coat pocket and the barrel of his pistol angled up as if he were glad to see someone. As he moved toward Ted, Rae was momentarily out of his line of sight. And that's when she acted.

Palmer cried out in surprise as her kick blew out his knee. As he toppled toward her, she grabbed his wrist, bending it downward so if the gun discharged, he'd be perforating himself instead of her or Ted. Then he glanced up to receive another unpleasant shock—Ted's night stick cracking against the side of his skull, putting out his lights like the flick of a switch.

As Ted dragged the motionless Palmer out of the car, he said without looking up, "Tell me I haven't just made the biggest mistake of my life."

"I'm a cop, and you just saved my life."

"Well, I guess that's only fair, since you and Mr. Flynn saved mine." He jerked a lamp cord from the wall and bound Palmer like a rodeo steer. Then, after wadding his handkerchief into Palmer's mouth to stifle any outcries, he tossed Rae the rogue cop's gun. "What can I do to help?"

"Get the hell out of here."

He gave her a steady look, impressed by the way she efficiently checked the weapon. "I don't think so."

"Think of your family."

"I am. And they wouldn't expect me to walk away from a friend in trouble."

Rae smiled and shook her head. "If I'd known you'd be this much trouble . . ." She reached into her pocket. "You can help."

Ted glanced at the key she pressed into his hand then back up in puzzlement.

"Go to the Copy Mart off Connecticut by the Zoo. Take the information in that box to a Marchand LaValois at this address." She wrote it out on the first piece of paper she could find in her purse. Then her throat closed up tight when she realized it was Nick's business card. Forcing that wad of emotion down was like swallowing one of her high-heeled hooker shoes. "I can handle things here, Ted, but I need to know this information is safe."

He took the card. "You can count on me. Do you want me to send reinforcements?"

"Page this number." She added Gabriel's cell phone to the card and then her own. "Tell the officer who answers everything. And then check with the area hospitals for Mr. Flynn. Call me as soon as you find out his condition."

Ted's features set in grim lines. "Is it bad?"

Dampness welled in her eyes. "Bad enough."

He squeezed her arm. "I'll take care of it."

Taking a stabilizing breath, she nodded. "Go on. And don't forget to send the elevator back up for me."

It seem to take forever for the elevator to return. Rae waited, calming her thoughts, training her focus to what awaited on the floor above. At her feet, trussed like a turkey, Palmer never stirred. He'd played his part in this masquerade badly, and for him it was over, while her own role had narrowed into a solo act again. She'd just gotten used to playing it as part of a team and now, here she was back on her own. She couldn't allow herself to think of Nick because, if those remembrances came back, she'd see again a wound too severe for a man to survive. And she couldn't confront the truth of that and do what had to be done for both their sakes.

With a quiet bing, the elevator opened for her.

As she rode up the final floor, she held Palmer's gun at ready. A gun that could do serious damage to Kaz Zanlos. But what did she have at her disposal to go up against Bianca Du Maurier and any other legions of the undead that she might have on hand to greet her?

A fine time to think of that now as the doors opened.

Naomi Bright sat working at her desk.

The sight so surprised Rae that she stood for a moment unsure of how to proceed. Until she saw how Naomi was working.

The girl sat in front of her computer monitor, staring at the nonsensical array of letters she typed with a rapid lack of precision onto the screen.

"Naomi?"

A glassy gaze turned in her direction. "May I help you?" Her voice was as mechanical as an automated phone message.

"Naomi, who's here with you?"

She registered no alarm at the sight of the gun, nor did she appear to recognize Rae until she said, "Mr. Zanlos is in conference, Detective Borden. He's expecting you."

A chill passed along the surface of Rae's skin. "Who's he in conference with?"

She just stared with eyes as blank as marbles. "I'll buzz him that you're here."

Rae stilled her hand before she could reach for the intercom. Her slender fingers were icy. "I'll let myself in, Naomi. Isn't it time for you to go home now?"

"Is it?" She stared, unblinking and without curiosity.

"Yes, it is. Get your purse and go home. Do it now, Naomi. I'll tell Mr. Zanlos you went home for the night."

A mild pucker of consternation creased her brow.

"It's all right. You go on. Mr. Zanlos won't need you for anything else tonight."

With robotic jerkiness, the girl reached into her desk drawer for her purse, picking it up by the bottom so that half the contents spilled out onto the floor. She stared at them incomprehensibly.

"Let me get that for you." Rae knelt and gathered the girl's belongs, pausing as she found a simple piece of silver jewelry. A crucifix. "This is lovely."

"Gabriel gave it to me, but I can't wear it to work. Mr. Zanlos doesn't like religious affectation in the office."

"Would you mind if I wore it just for tonight?"

No response.

Rae slipped the chain over her head. Strange how comforting that plain silver cross felt lying against her throat. Like armor, somehow. A knight's armor.

"Here are your things. I'll tell them good night for you."

Naomi stood and hesitated, mannequin-like until Rae slung the purse strap over her shoulder and gave her a nudge toward the elevator. She moved slowly, in a dazed shuffle while Rae waited impatiently to get her out of the line of possible fire. Finally, after Naomi pressed the call button, Rae turned her attention from the girl to the closed double doors leading into Zanlos' inner sanctum.

Who would she find in there with him? Bianca, most likely. But who else?

Just as she pushed the door open, she heard the distinctive jingle of a beeper.

Gabriel's.

A sudden shove from behind propelled her into the room at

a stumble. Zanlos sat behind his desk and Bianca on its corner. And kneeling on the floor in front of it, bound in shackles, was Gabriel McGraw.

Before she could regain her balance, one of the two men standing out of sight by the door stepped in to neatly snatch the gun from her.

"Thank you, Miss Bright," Zanlos announced casually. "You may return to your work now."

Woodenly, without any trace of remorse for the abrupt attack upon Rae, Naomi scuffled back to her desk.

"Detective Borden, you've caused us considerable aggravation.'

"It was my pleasure." She rubbed her wrist, aching from the goon's snatch and grab of the pistol. She exchanged a speaking look with Gabriel. His eyes were filled with guilt and apology. She forgave it with a slight nod. He didn't appear to be injured. But then he wasn't being held by the chains that bound him. He was kept captive by his love for Naomi. He wouldn't act if that action would bring her harm. If she was to count on his help, she'd have to get Naomi out of the equation.

"Is Mr. Flynn going to join us as well?"

At Zanlos's question, Rae's glare cut to Bianca who lounged on the desk like a chanteusse on a baby grand. "Didn't she tell you?"

"Tell me what?" He glanced at the enigmatic Anna/ Bianca and waited for a response.

"Mr. Flynn outlived his purpose," she stated in a bored tone. Rae bit the inside of her cheek to keep her fury and grief under control. Zanlos wasn't as successful. His face flushed a ruddy hue.

"Without retrieving the information he has? My dear, that was extremely careless of you."

Bianca's idle pose took on a slight stiffening. "I sent Palmer to fetch it."

Rae smiled. "Detective Palmer, unfortunately, outlived his purpose as well. The information is on its way to a source that will see your entire organization exposed. You won't be able to get as much as a beignet through customs in New Orleans.

And as for the *Noir*, consider your extortion days at an end."

"*Chienne!* Meddler!" Bianca was no longer cool and disdainful. Her features sharpened, becoming more angular and at the same time, less...human.

"Then I guess we have no further use for you, do we?" Zanlos drawled. "Time to get rid of the loose ends, right, darling?"

Bianca swivelled on the desktop, her smile chilling. "That's right, my love."

And before Zanlos had an inkling of what she meant to do, her hand flashed out to grip the back of his head, yanking him out of his chair and propelling him across the desk.

So Bianca could sink her teeth into his throat.

TWENTY-TWO

Thrashing arms and legs sent papers and *objects d'art* scattering to the floor as Bianca took Zanlos down to the desktop with her dark kiss. Rae watched in frozen horror as his eyes took on that same film of blankness covering Naomi's once-bright gaze.

When Bianca sat back, her chin stained crimson and her own gaze equally red and blazing, she used her thumb nail to cut a slit across her own wrist, then fed that gushing fount to her dying partner.

"There, my love. No more argument about who is in charge. And no more excuses for botching my best laid plans. Now I'll have all your connections and your brilliance without having to listen to your arrogance." She jerked her wrist from his greedy hold then purred, "Kazmir, my love, follow my voice back to a new life. Open your eyes and see your new master."

She stood and smoothed her hair and skirt, then took a tissue from her handbag to delicately wipe her mouth. No one would guess at the hideous monster hidden behind those affectations of gentility. As Zanlos slowly sat up and gazed about him as if seeing all for the first time, Bianca turned her attention back to Rae.

"You have become unforgivably bothersome. Have you any idea what plans you've interrupted?"

"Tell me."

"Oh, the set up at the *Noir* was paying off wonderfully well, but that wasn't the big plan."

"What were you planning to run through New Orleans that was worth the lives of the Grover family?"

She made a disparaging sound. "Their sacrifice was trivial."

"Not to me."

"Yes. I forget sometimes to take into account you humans' penchant for sentimental loyalties."

"Your only flaw, I'm sure."

The gorgeous facade of Bianca Du Maurier rippled like water when her fury was aroused. "You will regret your insolence."

"I doubt it. So, you were about to tell me about New Orleans. What difference does it make if you tell me now? Your plan will never know fruition."

"Perhaps not now, but soon, so why should I spoil everything?"

"Because you're going to kill me, and you want to boast about how clever and superior you are."

Bianca sneered at her summation. "You have no concept of my greatness, or the scope of my plan."

"Tell me. Amaze me. Woman to woman."

That made her snort. "No man would have the vision for such a coup. Yes, maybe you would appreciate my goal."

"Domination."

"Oh yes, but not just of a few puny mortals. Of a country."

Rae gaped at her. Either the woman was totally mad...or dangerously sane.

"You see, Kaz and I have been carefully plotting the overthrow of the government. Oh, not through violence or confrontation, but through a careful, quiet dissemination of our people in key places."

"By making Congressmen into vampires? I don't think the American people would understand why all the House and Senate meetings are suddenly held after sunset. Wouldn't they have a rather limited campaign trail?"

"Oh, we're not planning to create a new government. We're going to replace the existing one. With exact duplicates."

"I don't understand."

"Of course not. Your mind is too narrow, too constrained to accept the possibility of a breed of being capable of becoming the image of another. These replicants have been meticulously schooled to assume every nuance of the men they will replace. For months, they have been psychically tuned to their twin through the initiation of my bite. They've been seeing through their eyes, living in their thoughts. No one will ever suspect a thing. And when a daylight appearance is needed, the human half will be there to perform on cue."

Brilliant. Horrifying. Rae shuddered at the insidious plot, imagining the unsuspecting politicians being lured into Bianca's embrace and control in the pleasure booths of the *Noir.* And of the shipments coming into the port of New Orleans—inhuman cargo, familiar of face and ready to be plugged into Bianca's web of internal revolution.

And who would ever guess it was happening beyond those in this room, who would never carry the information beyond it?

"Why replace them? Why not just initiate those in power and control them?"

"Too tiresome. And initiates are slow to act, and unreliable. Like your Miss Bright, for instance. You knew right away that something was wrong with her. With these, no one will suspect, not even their spouses."

"It'll never work."

Bianca scoffed at Rae's claim. "Of course it will. Humankind doesn't want to recognize that we exist right beneath their noses. They never see the obvious or suspect the worst. My one goal, my one desire has always been to be the leader of men. And now, I shall be."

"But you forget, we know your plans."

Her laugh burned like acid. "Hardly. Do you think there was only one contingency? Oh, you and your lover and this boy here," she kicked at Gabriel, who, bound as he was, had no way to keep himself from toppling over, "have created an inconvenience, that's all. After you are repaid for that, we will simply move on and set up somewhere else. You cannot stop the tide, Detective Borden."

"But we can stop you."

All the arrogant power and confidence drained from Bianca's expression at the sound of the softly accented voice. "You." Her legs buckled, sending her back against the desk to find support.

"*Buona sera, cara mia.* It has been much too long."

Rae's knees nearly went out from under her as well. Not at the sight of the speaker, who, though darkly handsome, was unknown to her, but because Nick Flynn was with him, alive and whole. Or so she assumed at first. A sudden spear of confusion held her back from running to him. It was Nick...but then, it was not.

Nick Flynn and Kaz Zanlos stared at one another across the room, both recognizing what the other had become. And then Rae saw it, too. The icy fire burning behind their dark eyes, the sharper, somehow enhanced strength of their features that made them unnaturally beautiful. They were not the same two men they had been that morning.

They were both newly made vampires.

"You wanted revenge upon me," the elegant vampire with Nick told Bianca. "Here I am. I would have been content to forget our long-standing feud, but you cannot let any slight go, can you? Did you think you could harm my family and I would not act? You should have known better, *cara*. I am here, and we will end this now."

"Ever the dramatic, my dearest Gerardo. But you forget who you are dealing with."

The two guards at the door attacked as one, and the second they were distracted, Bianca was gone. There one instant, then absent. Unarmed and unneeded, Rae backed away from the melee to observe in breathless wonder what Nick had become.

He moved too fast for the eye to follow, with a lethal grace and purposeful viciousness that was both balletic and animalistic. He intercepted the rush from Zanlos's thug, side stepping it with ease then catching the man by the back of his coat to fling him to the far corner of the room. He closed that distance in a blur of motion to fall upon his crumpled victim...and to feed. In that act, he was nowhere near as fastidious as his friend Gerardo, who had neatly pinned his attacker to the wall with one hand and proceeded to drain the life from him with a deadly efficiency. Nick's approach was less controlled, more...bloody. And Rae looked away, her stomach roiling. And she and the still bound and helpless Gabriel were the only ones who saw Zanlos's attempt to flee the room.

She and Gabriel exchanged a brief speaking glance. Zanlos couldn't be allowed to escape. He had too much to atone for.

Without considering what she was grabbing onto, Rae launched herself at Zanlos, hooking him about the neck with the intention of bulldogging him to the floor. That was her intention. And she would have been successful had he still been the man he was that morning. But Zanlos was no longer a man who could be taken down and out of the equation like a common criminal. Her assault was as effective as it would have been against one of the monuments that propagated the city. He never so much as flinched, nor did he slow down his race for the door. He grabbed her by the back of the shirt and flicked her off like a bothersome flea. She hit the floor in a roll, bumping her brow on one of the uncomfortably formal chairs he favored. She swayed back up to hands and knees, meaning to give it another go when Naomi Bright stepped in and changed everything.

Zanlos encircled her throat with one hand, his other arm going about her middle to jerk her body in front of him as a shield. His hideously exposed fangs were inches from the artery in her neck.

"No!"

The cry came from Gabriel, who with one Herculean feat, ripped free of his shackles to become a dangerous force.

"Come near me and I snap her pretty neck."

Zanlos's coldly delivered threat stopped Gabriel like a ten-pound sledge between the eyes. He stood motionless yet aquiver with the pulse of his fury.

"Ms. Bright and I are leaving now. I wouldn't suggest that you think to follow immediately. But I will be disappointed if we don't meet again."

"Yes, we will." Gabriel's words hissed with all the poisonous promise of an adder hooded and ready to strike. "And when we do, I will kill you for putting your hands on her."

"You can try, boy. You can try."

And with his docile hostage, Zanlos backed from the room,

slamming the door to cover his departure.

Gabriel was instantly in motion. Rae had little more luck in slowing his advance until she stopped him with her words.

"Gabriel, it will be dawn soon. There's nothing you can do tonight except get yourself killed. Then what good will you be to her?"

Eyes wild with grief and rage, he drew upon her calming logic until it quieted the fever of his emotions to a dull pain. "She slipped out of Marchand's house before dawn. She left a note for me saying it was too dangerous for her to remain...too dangerous for me if the darkness inside her followed her to our door. She was worried about me, about me." His tone softened with the wonder of it. "I followed as soon as I could and rushed right into their trap"

"You should have called me." But someone had. Someone had called to Nick.

"I know, but I wasn't thinking with my head. I can't lose her again, Rae." His voice broke. "Not after searching for centuries."

She enfolded him easily, hugging him to her shoulder where he trembled with the violence of his forced inactivity. In that moment, she saw only a man tortured by love, nothing more. Not a preternatural being, not some alien creature to be feared and loathed. Just Gabriel McGraw, her partner. But those tender feelings took a labored twist when she glanced over his shoulder to see Nick straighten from his first kill. And her love for him tangled up in a confusion of other sentiments too complex to sort through.

But there was one emotion he saw clearly when their gazes met and held for the first time.

Fear.

***

They rode through the last moments of night in Gabriel's big Mercury. Rae was in front next to her partner leaving the backseat for Nick and his new-found relative...for his new-found heritage.

She was afraid of him.

He couldn't blame her. He was afraid of himself and what

he'd become.

All his strength had returned since Gerard brought him back from the brink of death. At the time, he hadn't known exactly what becoming a vampire might mean. When he'd opened his eyes, he'd discovered a world where his every sense had intensified but none of what he felt inside seemed to have altered. He was still desperately afraid for Rae. He was still driven by the same wants, the same needs, the same desires. Only they were...stronger. More compelling, harder to contain within the realm of self-discipline. He hadn't known just how hard until he'd been confronted by danger in Zanlos's office. An awesome fury and razor-edged hunger had taken hold of him, and that, combined with his new-found power, created a violent euphoria that was unstoppable. He hadn't realized what he was doing until he'd risen from the man's body to see the horror in Rae's eyes. He was that horror, bathed in blood and drunk on his own newly realized abilities.

Drinking down that man's life held all the irresistible appeal that he'd once found in a bottle. He'd lost his struggle against that need on more than one occasion, so how was he going to stay strong in his denial of this tenfold temptation? How easy to see how darkness might rule a man's desires when he had in his grasp such ungovernable power. He'd been accused of being a good man, though he didn't know how true that was. Even his father had feared he would succumb to the lure of unchecked greed–for success, for money, and now, for blood. Zanlos had seen him for what he was. How was he going to shore up that weakness to Zanlos...and himself wrong?

How was he going to be the kind of man deserving of Rae Borden's love and respect?

And therein he found his answer.

For her.

For her, he'd crossed the boundaries of life itself. She was the constant to keep him on the right course. Her love would keep his direction true and his motives pure. With her love as the compass, he would find his way through the treacherous waters ahead. He could not become in his need for blood the same thing her father had evolved into because of his dependence on alcohol. He would lose her if he did. She wouldn't go through that same hell again, so he had to prove to her that he would rise above it. The Nick Flynn who never thought beyond his next self-indulgence and outside the boundaries of his own goal was no more. Just as Nick Flynn the man was no more.

Then, he saw again the revulsion in her eyes. What if she could not love what he had become?

Nick closed his eyes and lifted his face to the wind, hoping the intensity of that experience would strip his melancholy away. The evening was alive with sensations, each vivid to the point of overwhelming, sharp to the brink of painful. The moment he'd been reborn to this altered state, he was swamped by sensory overload. Sights, keen and clear and too bright. Sounds, huge, echoing, cluttered. Scents, coming in a heavy bouquet to make his head spin. Flowers along the roadside. Rain soaking into greedy soil. Refuse too long unemptied. Rae's perfume, the shampoo in her hair as the breeze tore through it. The pungent aroma of excitement, fear and exertion upon her skin. The deep, erotic fragrance of the woman he had stirred to passion. And something new, something frightening.

The smell of blood.

Even from the backseat, he was atuned to the only human amongst them. He could scent her, could hear her pulse beats, could almost taste the salt on the curve of her throat and imagine the hot spurt of life flowing into him as he bit . . .

Nick sucked a startled breath, scattering the fantasy. A strange aching prompted him to put a hand to his mouth where he could feel the boldly aggressive shape of his feeding teeth.

Gerard touched his shoulder lightly, calling Nick's attention to his wry, knowing smile.

"You'll learn to control it."

"How?" His voice was low, rough with dark desires. Could he learn to curb the fierce urge to feed before he harmed the woman he loved? As much as he craved closeness with her, he would have to stay away, to keep her at a distance, until he was certain that primal appetite wouldn't get the better of his intentions. At the moment, his new basic nature ruled his thoughts, his impulses, tantalizing with the memory of the incredible burst of gratification and bliss he'd experienced at his victim's throat. How was he going to contain that driving instinct that even now clenched in his belly and growled for relief?

"It's like delaying self-gratification," Gerard offered by way of wisdom. "Think of something else."

"What? Baseball?"

Gerard didn't respond to the rather biting humor. Instead, his features grew angular and taut as his focus shifted. "Think about her."

Bianca.

"We need to know where she is, Nicholas."

"How should I know?'

"But you do know. Part of you will always know, just as part of me will always know. My link is ages old and weak from lack of use. Yours is fresh and strong."

The notion horrified him. "I thought you said she'd have no control over me."

"She won't. She does not. But the link is there. Just as the link between myself and your great great grandmother, Laure, my bride has passed through your generations, faint, unskilled, untried but always there."

"That's why my father was always so afraid."

"Yes. He was afraid you would be curious enough to seek us out and that the lure of darkness would be too much for you to resist."

"He wasn't wrong, was he?"

Gerard reacted to his bitterness with an empathetic smile. "But you, young friend, didn't seek it. It sought you, and therein lies the difference."

Nick supposed some day that difference would become tangible to him, but tonight on this first night of his new life, he couldn't discern it. "And my mother? Is she one of you?"

"Yes. I'm sure you will meet her soon."

"I don't know that I want to."

Gerard smirked at that. "Of course you do. There is no

reason for you to stay apart now."

"What reason was there?"

Gerard grew evasive. "Ask your father."

Nick gripped his forearm, drawing a haughty glance of objection until he let go. "I'm asking you."

"Your father discovered the family secret. He insisted that your mother sever all ties to us, including the fortune that comes with our name. She loved him and she loved you, so she complied. Until she was diagnosed with an inoperable tumor pressing against her brain. She would have died within a few months' time. So we presented her with an alternative, an alternative your father could not accept because she hadn't told him about the illness, only about the money and the exciting lifestyle. She had hoped he loved her enough to choose her. But it was not to be.

"So they made an agreement between them. He would keep our secret and you, and she would begin her new life absent from yours. Who can say he was right or wrong in what he did or her in what she did, but the bargain was kept until you were in danger, and he came to us for help."

But had the bargain been kept?

"She didn't stay away." Nick marveled softly. "I've always felt her near me. I didn't understand, and I never said anything to my dad because I didn't want to upset him."

Gerard shrugged philosophically. "A mother's bond to her child. I can think of no stronger tie. But now, I must ask you to think of something else, something decidedly less pleasant."

They were back to Bianca.

"What do I do?"

"Relax. Shut out all but thoughts of her. Reach inside for that essence, dark as it might be, and follow it to the source."

He shut his eyes, but they sprang back open. "I can't."

"Don't be afraid. She can't harm you or us."

"But she'll know I'm there."

"Not if you're careful, not if you reach slowly, quietly. Don't touch her mind. Reach out for her senses. What does she see? What does she smell? What does she hear?"

Nick took a deep breath and let his anxieties expel with it.

And then he started along the trail, a ribbon of sensations. He didn't try to analyze or concentrate too deeply. He followed, letting instinct draw him across the distance, out of his awareness in search of hers.

A sudden overpowering odor made him rear back against the seat.

"What is it?"

"I don't know."

"Explain to me what you're experiencing."

Hot smells. Wild. Rank.

"Animals."

"What kind of animals?"

"I don't know."

"Where are you, Nicholas? Look carefully. Don't let her know you're there."

A still fell over his actual body as his astral self grew more aware. Darkness and motion becoming light and silence. A cave? Water. He fought not to pull back from the smell. Against the sense of large, primitive life. A soft rumbling. A growl?

Where the hell was she?

Bars.

Then he knew.

"She's at the zoo."

"Ah," Gerard sighed, settling back with a thin smile. "I always enjoyed trips to the zoo. And that's where we will go. As soon as night falls once again."

TWENTY-THREE

Kisses, sweet and seductive, teased her from slumber. She didn't need to open her eyes to know who was in bed above her. Relief and want skirted the edges of her awareness in a deliciously tender welcome. Wordlessly, she lifted her arms to enfold him, drawing him closer, tighter, delighting in the weight of him upon her own body.

"Oh, Nick," she breathed into his increasingly avaricious kisses, "I thought I'd lost you." She looked up at him through a sheen of tears, reveling in the sight of his darkly handsome features, in the passion flaming in his dark, devouring stare.

"I want you, *cher.*" That claim growled from him, low and gruff and, excited by his intensity, Rae arched up against him. "Give yourself to me."

"You already have me, Nick. You had me from that first night."

"No," he argued softly.

Expecting husky petitions of love and desire, Rae smiled up at him, losing herself in the engulfing power of his gaze. Until something unknown erupted through that stare. Something harsh and ravenous.

"Not like I'm going to have you."

And with a snarl, he opened his mouth wide, baring glistening fangs.

Rae bolted from the dream with a gasp. She was alone in the unfamiliar bedroom with twilight still an hour or so away. Unconsciously, her hand went to the unmarked sides of her neck. Just a dream.

Not just a dream, she realized as the residue of fright yet crosscut her nervous system. A nightmare. A premonition of what she feared was to come.

What she feared from Nick Flynn.

She got up from the bed and moved restlessly to the window. Hot, lazy waves of waning daylight enveloped her as she perched there, rising her face to a sun she would never share with Nick again.

Don't leave me, she'd begged of him.

Perhaps she should have been more specific.

They'd arrived at the LaValois estate too close to dawn for many explanations. Nicole greeted Nick's friend Gerardo with a squeal of delight and hearty kiss, her husband with noticeably less enthusiasm. Without question, they recognized Nick for what he'd become.

Nick immediately recognized their hostess.

"You. It was you who spoke to me, warned me at the *Noir* and told me that Naomi had run away."

Nicole simply smiled and glanced chidingly at her husband. "A link from Gerard through me to you. We are like family."

In the elegant study, gathered like any normal group of reunited reminiscers, Rae nearly laughed hysterically as a quote from one of her favorite horror films, *The Lost Boys*, seemed to fit the moment so perfectly. The blood-sucking Brady Bunch. She'd thought that line incredibly funny at the time. Less so now.

"I had hoped to protect and guide you," Nicole continued. "Rae had Gabriel, but you were so all alone. It was the least I could do. I wish it had been more."

"Your friend arrived with the documentation needed to start an investigation into Meeker, Murray & Zanlos," Marchand told them. Unable to meet Nicole's challenge with argument or apology, he got right to business. "A legitimate investigation this time, led by some of ours and some of theirs. No cargo will enter through New Orleans." He nodded to Rae. "As I promised, they will get away with nothing."

"We have other priorities, Frenchman," Gerard Pasquale stated with a quiet ferocity. "She cannot be allowed to escape us."

"If she knows we're on to her, she'll stay one step ahead," Nicole mused from where she was seated on the arm of Pasquale's chair with her arm draped about his shoulders. Though her husband showed little pleasure in the situation, he said nothing to discourage her display of affection. Rae sensed great history among the three of them—four, if she included the wicked Bianca.

"Nicholas hasn't the skill to block her notice for long. The moment we begin searching for her, she'll feel our presence."

Marchand pondered Gerard's observation for a moment than said, "Not if we search by day."

"I thought your day-walking daughter was on the other side of the globe converting rogues like me from the dark side of our nature with her evangelical husband."

"I wasn't thinking of Frederica."

Then Marchand's gaze settled upon Rae once more, and the others turned their focus there as well.

With all their supernatural powers, it was the single human they sought for help.

"No." Nick had been silent to that point, but he spoke his opinion loud and clear. He glared at Marchand in open challenge and said, "You've asked enough of her already."

Considering all that she'd done, all that she'd risked, all that she'd lost, this seemed almost anticlimactical.

"What do you want me to do?"

After their plans were decided upon over Nick's objection, dawn forced them to go their separate ways, she to a bedroom upstairs, they to the sheltering darkness in chambers below. She couldn't shut out the images—of Nick lying back like one of the dead as a coffin lid closed above him, of his unnatural cycle of existence beginning on a clock that ran opposite to hers.

But he was alive! Wasn't that what she'd wanted? To be with him? To be loved by him? What she'd prayed for as he lay dying on his hotel room floor? That she wouldn't lose him? Would she prefer that he be nailed up in a coffin and lowered into a grave for the same endless eternity that Ginny and Thomas Grover shared?

Her yearning gaze detailed him. He was still Nick. Nothing all that discernable had changed. At least on the surface. Except for the sudden quicksilver movements he made without realizing it, movements too fast for her eyes to follow. Except for the odd glow in his gaze and the changeable state of his canine teeth. Except for his feeding and sleeping habits.

She shuddered as a confusion of emotions assailed her. Should she mourn the loss of the man he had been or learn to love what he had become? Could she?

As they passed in the doorway, Nick reached out to her for the first time, his hand tentative in its clasp of her own.

"Don't do this. You don't have to prove anything."

His touch was cold, his tone remote.

Rae pulled her hand away.

"I finish what I start."

She'd walked away from him, unwilling to decipher what moved behind his dark, masked stare. But the question continued to daunt her.

What about what she'd started with Nick? Was that finished now, or had she simply given up without a fight?

When she closed her eyes to sleep, she could see him rising up from his first kill, bloodlust blazing in his eyes, as he wallowed in the ecstacy of it. He'd killed a man in self-defense, to protect them all. It was something she would have done herself. But the manner in which it was completed, the pleasure that was taken in the accomplishment, those were what set this being apart from the man Nick Flynn had been.

Time was growing short. This wasn't the place to wax sentimental over expectations held and lost. She had a job to do.

It wasn't as if having nothing beyond the job was anything new to her.

While her friends slept below, Bianca Du Maurier was burrowed in at the zoo. It was her mission to find out where before sunset. Then, while Gabriel went in search of Zanlos and his kidnapped love, the others would join her to bring about the destruction of the woman Marchand so fondly called

Queen Bitch of the Universe.

Then her quest would be over. And she could return to...what? Detroit and the lonely dissatisfaction she'd found there? Despite all the pain, all the turmoil, these last few weeks in Washington were the first she'd truly felt alive and valuable. Through Marchand LaValois and his unconventional band of guardians, she had found the means to make a difference and, oddly, a way to fit in and be accepted.

Was this to be her future then? Living amongst these unnatural beings with their supernatural sense of right and justice?

Did it matter which wrongs she was righting as long as that justice was being served?

But there was more than herself to consider.

Did Nick have the right to know?

More food for thought to save for later.

Now, it was time to go to the zoo.

***

Someplace private. Someplace out of the light of day but artificially bright. Someplace subterranean, Nick had told them. With big animals and jungle sounds.

Despite the heat of late day, the zoo was crowded with families and tour groups. Amongst them, Rae was the only one with a purpose other than enjoyment. Starting at the visitor's center, she worked her way methodically along the paths, checking the panda habitat, the great ape exhibit, searching the gibbon house and monkey island for possible hiding places. Within the buildings, she found security or maintenance people who responded quickly to her questions once she flashed her badge.

And they all directed her to a single area at the very back of the zoo.

She placed her palm over her belly. "To the Bat Cave, Robin."

BATS Stop-22. It was a nocturnal dweller's paradise.

Rae shivered as she stepped into the climate-controlled area, from the steamy 90-degrees plus outside to a balmy 73. Home to over 400 night wings, the surroundings were pocked with nooks and crannies, artificial trees and even a pond and waterfall. She listened briefly to one of the enthusiastic guides describe their system of reverse daylight. From 10:00 p.m. until 9:30 a.m., all the lights were kept on to simulate daylight so the bats would be fooled into sleeping while the zoo was closed. Then, during the day, the interior lights were dimmed so visitors could observe them when they were active—the short-tailed bats from Central and South America grooming one another or snuggling for warmth. The giant fruit bats dining on fresh produce or squabbling over the prime roosting spots which most of them were busy doing as their false daylight hours approached.

Rae walked slowly through the habitat, ignoring the noisy squeaks and shrieks of both inhabitants and visitors. She studied the topography, searching for a shadowed nave, a dark recess, a crevice big enough to hide a member of the most night dangerous breed.

And then she found it, tucked up behind the waterfall, niched into the wall to hint at secrets untold. Just the suggestion of a cave that went far enough back to harbor one inverted sleeper. She couldn't be sure. It was too far, too dark.

But, knowing she'd be searching in the dark, she'd come prepared.

The powerful flashlight beam startled the lair's occupants into a frenzy of flight.

"Hey, turn that off."

Just before her arms were gripped at the elbows and pinned behind her, the area behind the falls was illuminated for an instant. Long enough for her to distinguish a downward spill of blonde hair as gleaming red eyes opened and lips drew back from pointed teeth.

Then the flashlight was shaken from her hand to shatter on the ground.

"I'm sorry," Rae began to explain. "I'm a police officer. I thought I saw a child back there."

"Well, I'm a police officer, too, and I know exactly what you were looking for."

Palmer.

He kept her elbows notched up high to propel her up the steps and out of the bat cave. In the fading light, he looked none to pleased to see her. Or perhaps that was due to the huge discoloration swelling like a noxious puffball on the side of his brow. He was hurting her, but she refused to let him know it as he marched her out into the Great Cats exhibit near the lions habitat.

"You've made a lot of trouble for me, Borden, you and that boyfriend of yours. It's not going to hurt *my* feelings at all to get rid of you."

"About as much as it's going to disturb them when you screw up one too many times. I don't think they offer a vampire toadie retirement plan. Then who'll put your kids through school?"

"Shut up."

He shoved her forward, forcing her into the cement wall that surrounded Lion/Tiger Hill, Stop-17 on the zoo tour. Palmer gestured into the hilly habitat with his gun barrel before digging it into her side.

"They're out there prowling tonight," he told her with a low viciousness. "Usually they bring the big cats in at six for their feeding, but somehow, a rather toxic chemical was released in their den. So tonight, they roam free. One of those big kitties can weigh up to 600 pounds and goes through sixty-five pounds of horsemeat and oxtails a week, or so my helpful tour guide told me. They're creatures of habit, and they're wondering about now why no one's rung the dinner bell."

Rae gasped as a sudden pain scissored up her forearm. When Palmer held it out in front of her, she could see he'd cut a long slice from elbow to wrist. Extended over the restraining wall, her blood began to drip into the moat circling the exhibit. It wouldn't take long for the cats to pick up the scent.

Nor would other predators miss it.

Palmer chuckled.

"Feeding time at the zoo."

***

Blood. Human blood.

From the way Gerard's eyes glittered in the gathering

darkness, Nick knew he smelled it, too. But what his relative may not have picked up was a subtle nuance entwined with that intoxicating scent, that of Rae Borden's perfume.

A low growl rippled up through Nick. Someone was going to pay dearly this night if any harm had come to Rae. He'd been against this plan, against thrusting her back into the jaws of danger. But he couldn't stop her from doing what she'd been trained to do, from what she was driven to do. All he could do was the best he could to see that she was safe.

And so far, he wasn't doing a very good job.

"Since we haven't heard from her, we'll have to assume they have her."

Marchand's brutally blunt summation was a stake to the heart.

"We don't know that for sure," he argued softly, as if saying it could make it so.

"No, we don't." The Frenchman placed a reassuring hand upon his shoulder. "We can't afford to assume anything. And we can't let that blonde bitch escape us. Agreed?"

The consensus was unanimous.

"We'll separate here. We can cover more ground that way. I don't have to tell any of you that we're dealing with a clever and completely ruthless killer. Be careful."

The four of them, Marchand, Nicole, Gerard and Nick split and swept down different paths in search of a demon and the human who might now be her captive. Nick didn't want to consider that possibility. Since his transition, he hadn't had a chance to give much thought to the future—or to a future for him and Rae, but he knew he didn't want her trapped in darkness the way he was now. He wanted her to have all her options open for a normal life, even if that meant a life without him in it.

I want to grow old with you.

Impossible now.

She had to be alive, and he had to keep her safe from...from those like him.

He moved down the walk, his agitation hurrying his pace so that he was all but invisible to the human eye. But the animals sensed him. A chaos ensued in their cages and houses. Howling and banging quickened at his passing, for they knew one of their own was on the hunt and death was in the air.

He honed in on the scent, the dark, compelling fragrance that had his appetite pounding and his senses razor sharp. He could feel Bianca Du Maurier close by but was careful not to explore that prickling awareness lest he give them all away.

As if she didn't know they were coming for her.

He hoped Rae knew. He hoped she wasn't afraid.

And then he saw her, and terror bobbed up in his throat as big as the Times Square ball on New Year's Eve.

The obnoxious detective. Gabriel's partner...what was his name? Palmer. Palmer had Rae bent over the cement wall, hanging head first over the water below. Only his balancing grip on the waistband of her jeans kept her from plunging the twenty feet. And if the fall wasn't bad enough, the audience observing them looked to be tough to play to. Two Sumatran tigers paced the edge of the water, drawn by the same scent that called to Nick. Rae's blood.

"Stop right there, Flynn, or your girlfriend here will need a mortician, not a lawyer."

Palmer didn't know about his altered state.

"You drop her, and I'll drop you one second later," he promised as he continued his approach.

Rae met his gaze. There was no fear in her eyes, only anger and concern...for him. "Nick, he's not alone."

Her warning wasn't necessary. His instincts shivered with Bianca's presence, though she'd yet to put in an appearance. She was close, probably watching to see how things would unfold before she chose to involve herself. Let her underlings take the risk. That's how she'd lived so long.

Too long.

He had to act. He had to get Rae out of their hands. But was he overestimating his untested skill at the risk of her life? He didn't have time to wonder. It was time to trust himself.

"Go ahead and drop her, you son of a bitch. Or do you have to hide behind a woman to consider yourself a man?"

Nick's acidic drawl was an insult that could not go

unanswered to a man of Palmer's ego. While he sneered at Nick, he gripped Rae's feet and flipped her over the wall.

Before she had time to cry out, before she touched the water, Nick had her safe in his embrace.

"I've got you, *cher.*"

And she had him, tightly about the neck in a near stranglehold as he hovered a scant inch above the water's surface.

His highly sensitized faculties filled up with her—the way she fit his body with a lush strength, the way her quickened breathing made her breasts surge against him in a primal rhythm, the way the scent of her blood dazzled his thinking into a frenzy of want and need and urgency. But it was the way his heart swelled up with love that overwhelmed his new exaggerated responses.

And he knew right then that she would never have any reason to fear him.

"You took your sweet time getting here," she complained weakly. "What? Was there traffic?"

Relief shuddered through him as he hugged her close. "I came as quickly as I could."

The soft stroke of her shaky laughter teased against his neck. "I guess in this case, quick is good." Then her tone sobered. "She's in the bat house behind the water fall."

"Can I trust you to stay out of trouble while I deal with her?"

She leaned back far enough to capture his dark gaze with the intensity of her own. "I trust you, Nick." Then she glanced down to see their feet caressing the surface of the pond. "Just don't let me go."

"I won't."

With that husky two-fold promise, he begin to rise up, bringing both of them up to the level of the wall.

Where Palmer was waiting with gun drawn.

His finger spasmed on the trigger, but just when the bullet should have sped from the chamber to burrow into Rae Borden's back, a slender hand gripped the barrel, crushing it shut.

"Have you no respect for true love?"

And he screamed silently as Nicole LaValois went into his veins. She stepped away, delicately dabbing at the sides of her mouth as Nick and Rae settled beside her. Palmer crumpled boneless to the walk. At Rae's questioning glance, the other woman smiled.

"Don't worry. My appetite never runs big enough for the kill—even if they deserve it. He'll be a little less of a problem when he wakes up."

"Nicole, keep her safe for me."

When Rae understood that he was leaving her, her grip on him tightened. But the fear in that action, the fear that steeped dark and desperate in her gaze, never transitioned to speech. Her words were brave and encouraging.

"Be careful. Come back to me."

"Always." To both things.

She hugged him about the neck, unwilling and momentarily unable to let him go. He was pleased to oblige her and gloried in their embrace for another long minute.

The bastard had cut her.

The wound wasn't severe, but it still seeped blood. With her arms wound about him, the opportunity was too tempting. He had to know. He turned his head slightly to move his lips upon that gash, not to drink but to lave along the cut in a slow, sensuous stroke. The taste of her was close to orgasmic. He'd expected his control to falter, but what pushed him to the brink was a deep, desperate desire. Desire for this woman, this brave, reckless woman whose sweet richness danced upon his tongue. Then his head canted slightly as he puzzled over a variation in that essence that he couldn't quite grasp. He pondered over it as Rae eased back from his arms. Her look was guarded and confused, too. But there was no fear of him in that steady stare.

"Stay with Nicole."

She nodded. Then bit her lip to hold back her cry for him to stay, too. But he was gone, a blur of motion streaking down the steps into the bat cave. And all she could think was not how much he'd changed when he'd become something foreign and somewhat frightening, but how much—*more*—he was. Gone was the hesitancy, the uncertainty, the unwillingness to commit to anyone or anything. He was a man of purpose and focused power. And, strange as it might be, she found that irresistibly arousing. The gash on her arm, instead of aching from the abuse, tingled where he'd licked the blood away. It made her think of the ancient childhood ritual of becoming blood brothers. Is that what they were now, bound by the primitive sharing, or had only the first step been taken? Would she find the courage to continue down that forbidden path of promise and dark passions with Nick Flynn as her guide?

"Men. Always in such a rush to plunge into danger while we women know that survival is found in restraint."

The purr of Bianca's voice startled Rae from her flirtation with the unknown. Confronting her now was an evil that might well end any chance of exploring those possibilities.

"*Bonsoir,* Nicole, my dear friend and pupil."

Nicole met her congenial greeting with a rightful contempt. "We were never friends, and the only things you taught me were lies and the bitter taste of revenge."

"You learned those lessons well, my dear, but perhaps you did not pay close enough attention."

She struck with a stunning viciousness, gripping Nicole by the shoulders and flinging her back into the retaining wall with a force that sapped her breath. Then Bianca had the younger woman by either side of her head, smashing it again and again into the cement until Nicole ceased to struggle. She stood, wiping her hands on her snug silk skirt as she smiled down at the limp figure in satisfaction.

"There. That ought to distract your brutish husband long enough for me to deal with our meddling human friend." She turned to Rae with a hiss and a display of her fangs. "Time to make final payment for all the inconvenience you've caused me."

"I pay as I go," Rae stated. She gripped the silver crucifix and yanked to break the slender chain. Then, as the snarling vampiress leapt toward her, Rae dropped the cross and chain down the low vee neckline of Bianca's blouse.

With a screech of agony, Bianca's thoughts of retribution became a writhing need to rid herself of the object that burned her breasts and belly.

With Bianca momentarily distracted, Rae took the surest and riskiest means of escape. Hoping her knowledge of late night vampire lore was correct that they loathed the water, she vaulted over the wall and cannonballed into the moat below. Stunned by the shock of the water, she pushed off the bottom to find herself treading to stay afloat. Above, Bianca's shrieking stopped. It was then she heard the hungry growls from the shore. The tigers paced restlessly, their cunning yellow eyes assessing the distance between them and supper. Knowing the cats had no such aversion to water, Rae began to swim.

***

Bianca's sonic screams drew them back for a rendevzous at the point where they'd left the women.

"Mon Dieu!"

Marchand rushed to the crumpled Nicole, his features stark with terror and rage when he saw the blood on the wall behind her head.

"Is she all right?"

It was a long moment before Marchand replied to Gerard's worried question.

"Just stunned."

"Rae?" Nick scanned the area frantically. No sign of her.

Nicole moaned softly and forced her eyes open. Her anguished gaze sought Nick's. "I'm sorry. It was Bianca. She's after Rae. Hurry."

Marchand looked to the others, obviously torn between his duties.

"We'll handle this, Frenchman," Gerard assured him with a grim smile.

"Her evil must end."

"It will." Nick's promise finished the discussion.

Then they hunted the night.

Nick led, his senses tuned in two directions, one being the dark vibrations from Bianca and the other to the uniquely human essence of the woman he loved. They were close, almost one. Struggling to suppress his raging fear for Rae's safety so he could accurately read the signs, he skirted the cement walls next to the pond. There, he nearly lost the trail, overwhelmed by the strong musky odor that stained the walls—scent marks freshened by the tigers each day to claim their territory. A bold reminder that they were on the big cats' turf and the blonde demon was not the only one following the scent of live blood along the terraced hills, under spreading oaks and Himalayan pines.

Tangled impressions fought for dominance— the sharp throb of Bianca's hunger, the luring pulse of Rae's heartbeats, so fast and furious, the wildly dangerous scent of the cats all intermingling. He couldn't separate one from the others. And then he understood why.

A shrill female scream brought the hairs of his nape up on end.

"Rae."

TWENTY-FOUR

Rae pushed her way through the bamboo thicket, shoving between the canes as threatening sounds pursued her. She had no hope of outdistancing that relentless predator, nor could she simply hide and wait for the saving grace of dawn. The only chance she had was staying on the move, becoming a difficult target until Nick arrived to rescue her. A sobbing laugh escaped her. Yes, she the intrepid loner, the fiercely independent female, wanted...desperately needed help.

She'd torn a strip from the bottom of her shirt to bind her arm, stopping the bleeding that was like a beacon to those who followed. It ached incessantly now, a dull reminder that she alone was human and vulnerable in this game of cat and mouse. Or big cats and deadly rat.

She pushed through the last of the canes to find herself in a small clearing. She surveyed her surroundings as she leaned forward, palms on knees, to catch her breath. Her advance was blocked by a high wall. Large openings had been scooped out of its surface.

Tiger dens.

Great.

"Nick, save my ass," she panted softly.

"I'm sorry. You'll have to settle for me."

Too weary to straighten, too realistic to assume a fighting pose, Rae glared at her in defiance. There was a small satisfaction in knowing that Bianca looked as bad as she felt. Gone was the coolly elegant sophisticate. Her blonde hair was disheveled, and her silk clothing torn and stained. The pale skin of her bosom revealed by the low scoop of her blouse was blistered and burned from contact with the silver cross and chain. There was nothing lovely about the gaunt, pain-ravaged features that confronted her.

She looked pissed.

"If I take no other pleasure this night, it will be the joy of tearing out your throat and drinking down your miserable life."

Rae braced for the attack as a powerful roar announced the end.

But the sound didn't come from Bianca.

Rae stumbled back with an involuntary cry as two huge paws settled on Bianca's shoulders. The tiger's weight carried her to the ground, then they were struggling—fang to fang, claw to claw—a beast of the jungle versus a demon of the supernatural. Rae shrank away from the horrible sounds, snarls, yeowls and finally a wail of pain as the victor found the other's jugular then tottered upright, bathed in the other's blood.

"Prepare to die, bitch," Bianca promised, wiping the gore from her face with a yet taloned hand.

A mocking chuckle from behind her jerked her focus from her human nemesis.

"Cara mia, look at you. Such a sight I never thought to see. You are...a mess."

Her clothing torn, her shoulders clawed and skin shredded, the demon tried nonetheless to assume a haughty attitude. "So cruel with your comments, Gerardo, my love. Take pity on me in the name of the fondness we once shared."

"Pity? Like the pity you felt when you left me chained to a wall to face the light of day? I think I can manage an equal compassion."

"Gerard, don't be mean. Your disloyalty wounded me deeply. I was angry with you. It was a lover's tiff, that's all. I would have taken you back. I would take you back now. Remember how you once loved me."

His smile made him at once beautiful and brutal. "I remember how your greedy act cost me all that I once loved."

"Surely you've forgiven me for that. After all," she goaded, "you've done worse yourself."

"I've atoned for my sins. Time for you to atone for yours."

"Perhaps, but I will not go alone."

With a manic shriek, Bianca whirled to rush at Rae...and found herself impaled upon the bamboo stake Nick braced before him. She stared at the two of them in surprise, at the small-change lawyer and his tough-minded lover and then down at the length of wood piercing her black heart. She laughed faintly at the ridiculousness of being defeated by such a pair. Then she collapsed under the weight of souls she'd stolen over the centuries.

There was no dramatic flash of fire. No rending of the heavens to announce her demise. Just a crumbling from corpse to cinder-like ash that scattered on the breeze as the once reigning queen of the night was no more.

***

Rae had known it would be difficult to say good-bye, but she hadn't expected it to tear her heart in two.

They stood in the drive at the LaValois's big estate as she swiped unashamedly at her tears. She'd managed some degree of dignity until he turned to her with a final smile.

"It's not like we won't see each other again. We're partners, Sugar Rae."

With a wail, Rae launched herself into Gabriel McGraw's arms, hugging him fiercely as she sobbed over the friend she was losing and the love he had lost. He simply held her for a long moment until she got her careening emotions under control. She dried her eyes on the shoulder of his gaudy shirt and stepped away with an apologetic, "I'm sorry. I'm usually not such a basket case."

"You're a mother-to-be. It's allowed." Then he clamped his jaw shut at her look of dismay. "Oops. Was it a secret?"

"How did you know?"

"Nick told me."

"How did *he* know? I wasn't even sure myself."

"Something about a blood test."

She flashed back to Nick's sensuous kiss on her injured arm. "Oh."

Gabriel touched her damp cheek. "You've got what you want, Rae. Don't let go. Don't let pride get the best of love and push you to making the same mistake I did."

She covered his hand with her own. "You'll have your happiness, too. I know it."

His smile was bittersweet. "I haven't searched so long to give up easily. I'll find her and I'll find Zanlos. And I'll settle things with him for the both of us."

He leaned forward to place a kiss upon her other cheek then turned to vault into the big Mercury. It started with a roar and sped down the drive toward a different destiny. Rae hugged to herself as she saw him lift a hand in farewell.

"Godspeed, Gabriel."

She took a deep breath. Time to secure her own destiny.

They watched the parting scene from the house. Gerard looped a companionable arm about his brooding relative's shoulders.

"Do not worry, my friend. She has eyes for only one man."

"Who's no longer a man."

Gerard's laughter mocked his sober statement. "It depends upon your definition of man. Do you love her any less now?"

"No."

"Do you want her any less than before?"

"No." A passionate growl that made Gerard grin.

"Then what is the problem? *Non capisco.*"

"What could I possibly give her the way I am now?"

"Why, anything but an afternoon wedding. And, of course, she'll have to adjust to the changes in your...um, personal life."

More alarmed than embarrassed, he gasped, "No sex?"

"Only about a dozen or so times between dusk and dawn, depending upon her stamina." He winked. "Like I said, an adjustment." He embraced his stunned relative, kissing him fondly in European fashion upon either cheek. "I must go. My wife prefers me home. She fears I will fall into bad habits if on my own for too long. Bid the Frenchman and his lovely Nicole good-bye for me. And I shall expect a visit soon. Don't forget your family, both new and growing and old."

And Gerard was gone, hurrying to beat the dawn back to New Orleans and eager for the arms awaiting him there.

Leaving Nick to wait with equal parts eagerness and

apprehension as Rae came inside. She paused when she saw him, her expression unreadable except for the edge of caution. She knew he knew.

"When were you going to tell me?" He nodded toward her belly for clarification, as if it was needed.

"I don't know. So many things...changed all at once. I haven't had a chance to get used to the idea yet."

"You'll have about nine months." His smile faltered and faded. "You do like the idea, don't you?"

"Of having the baby? Yes."

"And the father?"

There was a long silence, the kind of suspense that was like crawling over an acre of broken glass. And then her answer.

"Yes."

He held out his hand to her, palm outstretched. Slowly, hers crossed it. He kept his grip loose so she could pull free if she chose to. She clung tightly.

"What are you going to do now?" She began with an impossibly broad question that encompassed their entire future.

"Well, I think I've officially resigned from Meeker, Murray & Zanlos."

They shared a rather strained laugh and a long, compelling look. His tone grew serious.

"I've made a lot of bad choices in the past. I've done things for the wrong reasons and only for myself. It's time I did some *pro bono* work if Marchand will have me. I'm sure I can put this law degree to some use, even if my clients have to get used to the odd hours." He needed to work. His first order of business would be to set up a trust fund in New Orleans for two little girls who'd lost their mother. His mood deepened. "And you...and the baby?"

"Robin."

"Robin?"

"The baby's name. Kind of an inside joke between the two of us."

The two of us. Her and the child. Not promising.

"Will you go back home?"

"I am home. This is where all my ghosts are buried. I just

heard that Bette Grover's condition is improving, and I want to be there for her. It might take some time before she gets the okay, but when she's released, I intend to see she gets all the TLC a mother would get from a daughter. I owe that to her and to Ginny. We've got some fences to mend. I'm not walking away from those I love any more."

"Really?"

She lifted his hand so that his palm spread open above her heart. Its strong, determined beat spoke of a truth she had yet to confirm.

He took a breath and took a chance. "I need to hear you say you love me."

Never breaking their intense gaze, she brought his hand to her lips for a soft press. "I have always loved you, and I have always believed in you."

His kiss-dampened knuckles glided along her cheek. "And that's what saved me."

"I guess that settles it, doesn't it? Marchand will have to take the both of us, then. Someone who can investigate in the daylight isn't a bad thing." At the questioning lift of his dark brow, she assumed an independent stance. "You have a problem with a working mother?"

"No problem at all as long as she exercises a little self-restraint."

She stepped in closer. His senses filled up with her, with her fragrance, with her heat, with the excitement stirred by her rapid heart beats.

"Does that self-restraint have to start now?"

"Perhaps not."

She rubbed his jawline with her knuckles and, once she'd touched him, felt the familiar line of his strong chin, she couldn't stop. She caressed his cheek, his brows, the shape of his mouth with her fingertips while her steady gaze adored him and asked for more. She wanted his kisses, to embrace all that he had become without regret or reluctance. But she waited, sensing there was more he wanted to say.

"Before we see if what Gerard told me is true, there's something you need to take care of first."

Cautioned by his rather remote tone, Rae took a step back. "What?"

He grinned, all wolfish charm and dazzle.

"I'm ready for that apology now."